A Home Subscription! It's the easiest and most convenient way to get every one of the exciting Coventry Romance Novels! ...And you get 4 of them FREE!

You pay nothing extra for this convenience: there are no additional charges...you don't even pay for postage! Fill out and send us the handy coupon now, and we'll send you 4 exciting Coventry Romance novels absolutely FREE!

SEND NO MONEY, GET THESE
FOUR BOOKS FREE!

▬▬▬▬▬▬▬▬▬▬▬▬▬▬▬▬▬▬

PEGASUS

by

Eleanor Anne Cox

FAWCETT COVENTRY • NEW YORK

PEGASUS

Published by Fawcett Coventry Books, a unit of CBS Publications, the Consumer Publishing Division of CBS Inc.

Copyright © 1981 by Eleanor Anne Cox Company

ISBN: 0-449-50195-7

Printed in the United States of America

First Fawcett Coventry printing: July 1981

10   9   8   7   6   5   4   3   2   1

Chapter 1

Margaret Mellicent Gorham had been neither in appearance
nor in disposition the sort of child one supposes destined to
become a romantic heroine. Margaret was neither wealthy
nor beautiful. She was merely the oldest of five children of
an impoverished, if genteel, military gentleman. Moreover,
as a child she had been a large plain sort of girl and, although
she had matured into a woman of only average size and of
very tolerable appearance, the lessons of her youth were well
learned and she continued to think of herself as both very
large and very plain. Being an unusually strong-willed person, Miss Gorham had no difficulty convincing the rest of the
world to accept her own appraisal of her person.

Her father was often abroad, and her mother, although a
pleasant woman, was singularly lacking in intelligence and
had no sense of economy. Consequently Margaret was, from
an early age, left to manage the family's meager resources
and to raise her younger siblings.

Captain Gorham died when Margaret was twenty. The
Gorhams, while never well-to-do, were now almost reduced
to penury, and it seemed natural that they should all turn
to Margaret in the expectation that she, even in these strai-
tened circumstances, would somehow manage to arrange for
their secure futures.

Nor did she intend to fail them. Due to the beneficence of
a distant relative, she was able to see the older and dearer
brother, Michael, acquire a commission as a second lieutenant in the navy, and, with great economies on Miss Gorham's
part, the younger son, Phillip, had been sent off to Oxford,
where he had begun the pursuit of a career in the clergy.
Margaret's two sisters, at fifteen and sixteen, were still safely
in the schoolroom, but would soon be cast out into the world.
Their mother's meager jointure, however, would not suffice
to support all three sisters, in the career to which every young
lady was taught to aspire—marriage. Marriage required a

pleasant appearance, a docile nature, and a reasonable portion. Margaret Gorham argued to herself that since she did not have a pleasant appearance, a docile nature, nor a portion of any sort, and since, moreover, she had not in years encountered a man who excited either her affections or her profound respect, it would be better for her to abandon all thought of marriage in favor of a more direct method of attaining financial security.

Miss Gorham was exploring various such possibilities with her friend Rachel Woodruff one evening when the both of them were sitting before the fire in the schoolroom of Mansfield Manor.

"My dearest Woody, the family Gorham is simply being stretched *too* thin. I *must* discover some way of earning my own way and perhaps even contributing to the support of my sisters."

Miss Woodruff was not surprised. She had been Margaret's governess and was governess to all the Mansfield and Gorham children, and she was well aware of Margaret's notions of responsibility. Rachel Woodruff merely looked up from her knitting and raised her eyebrows in a question. "And how, Pegasus, do you expect to do that?"

"I do have *some* talents, you know. I can manage even the *most* difficult of children, and I can manage money. I do not suppose there is a *vast* market for women employed to manage money, outside of marriage that is, so I suppose I had better concentrate on the management of children."

Miss Woodruff pearled half a row before responding, "Don't be a goose, my dear. *You* would not be suited to years and years of submission in someone else's home as a governess."

"True, Woody, true. Of course I can, if the need arises, *appear* to be submissive for several days running, but I could never manage to do so for years on end." Margaret continued to unwind skeins for several minutes before attempting another suggestion. "It will have to be the horses, then."

Miss Woodruff completed a few more stitches. "Without a doubt you do know horses, but Pegasus, dearest, do you really think you would be able to succeed in passing yourself off as a groom?"

"Actually, I believe I might play the part of a boy with greater success than I would play the part of a submissive female, but I do not suppose that I could maintain the disguise *indefinitely*. The pity of it is that I would make an excellent

6

trainer. Still, it won't answer, I would be immediately disqualified, if only because my style is *so* unconventional."

"Rather say 'heathen' and be done with it. Steven Mansfield should never have brought that savage back from America. I never thought to see my Margaret Gorham requesting instruction from an American aborigine. There you were—riding about the countryside negotiating a horse with what appeared, to all of us, to be the tips of your toes and your pinky fingers—as you were hanging precariously from the side of the animal. We could see nothing else of you at all. Fortunately, this is quite an enlightened age and you have been very well liked and respected among the community, or I am certain they would have handed you over to the authorities as a witch."

"A nine-year-old witch?"

"Do not laugh. It was remarkably fortunate that your Silver Fox grew homesick and returned within a year to his grim America. I shudder to think what would have become of you had he remained longer."

Margaret, who seemed deep in thought, appeared to have ignored the better part of this attack. Miss Woodruff was not deceived, however. Her former charge's eyes were gleaming with mischief as that young lady continued to dwell on possible opportunities for employment.

Finally, Miss Gorham, with her hands folded primly in her lap, broke the silence. "I suppose I might apprentice myself to a circus."

The knitting had stopped completely, and Miss Gorham grinned and reached over to reassure her friend, "No, no, don't fly up into the boughs, Woody. I am not thinking *seriously* of the circus. It is a possibility to be sure, but I am quite certain that the remuneration would be inadequate, and, besides, a daughter in the circus would surely break poor Mama's heart." Margaret chuckled to herself. "And you know I believe Phillip would have spasms if he knew I had entertained the thought for even a moment." For a few precious moments Margaret appeared lost in the almost pleasant contemplation of her brother Phillip's spasms.

Woody recalled her to the present. "I do not mean to *pry*, Pegasus, but have you given any consideration to the possibility of marriage?"

"Woody, my love, we are speaking of *feasible* alternatives. Marriage is a very very remote possibility indeed... why, I could sooner become a writer of gothic novels." The gleam of

7

mischief had ripened into a wicked smile as she continued, "Yes, I *could* write novels."

Miss Woodruff set aside her knitting. "Yes, I believe you could. We have known for years what a deadly pen you wield, my dear, but one must be exceedingly careful how one uses such a weapon."

"Pooh! And you, Woody, were my greatest supporter when I set to work exposing the horrible conditions at Bishop Russell's Home for Impoverished Foundlings."

"To be sure, Pegasus, I was very proud of you. Who would not have been proud of a fifteen-year-old girl able to remedy such a monstrous evil?"

"Yes, but those evils were not remedied by a fifteen-year-old girl. As you will recall, the letters to the *Yorkshire Post* were signed by a Reverend James Higby the Third."

"To be sure. And when the dust had settled no one could discover who the Reverend James Higby the Third was. Now *that* was a *worthy* piece of work, my dear."

"Yes, Woody, but do you think that there is an income to be had in the exposure of evil unless such exposure happens to come clothed in lurid prose—and is liberally sprinkled with romance, death-defying acts of courage, and incredibly beautiful silly heroines? No, if I am to earn my keep, I will have to concentrate my energies on the novel. I shall become a scribbler of lurid romances.... Yes, yes, Woody, you will warn me of the dangers of exposure. But no one, save yourself, of course, need know of my identity. I am convinced that I will be able to write quite lethal novels about the follies and the weaknesses of our more eccentric brethren. And the novels *would* sell, Woody. I know they would. I shall use a garish *nom de plume* and I will earn seas of money, and one day, Woody, you and I and a horse or two will retire to a pleasant cottage in the country.... To begin with, I think I will become a governess. Have you noticed that the insufferable adults of this world are always to be found where there are particularly unruly children? I shall reform my households, write scathing novels about their occupants, and then move on to another tableau. Yes, Woody, I believe that you have hit upon the perfect scheme—you are a positive genius, dearest."

The perfect scheme had been working perfectly for something over four years now. In the interim the second lieutenant had become a first lieutenant and the aspiring clergyman had become a curate; one of the younger sisters was married and the other was betrothed. And since her mama, living alone, could manage on her limited income, Miss Gorham was well on her way to becoming not only a famous authoress under the preposterous name of Madame Fleur de la Coeur, but also a modestly wealthy young woman.

In those four years, Margaret Mellicent Gorham had also become a frightfully expensive governess. Miss Gorham could and did command exorbitant wages simply because she had developed a reputation for dealing with even the most obstreperous members of the infantry. In fact, Miss Gorham's services were regularly bid on by any number of distracted mamas, all of them totally unaware of Miss Gorham's secret activities as a chronicler of human foibles.

Currently Miss Gorham was employed at Pemmfield Manor, the home of Julia Pemmrington, widowed wife of Sir Scott Pemmrington. Lady Julia had herself been a pampered child of a viscount. She had been very sweet, quite beautiful, and remarkably silly—and with these qualities she seemed destined, almost from birth, for a splendid marriage. For a very short while Lady Julia had even managed to fulfill that destiny. Sir Scott had not himself been a member of the peerage, but he *was* quite wealthy and he was a grandson of the Earl of Barth and the cousin of several prominent land holders in Devonshire. Fortunately, Scott Pemmrington had never been quite so very silly as his wife, and so they would have muddled along fairly well had not Sir Scott carelessly succumbed to a fever shortly after having been blessed with the last of his three children, none of whom either he or his wife had ever been able to manage. The Pemmrington children had inherited both the best and the worst in their parents—they were all of them remarkably good-looking and rather silly—in addition to being wild to a fault.

In every way, it was a perfect situation for Margaret Gorham, and within two weeks of her arrival the indomitable Miss Gorham was in full control of the household.

At the end of her first month at Pemmfield, Margaret took a few moments from her work to report to Rachel Woodruff:

My Dearest Woody,

What a superb setting I have found here. It could not have been better. I am being paid an outrageous 140 pounds per annum and I have a great deal of liberty. The children are horrid beyond description but not, I think, beyond redemption. The mother is a very sweet featherheaded suffle-like creature and the relatives in the neighborhood—the Dillinghams—are exquisitely obnoxious.

Lady Julia is the sort of woman who is eager to be dependent and already I find myself with a rather disproportionate share of the management of the household. I have accomplished a great deal thus far. A month ago Pemmfield Manor was in a state of chaos and it is now a place of decorum and control.

We are currently up to our ears in plans for the arrival of my lady's cousins—the Misses Campbell. The older Miss Campbell is reputed to be one of the most beautiful young women in London and I am told that the younger Miss Campbell is "a sweet little thing." Miss Gwendolyn Campbell, the beauty, is coming, I believe, to further an acquaintance with the trustee of Sir Scott's estate, who is himself scheduled for a visit to Pemmfield.

And I have saved the best for last! The trustee of Sir Scott's estate, the guardian of his children, and by inference my employer, is none other than Sir Hillary Pendragon. Even in the wilds of Yorkshire I know you will have heard of *the* Sir Hillary Pendragon, and I, Madame Fleur de la Coeur, will have the great honor of immortalizing that gentleman. The very same Sir Hillary who, single-handedly, it is said, seems to, at any given time, juggle the hearts of half a dozen ravishing females while simultaneously engaging in slews of death-defying acts, every single one of which is totally lacking in rational purpose.

How curious it is, to be sure. I sit in Devonshire and my characters are coming to search me out. What fun I shall have with the next manuscript.

You will tell me, dearest Woody, that I *ought* to feel some slight twinges of guilt to be so exploiting my employers, but it is all *quite* innocent. They will never know and are as likely as anyone to enjoy my novels without recognizing themselves buried in the labyrinth of a gothic plot.

10

Take care, Woody. Two more novels and I believe we will retire and breed horses.

Yours,

Pegasus

The residents of Pemmfield Manor were awaiting Sir Hillary's sojurn into Devonshire with a great deal more enthusiasm than was that gentleman himself.

As Miss Gorham was writing her letter to Miss Woodruff,
Sir Hillary was seated with his man of business in the library
of an impressive residence on Grosvenor Square. Hillary Pendragon was engaged in attending to those items of business
which must be successfully resolved before an extended jaunt
into the country could be embarked upon. A casual observer,
however, might not have thought that Sir Hillary was either
capable of or remotely interested in deciphering such mundane matters as the vacillating interest rates being offered
in Consols, the complaints of several of his own tenants in
Somerset, and the recent address in the Lords on the subject
of the Corn Laws. Sir Hillary seemed, in the words of one
admiring miss, almost "too divine" for such earthly concerns.
But Hillary Pendragon, the admiring miss not withstanding,
was not divine. His appearance was good but not remarkable
either for Byronic abandon or for Adonis-like beauty. Hillary
Pendragon was rather too big for either of those roles. His
hair was an undistinguished light brown—neither golden nor
coal black—and although he was very tall he was also rather
large, thus robbing his six-foot-three frame of the aesthetic
graces of a starving hero. In fact there was in Sir Hillary an
extraordinary vitality, and it was that vitality which was the
true source of his great appeal. Hillary Pendragon was almost
irresistible to both men and women. He moved with a casual
animal grace and he radiated a sort of effortless virility in
the same sort of way that some men radiate intense suffering
and some women radiate maternal love. In his gestures—the
sauntering march across a room, the slow smile, the compelling gray eyes—Sir Hillary Pendragon was both the perfect aristocrat and the quintessential male animal.

At thirty, Sir Hillary was also one of the most sought-after
bachelors in London. And, as everyone in the ton knew, this
unenviable status was only in part due to his very considerable fortune. Sir Hillary, without a sou, would still have

11

been a magnificent being. *Fortunately,* he was *not* of the peerage. Had a "lord" attached itself to his name, the mamas would never have let him be, and their daughters would have devoured him like a plague of locusts. Sir Hillary's grandfather had been the Earl of Barth but his father, Sir Joshua Pendragon, only a second son, had, with great foresight, made a brilliant marriage and, as a result, Sir Hillary had inherited a modest fortune from his father and an enormous fortune from his mother, as well as a lavish fortune from his paternal grandmother, who had favored her second son and his only child over all her other various and sundry progeny.

The present holder of the title, his Uncle Geoffrey, had, after many years of dissipating both his fortune and his body, retired to his estates in Cornwall with a young bride, where, it was devoutly to be hoped, he would father a son so as to avoid, for Sir Hillary, the added onus of inheriting an almost worthless title.

Hillary Pendragon was not himself interested either in marriage or in the begetting of heirs, although as a very young man he had been quite interested in women in general and several women in particular. Sir Hillary's profound love of life was matched only by his equally profound love of danger, and in his early years he had somehow come to think that women were the purveyors of both these precious commodities. But after a brief although extraordinarily colorful career as a rake, he lost interest, almost entirely, in the pursuit of Venus. Women, he decided—all women with the exception of his mother and grandmother—were either grasping or stupid, qualities which he found personally offensive. He had, of course, not entirely abandoned women, but from the age of twenty-two he had used his women as a sort of condiment rather than as a major source of sustenance.

Directly after his stint as a rake, Hillary Pendragon became addicted to danger and to heroism in almost all of its various manifestations. In an age of war and of great recklessness, it appeared that he would be able to indulge this addiction indefinitely. And so began a short career of extravagant folly. Hillary became one of those young men who enjoyed such things as wild races from London to places unknown in blinding snowstorms with one hand tied behind their back. Eventually, however, he came to see that all such pursuits were fundamentally trivial, and the enjoyment of them paled. The ton, in its ignorance, still perceived Hillary Pendragon as a rake and as a hell-or-nothing Corinthian, and he saw no reason to deny the members of the ton their illusions. Actually, however, he had for the last few years been engaged in very serious endeavors. Five years ago, he had quietly put aside the follies of his youth and had joined forces with Wellington to defeat Napoleon. Sir Hillary Pendragon had become a courier and an agent extraordinaire behind French lines. The tales of his exploits, perilous escapes, and hair-raising sang froid in the face of enemy fire were slowly becoming legend among military men. He was admired by the men he worked with not only because he was such a magnificent fighting man, but because he managed even in an army of lock-step conformists to be a blazing individualist and because, of course, he had the reckless wild sort of courage of those who not only love danger and freedom but fear nothing of this world.

Sir Hillary Pendragon had it all. A reputation for devil-may-care heroics, a mild resistance to the blandishments of women, and an aura of danger. All of this capped by that *sine qua non* of social requirements—an immense personal fortune. Moreover, no one disliked Sir Hillary, because he had always, even in his raking youth, been exceedingly careful of the feelings of others. Hillary Pendragon did not care to have the sour odor of animosity attached to his person, and so he was never less than totally charming even when disengaging himself from the grasp of the most mercenary of females. Except to those observing him in the battlefield, charm seemed almost to be his defining characteristic. In fact, Sir Hillary had always felt that to be less than charming to his friends, servants, lovers—to anyone—would be ungentlemanly. It would constitute an abuse of his position.

The world seldom saw beyond Sir Hillary's mask of seemingly effortless charm and flawless manners. And, in particular, none of his own family was ever allowed to see with what singular lack of enthusiasm Hillary Pendragon shouldered many of the burdens of his position within society and within his family.

Hillary was, for example, almost dreading this planned jaunt into Devonshire. Julia was a dear sweet little creature, but she had about her an excess of dependency that tended to suffocate Sir Hillary. He would, of course, have to settle all her little problems, humor her, and then, after dealing with the bailiff, he would return to London to forget, for as long as possible, that he, Hillary Pendragon, was responsible for the care of one widow and her three almost impossible children. Really it was extraordinarily shabby of his cousin Scott to have married such a silly creature and, once having married her, to have died so inconveniently, foisting the responsibilities for his mistake on his cousin's broad shoulders.

Still, whatever Sir Hillary's faults, and he himself knew them to be many, he did not shirk his responsibilities. He might shoulder these same responsibilities with what the world took to be a sad lack of seriousness and a careless flamboyance, but Hillary Pendragon nevertheless met all his obligations to the very best of his very considerable abilities. And so, with a sigh of resignation, he completed the work at hand and set out, two days later, for Devonshire.

Chapter 2

For a man of Sir Hillary's notoriety, the ability to appear and disappear almost unnoticed was a great luxury, and so whenever possible he traveled on horseback, allowing his valet and groom to follow at their convenience with whatever equipage he would need. Without the encumbrance of a carriage and servants he was able to travel both quickly and quietly, appearing in one place or another with a minimum of fanfare.

So it was that several days later Sir Hillary was quietly riding along the outside of a hawthorn hedge which bounded the Pemmfield manor house to the east.

Suddenly, he was pulled up short by the harsh screech of a whistle—a military sort of whistle. Himself concealed behind the hedge, Hillary quite naturally looked over to see the cause of the disturbance, half expecting to find the servants of Pemmfield engaged in the now common practice of militia drill. Although Hillary Pendragon, in his official capacity, could not believe that Napoleon would choose to land in this part of Devonshire, he knew that all of England was being mobilized to repel the invader.

Peering over the hedge, he saw that this was no ordinary militia. The person attached to the whistle was a woman—an awesome woman with an almost military bearing and all the femininity, Sir Hillary thought, of a seasoned sergeant major. He saw her face for only a moment before she turned to address her troops. And, instead of the local yeomen Hillary had expected, he saw three small children dressed in quasimilitary uniformity. Not, Sir Hillary thought with a grim little smile, that my darling wards would not constitute a grave threat even to Bonaparte himself.

"Attention!" the sergeant major ordered, and the three small children came to a halt and stood at an almost rigid attention. Slowly the woman moved from one to the other in a silent inspection. The inspection completed, she began to address them each individually.

"Master Thomas, you were left with a composition to complete. It has not been completed. Why not?"

"The composition, Miss Gorham? I didn't know you expected it this afternoon. I really truly didn't. I thought it was to be completed for tomorrow's class," the eight-year-old Thomas answered hesitantly, squirming about in his collar.

"That will be six demerits, Thomas."

"For not completing the composition, Miss Gorham?"

"No. Had you simply not completed your work you would have received a single demerit. You have received five demerits for lying. And why is your coat missing a button?"

"It was Richard, Miss Gorham. Richard fell on me and beat me and ripped off my button." Thomas was glancing with some fear and a hint of malice at his older brother.

"Is that true, Master Richard?" The ten-year-old was being scrutinized.

"Yes, Miss Gorham, it is true, but he *deserved* it. He stole my favorite tin soldiers."

"Master Richard, you will repair your brother's coat yourself and you will receive three demerits. The tin soldiers in dispute will be in my sole possession for two weeks—until you young men learn to settle such conflicts rationally."

The two boys hung their heads silently and waited. Clearly they expected her to continue.

"Master Richard, cook has reported to me that you called the little Tate boy 'freaky face,' and threw rocks at him. Is that true?"

"But Miss Gorham, Jamey Tate *is* an idiot. *Everyone* knows he was born an idiot. *Everyone* calls him 'freaky face,' and I did not throw rocks, only little stones, and not precisely at him, just to make him run. *Everyone* does it."

For a brief moment Sir Hillary saw the woman's shoulders

begin to slump, but she rallied herself and her voice was perhaps a shade less strident but nevertheless very firm when she answered.

"I had hoped for better from you, Richard. I am ashamed for you. To call that child names and to abuse him is very wrong. It is so wrong it cannot be atoned for with demerits. I expect to hear you apologize to Mrs. Tate and to her son, and you will assist Mrs. Tate in the peeling of potatoes during all your free time for the next two days."

"Peeling potatoes! Miss Gorham, I am a *gentleman!*"

"On the contrary, you, Master Richard, are not a gentleman, you are an aspiring Mohawk, and I am determined to see you reformed, young man."

Richard, knowing it was of no use to appeal to his mama, who was only too happy to leave all such matters in the hands of "the General," merely hung his head. Thomas, on the other hand, was looking excessively pleased with himself when Miss Gorham turned back to him and awarded him an extra demerit for tale-bearing.

Thus far the youngest member of the group, six-year-old Pamela, had escaped notice. Now the eagle eyes of Miss Gorham were fastened on that young lady.

"Miss Pamela, two hours ago I left you in your room for a nap, and at that time you had all the appearance of a normal well-bred young lady. What has happened to your face?"

The little face before her colored up rapidly, and the eyes were downcast.

"Yes, I can see how you are justified in blushing, but not all that color is contrition. You have rouged your face, young lady. Whatever for?"

"I want to look beautiful."

"Rubbish, you are beautiful. You are told you are beautiful, which is no more than the simple truth, no less than ten times a day."

"Oh, I know I am pretty, but I want to be *ravishing.*"

"Six and ravishing, I believe, is an almost impossible combination."

"Miss Gorham, don't you understand, Uncle Hillary is coming, and he is the most *divinely attractive* man in England. I *must look ravishing.*"

"Miss Pamela, you have at least ten years before it is socially acceptable for you to either ravish or be ravished by men no matter how divinely attractive. Presently nurse and I will scrub your face with lye soap, Mistress Vanity."

Then she raised the whistle to her lips and there was another sharp screech, and the children were dismissed to the schoolroom, where they were instructed classes would begin in precisely ten minutes.

The children turned and ran, but for a few moments the woman remained in the garden, with her back to the hedge. Then, without so much as turning, the woman in brown bombazine spoke again. "And you behind the hedge—whoever you may be—would do well to learn either not to spy or to do so without the assistance of a horse. Good day to you." Then Miss Gorham marched off toward the house, leaving an abashed and irritated Sir Hillary still framing an adequate reply.

Sir Hillary was announced in the blue saloon a half hour later. As he came toward her, Julia Pemmrington looked up with a studied moue—half surprise and half genuine delight. Then she fluttered beguilingly as she moved into the arms of that man who was not only one of the most sought-after bachelors in all England but also the trustee of her affairs and guardian of her children.

"Oh, Hillary, how happy I am to see you." She smiled up into his eyes.

He held her from him, looking down from his own considerable height into the familiar face of his Cousin Julia. Julia with the unbelievably blond curls, and the rose-colored cheeks. Somehow, almost against his will, Hillary found himself visualizing the six-year-old Mistress Vanity in the schoolroom above the stairs. It was not a pleasant sort of thought, and, as if in repentance, he smiled down at Julia even more lovingly before addressing her. "Julia, you are looking very well—young and radiant, like a breath of spring." Then, bowing low, he took her hand and kissed it tenderly, chuckling at her own harmless imitation of a bashful debutante.

"La, Hillary, we are both too old for such dalliance."

"My dearest Julia, perhaps you are correct. I have always believed that the French greatly overestimated the value of that particular form of salutation. I could think of a great many more pleasant and more direct methods of address."

"I'm certain you could, Hillary." And she began to giggle.

He patted her indulgently on the top of her head. And, after a few more minutes of dilatory conversation, he asked, "Well, Julia, and how have you been going on here at Pemmfield?"

17

"Quite well, I suppose. Oh, but Hillary, I am so incredibly bored. I have become convinced that I *must* get to town for the season this year or I will wither away into my dotage twenty years before my time."

"No fear of that, Julia. But *I* do not keep you from town—never have. Do you mean to take the children?"

"Of course not. Why ever should I? By the by, Hillary, I have engaged the most *marvelous* governess. Miss Gorham is beyond price. Although you may think one hundred and forty pounds a trifle steep for a governess, I can assure you that it is very reasonable indeed. She has done wonders with the Wolverhampton children and the Twining brood, and she comes to us from Lord Gales. I cannot tell you what a source of strength she is. You would not recognize the children."

Sir Hilary held his peace. Had he met them on the street he would indeed not have recognized his three wards in the dourly uniformed threesome of the garden; nor was he at all certain Miss Gorham's alterations in their appearance and behavior had been for the best.

Julia continued. "No, Hillary, I shall leave the children with Miss Gorham—if she is still here. Her one disadvantage, you see, is that she tends to get miffed when crossed and has stayed nowhere longer than six or eight months."

"Come now, Julia, if Miss Gorham should decide to leave I am certain I can find an adequate replacement and you will have your London season unencumbered."

Julia threw her arms around him and thanked him profusely. He acknowledged her thanks with a smile, while hoping that she *would* trap a husband during that season and so, to some extent, relieve him of his own responsibilities to her family.

Women, thought Sir Hillary, were delightful creatures, but only when the spirit moved one to seek their company. At other times they tended to be very tedious companions.

Aloud he said, "And now, Julia, before I begin with all the latest *on dits,* you will tell me where I shall find Mr. Duffy, your bailiff, so that I will lose no time in familiarizing myself with the state of your lands."

"To be sure—Duffy. I believe he planned to come and meet you tomorrow morning. There are so many decisions to make every day, and it is just too difficult for me, you know. Miss Gorham has been a great help and has made a great many decisions, but for some reason she refuses to have anything to do with Duffy. I don't know why."

"But surely, Julia, you must realize how inappropriate it would be for a governess to deal with a bailiff."

"Oh, Hillary, do not *you* scold me. I just don't know how to manage. I so need my darling Scott. Pemmfield is just too much for one silly woman. Please don't scold."

Hillary sighed and, still smiling, reassured her, "Of course not, Julia. Perhaps on those small day-to-day matters you might turn to the colonel. Our Uncle Dillingham is not wonderfully wise, but he *is* capable of distinguishing a hawk from a handsaw."

"Yes, I suppose I *should* turn to him more often. He is a pleasant sort of person, but one has only to ask the Dillinghams for advice of what sort of hens to purchase for the egg house and our Aunt Augusta will begin to make all sorts of decisions about how one is to raise one's children and what color bonnet to wear. I may not know everything there is to know about raising children, Hillary, but I am quite certain that I know a great deal more than Aunt Dillingham about bonnets."

"Infinitely more, little Julia. Infinitely more. Is our aunt still favoring puce this season?"

"No, she has decided that chartreuse is to be the newest rage. Really, Hillary—chartreuse on an aging redhead. Can you imagine!"

"I shudder to think of it. No, you must not ask advice of the Dillinghams unless absolutely necessary."

"Yes, so *you* must convince Miss Gorham to decide on things like the hens, for I am convinced she is quite capable of it. Ernesta Twining says she managed their estates for the better part of a year, and they were far more profitable than at any time Lord Twining had the handling of them. Even the tenants were very sad to see her go."

"I will have to judge this Miss Gorham for myself, Julia. Meanwhile, let me give you the news from town."

And the next half hour was spent in the delightful activity of hashing through all the current gossip circulating through the drawing rooms of London's elite. Some time later, having thoroughly enjoyed the vilification of Byron, Caro Lamb, Brummell, and half a dozen other exalted leaders of the ton, Julia turned to Sir Hillary and, sipping her tea, her face a mask of innocence, she asked, "And you, Hillary. No marriage on the horizon yet?"

"Et tu, Julia. Have you turned on me as well? Hillary

Pendragon is a confirmed bachelor and quite content with his lot."

"You a bachelor! No, the world will never let you be. Hillary Pendragon is far too wealthy and far too handsome to remain a bachelor. Every season we hear rumors of your pending marriage to any number of delicious young lovelies."

"And rumors they will remain, Cousin Julia."

"And those are not the *only* rumors about you to reach Devonshire."

"Out with it, imp—what sort of vicious gossip have you been attending to?"

"Did you really fight a duel with Marchpane last spring? Who did what? And who shot whom? And was his wife your mistress?"

"Too many questions at once, and I fail to see that you have a right to *any* answers."

"Cousin Hillary!"

Laughing, he answered, "It is not near so romantic as you seem to imagine, Julia. I did fight a duel with Marchpane, who believed for some reason that I was interested in his wife. I was not and have never been involved with that lady."

Actually Lady Julia already knew, as did everyone else save Marchpane, that the lady had offered and had been refused. Hillary Pendragon, at thirty, was known to have become very discriminating in his tastes.

"In any case, Marchpane was quite foxed when he challenged me and even more intoxicated the morning of the duel. It was a wonder he could remain standing to the count of ten, and his collapse, immediately thereafter, was due to the alcohol in his blood and not to any bullet of mine, which in fact only grazed his sleeve. I understand he was brought home on a stretcher to his temporarily reformed wife, who has sworn to be true to him alone."

"Yes, Hillary, and knowing Emilia Marchpane, I am certain she will be forsworn in six months."

"Cynic."

"Am I? Well, I don't quite know what a cynic is, but I know very well what Emilia Marchpane is, and you were wise to avoid her. Gwendolyn will suit you far better."

"Gwendolyn Campbell? Good God, what gave you that idea?"

"Gwendolyn is beautiful and intelligent— which I am not and know very well I am not, but I can recognize intelligence,

Hillary. Gwendolyn will be a perfect wife for you, and I am sure that is in her papa's mind in sending her to visit me when everyone knows you will be in the neighborhood."

"A matchmaking papa and a matchmaking cousin. I will guard myself and proceed with exceeding care." Then, chucking her under the chin, he continued, "Whatever your intentions, my dear Cousin Julia, I warn you I will not be caught. Someday I will marry, out of a species of necessity, I suppose, but I will do nothing to hasten that day. I enjoy my freedom."

"We all know how well you enjoy your freedom, but you cannot be allowed to win out. Hillary, you are a challenge to every matchmaking mama in Britain."

Before Sir Hillary could answer, they were interrupted by Thackery, the butler, who had come to ask if Sir Hillary would be staying for dinner.

"No, I do not think so, Thackery. I dine tonight at Dillingham Hall, where I will be staying for the next week or so. Thank you."

"Very good, sir." Thackery bowed his way out of the room. Shortly thereafter, Sir Hillary gathered together his hat and cape, took his leave of Julia, and made his way to his Aunt Dillingham's.

That evening Miss Gorham and Lady Julia dined together without benefit of his company. Julia, who had a horror of being alone, had insisted on Miss Gorham's company at dinner, and so the children were allowed to eat with nurse in the schoolroom while Margaret Gorham was treated, nightly, to a lengthy monologue on various and sundry topics of general feminine interest. Almost invariably, Miss Gorham, who was genuinely fond of Lady Julia, would listen quietly, only adding here and there a few words of restraint and wisdom. But that evening there was no restraint or wisdom tolerated, for Julia was holding forth on the wonders, abilities, and charm of Hillary Pendragon. Miss Gorham was listening quietly but all the while taking mental notes for the character of the villain in her next novel.

Although Hillary Pendragon would undoubtedly have been embarrassed by the extraordinary praise being heaped upon him in the Pemmrington dining saloon, he would still quite possibly have preferred Julia's chatter to the orchestrated irritation of dinner at the Dillinghams.

Augusta Dillingham was a very formidable woman. She had been formidable as a girl as well, and that is perhaps why, despite her position as the eldest of the Earl of Barth's children and her own modest fortune, she had not taken in her first London season. Nor in her second and third and fourth seasons. In fact, Augusta did not find a husband until chancing upon the innocent Captain Dillingham during a country visit in her twenty-eighth year. It was not, from her standpoint, an ideal match. Socially and financially it was just barely tolerable. Had Reginald Dillingham been a more sensitive individual the marriage would have been for both of them totally intolerable, but as he was a placid, large, drinking man, he had managed to bumble through thirty-some years with Lady Augusta without once attempting to strangle her. As a consequence, he was universally admired for his forbearance, and his various peccadilloes, all inspired by an appreciation for aged wine and full-blown women, were viewed, in general, with a generous complacency.

The Dillinghams had settled in close proximity to Augusta's younger sister, Olivia Pemmrington, and the daughters of the Earl of Barth had come to dominate the neighborhood. In the first few years of her marriage, Augusta had managed to produce two sons, neither of whom seemed destined ever to escape the iron control of their mama. Each son, in his own way, had learned to simultaneously hate and depend on that awesome mother, and so despite their brief forays into the outside world, the Dillingham sons invariably returned to the Dillingham hearth to prey on each other and to be preyed upon in turn.

The younger son, Claude, was, like his father, phlegmatic and therefore relatively impervious to his mother's insistence that she manage his life. But, unlike his father, Claude was a smallish delicate sort of man, and he would never have sought refuge either in wine or in women. Claude's passion was clothes. He lived always in a foppish world of color and fashion to which he devoted himself with heroic fortitude, in part at least because he sensed that in doing so he was greatly irritating his mother.

Anthony, the older son, had once been a handsome man, but the years had not been kind to him. It was not clear to what sort of dissipations Anthony was primarily devoted, but at thirty-two his body had begun to bear the scars of decadence. His hair had thinned and had lost its luster, his skin was sallow, his teeth had darkened. The entire effect was to make a man, who had once appeared rakishly handsome, seem at thirty-two merely a tall thin middle-aged gentleman with only a thin veneer of sophistication which did little to conceal a deep well of cynicism.

Anthony had been married at an early age to a local beauty whom he had systematically set out to destroy, until she, relieved finally to escape him, lapsed into death, leaving the Dillinghams with two children—Sarah, now aged ten, and Luke, now aged nine. The children had been reared with a toxic combination of their father's cynicism and their grandmother's intrusions. They were shy, reserved, and very frightened children, and they were the only members of the Dillingham ménage whom Sir Hillary could truthfully say he was fond of.

Unfortunately, while Sarah and Luke ate in the nursery, Augusta Dillingham was allowed to hold sway, unchallenged and seldom interrupted, in the dining saloon.

"Anthony, dearest, do eat your flambeau. You must know cook has made it particularly because you are so fond of flambeau, and you *are* becoming quite thin."

Anthony stared sullenly at his mother before slowly and methodically pushing the flambeau from him.

Augusta Dillingham had turned to her nephew and addressed him almost as though Anthony were not in the room. "Anthony is such a *fragile* young man. He has not really recovered from poor Louisa's death and he does not eat as he should. I *must* keep reminding him."

"Mother, Louisa died five years ago. I had fully recovered within a week."

"Of course you did, my dear, and I am particularly pleased with how very well you have been doing just lately. You must know, Hillary, that Anthony has been taking a remarkable amount of the responsibilities from his father's shoulders. My son has become very involved in the management of the estate and even in accepting some of the duties of magistrate. He is also, I might add, spending a prodigious amount of time supervising the education of his children. I used to think he would never be properly interested in such matters, but Anthony has spent hours explaining to our Miss Porter precisely how she is to carry on with Sarah and Luke. There will be no more novels; the children will be read sermons as they should. It is a great pity that my Anthony was not made guardian to Scott's children. If he had been, you would not have had to come from London so often. It must be quite a burden for you—although I have always said that Hillary Pendragon does not shirk his responsibilities."

"Thank you, Aunt Augusta," Hillary murmured. His Aunt Augusta took a moment to catch her breath and finish her flambeau. "To be sure we all, as members of the aristocracy, must accept responsibility, and I know I need not tell you how onerous those responsibilities can become. Many a time I have to literally *force* myself to visit the sick and dying among our people—as undeserving and as slovenly as they usually are. And although they are *quite* deaf to any suggestion of reform, I visit them nonetheless and I never tire of my commitment to improve their lives if only by pious example and Christian charity.

"Unfortunately, Hillary, I cannot honestly say that Lady Julia has shouldered her fair share of *that* burden. She handles her duties toward the villagers with a species of levity of which I cannot approve. But then Julia is sadly lacking in judgment, don't you think?"

Through long experience Hillary had learned never to attempt an answer to one of those rhetorical questions which punctuated his aunt's monologues. Claude, however, who seemed completely impervious to his mother's superficial irritations, answered for Hillary.

"No, no, Maman! I cannot agree. My Cousin Julia is a genius, a veritable genius, and is surpassed by no woman in her judgment of color and cut."

Claude's mother favored him with a gimlet-eyed stare. Sniffing, she responded to him, "Claude, need you always be reminding one of your preoccupation with such things? Is it not enough that you parade about your home dressed in such *excessive* fashion? I blanch to think that one of *my* children— the grandson of the fourth Earl of Barth—should have become a fop."

"Please not a fop, *ma mère*. I am a dandy. The grandson of the fourth Earl of Barth has become a dandy, and there is no avoiding the fact, dearest *ma mère*. My soul does not venture above buttons. You were always wont to tell me that I must recognize my grave limitations, and I have—I have limited myself quite nicely to matters of fashion. And my Cousin Julia's eye *is* excellent. Is it not, Hillary?"

"To be sure, Claude, Julia's eye is perfection itself," Hillary answered, sipping his coffee.

"See, I told you so, Mother, and Hillary agrees, which must be the clincher, because Hillary *does* understand these things."

"I will not contradict our guest, Claude, but even you must realize that when I speak of judgment I am not restricting myself to superficialities of fashion. Julia Pemmrington has found herself a widow in a position where she *must* manage a considerable estate and three poorly behaved children. She is by nature totally unequipped to manage either."

"Too true, Maman, but Julia has always been quite successful at attracting helpers. She has now got Miss Gorham, and there is no doubt at all that Miss Margaret Gorham could manage Pemmfield and twice the number of poorly behaved children with absolutely no loss of composure."

"True, Julia is more fortunate than she deserves to be in her choice of governess." Augusta sat back and laid her napkin on the table, thus effectively punctuating her sentence and announcing that her dinner had been completed.

The gentlemen stood as Lady Augusta sailed from the room, leaving them to their port.

Sir Hillary savored the truly excellent port as Anthony continued the discussion. "Yes, dear Miss Gorham has invaded Pemmfield Manor. She came, she saw, and she conquered, and, like Caesar before her, she took the barbarians and organized them into a smoothly functioning military unit."

"I take it, Anthony, that you do not share your mother's enthusiasm for the new governess." Hillary smiled.

"Splendid woman, indeed." Colonel Dillingham belched discreetly as he placed his goblet on the table. "Splendid woman, Miss Gorham."

"I am reluctant to contradict either of my esteemed parents, coz. In any case, the 'splendid woman' has never condescended to exchange two words with me. I prefer my governesses less competent at running a household and more competent at tending to a man's creature comforts."

Claude, who was never a drinking man, had wandered off, and the colonel seemed lost either in thought or in drink, and so, for the next hour, Anthony and Hillary exchanged gossip from London and Hillary was brought up to date on events in the neighborhood. As Sir Hillary had had a long hard day, he excused himself rather early from the two gentlemen. He was nearly out the door when he turned back to address his uncle. "Incidentally, Reginald, I do not believe

I will be abusing your hospitality for above a week. I am expecting to be joined by a comrade-in-arms. A young man name of Robert Mansfield—he served with me in the Peninsula, you know. And we shouldn't dream of burdening your household with two guests. I have arranged to stay at the inn with Mr. Mansfield."

His uncle shook his head, partly to clear it and partly to dissent. "Never hear of it, my boy. It shall never be said that I closed my door in the face of a military man. You will both come and stay with us. Augusta, I am certain, will insist upon it. Likes to keep her hand in things, don't you know."

Hillary knew only too well, but he resigned himself to the inevitable and excused himself from the room.

Chapter 3

The next morning Sir Hillary managed to escape from Dillingham Hall well before the rest of the household had made their way to the breakfast table. Arriving quietly at Pemmfield, Hillary stabled his horse and informed Thackery that he would remain sequestered in the library studying the accounts and awaiting the arrival of Mr. Duffy, the bailiff. That gentleman arrived promptly at nine and was shown into the library, where he spent a harrowing morning with Hillary Pendragon poring over the books of the estate. Sir Hillary was not entirely satisfied with the meeting, and so more meetings were scheduled before Mr. Duffy was dismissed at one o'clock, when Thackery knocked on the door to announce luncheon.

During luncheon, Hillary and his hostess were exchanging particularly salty *on dits* when Julia's youngest, little Pamela, burst into the room and literally threw herself at Sir Hillary. "La, Uncle Hillary, we are *so* happy you have come. We saw your horse in the stable, and *even* Miss Gorham said it was a *very* fine horse and I *could* not wait to see you. What have you brought me from town? You *have* brought me a present, haven't you, Uncle Hillary?"—all of this punctuated with kisses, making it impossible for the assaulted gentleman to attempt a response even had he chosen to do so.

Margaret Gorham had appeared in the arched doorway of the saloon, and without raising her voice even a fraction she brought her charge to heel.

"Miss Pemmrington, if you are quite finished distributing turtle soup on the gentleman's coat you will release him sufficiently so that he may answer your inquiry, and then, young lady, you will leave your mama and her company to their luncheon. Have I made myself clear?"

"Yes, Miss Gorham," the little voice said, and Pamela dropped away from Sir Hillary, apologized with a curtsy for the stained coat, and then, with a very quick glance at the doorway, asked, very sweetly, whether he had brought her a gift from town.

At this last request Sir Hillary noticed Miss Gorham wince almost imperceptibly, and looking down at the little face he answered with his most devastating smile.

"But of course, my little beauty, I have brought you *several* treasures. A new dress, two dolls, and pounds and pounds of the very latest in bonbons." Then slowly ruffling her hair, he dismissed her into the iron grip of her governess.

With the door closed behind them, Julia spoke.

"I do wish, Hillary, you had not handled the matter quite as you did. I think you may have upset Miss Gorham, who does not, you know, approve of any interference in her disciplining of the children."

"Julia, that woman, if I may call her so, is your employee. It is what you countenance that is of concern. You *must* learn to assert yourself."

"But it *was* wrong and quite the worst of manners for Pamela to nag at you for gifts."

"It is also wrong for you to be ruled by a mere governess."

"Quite true, Hillary, when you put it that way—but you see, before Miss Gorham came to us there was so very much chaos in this house. We were *all* miserable, I am sure, and the children did not love me at all. Since Miss Gorham has taken a hand to things, everything is going smoothly, and you know I believe the children have discovered a great affection for their silly widgeon of a mother now that she need not be constantly screaming at them to keep order."

"Nevertheless, Pamela was merely being honest, if a trifle overenthusiastic, in asking for her gifts. I can assure you that most women of my acquantance would have raised the same question within ten minutes of meeting me, and although they might have used a bit of subterfuge we should not fault Pamela for honesty. Your daughter is only a child."

"True, Hillary, she is only a child, but I think if she were to be left to my guidance exclusively she would remain a child all her life. I often wish I had had a governess like Miss Gorham. Had I had Miss Gorham, I doubt that I would have been allowed to grow into such a silly ninny as I am. Please, Hillary, you *must* make peace with her!"

Julia seemed almost on the verge of tears, and so, with a sigh, Sir Hillary reached over and patted her hand. "Peace, Julia, peace. I will make everything right with the Gorgon. Do not upset yourself. It is really a very simple matter." And saying this he guided the conversation back to Lord Byron and Caro Lamb.

Shortly after lunch, Sir Hillary braced himself for the unpleasant task of confronting the governess. He anticipated no problem in overcoming what he thought of as Miss Gorham's miff, but he did not relish the thought of the interview. Unfortunately, it appeared to him that his life in England had degenerated into a never-ending endeavor to smooth the ruffled feathers of one female or another. And while he did not for a single moment doubt his own ability to soothe any female, he was becoming a trifle bored with the entire enterprise.

Hillary braced himself and, almost automatically, pinned a smile to his face. Life had taught Hillary Pendragon that he could nearly always turn away feminine wrath with a carefree smile and caressing eyes. Even his grandmother and his mother, women who were exceptionally strong-minded in their own right, had always been vanquished by that smile.

The one exception, an exception still burned into his mind, had been a Miss Agitha Smith, a sixty-year-old ogre employed as governess to his maternal cousins the Cavenaughs. Hillary had been seven and was visiting his cousins one spring when Miss Smith had asked him to assemble a pressed-leaf collection. He had not completed the leaf collection but, armed with that smile which proclaimed him a truly good-natured child, he had very sweetly apologized to Miss Smith and promised to have the collection completed for the next day. The young Hillary had executed his pretty apology only to see that remarkable block of ice Miss Agitha Smith, become, if it were possible, even more glacial than she had been prior to the apology. Then Miss Smith had leveled the boy with her blank stare and read him a lecture on doing one's duty and on accepting responsibility. Hillary had always been a well-mannered child, and so he had listened quietly, attempting to mask his own chagrin. At first he had merely been shocked, but as she continued, he had experienced, almost simultaneously, both a great resentment toward Miss Smith and a deep disappointment in himself.

In all the intervening years Sir Hillary had never forgotten her words or the granite promontories of her face. At times, in his dreams during those long dangerous jaunts into France when he had been trying desperately to break back across enemy lines with some vital information, he would dream of that blasted leaf collection. The leaf collection which had never been completed and could now never be completed because Miss Agitha Smith did not allow for second chances.

With a shake of the head, Hillary banished Miss Smith from his mind. Miss Margaret Gorham was the problem at hand, and she was not a sixty-year-old gray woman confronting a seven-year-old child. He was no longer a child, he was now Sir Hillary Pendragon, hero, adventurer, and, by common consent, irresistible to all members of the female sex.

The smile in place, he knocked on the door of the schoolroom, and a voice bid him enter.

Miss Gorham was in the midst of a lesson, and so, smiling, he asked her to continue. His business could wait a few minutes.

"Very good, Sir Hillary. Please be seated." He noticed that his smile was not being returned.

As Miss Gorham was occupying the only full-size chair in the room, Sir Hillary was forced to fold his very considerable length into the confines of a child's chair. He could have minimized his discomfort by relaxing his long legs out before him, but he realized, intuitively, that such a casual posture would not be tolerated in Miss Gorham's class. And so he continued to sit cramped and uncomfortable while he quietly observed the lesson in progress and smiled occasionally at the instructor until he slowly came to realize that Miss Gorham was paying him no attention at all.

Sir Hillary had interrupted a session devoted to the appreciation of English literature. In her manner, Miss Gorham was, as he had expected, strict, unyielding, and totally immune to any attempt by the children to lighten the atmosphere. Each child was asked to recite a verse from memory and then to interpret that verse for the class. Miss Gorham asked a question now and again to focus the child's attention on this or that part of the poem, but for the most part both Pamela and Thomas completed their work almost mechanically. Unlike the others, young Richard actually seemed to have enjoyed the Shakespeare sonnet he had selected, and Hillary was surprised to hear the boy interpret the dominant metaphor of the sonnet in an original and imaginative way. During Richard's recital, Sir Hillary was not glancing at Miss Gorham, and so he missed her short simple smile of approval. Master Richard did not miss that smile, however, and he was beaming with pride as he completed his interpretation.

Then the omnipresent whistle announced the end of the session—just as Sir Hillary thought his knees would crack—and the three children were very formally dismissed for a twenty-minute unscheduled recess.

The children filed from the room while Miss Gorham remained seated with her hands folded quietly in her lap, and as she admonished Sir Hillary to please remain seated as well, he could not, as he wished, escape the confines of his stool.

"You wish to discuss some matter with me, Sir Hillary?" She graciously nodded her head and then, with her hands still folded and her features quite motionless, she waited for him to begin.

It was not the atmosphere he would have chosen, but seeing no alternative, he began. "Miss Gorham, you must know how very much your work is appreciated here at Pemmfield. Lady Julia has repeatedly assured me of your great worth not only as a governess but also as an assistant to her in other respects." He punctuated this remark with one of his charming but respectful smiles and was somewhat surprised to see no reflection of that smile in her countenance. In fact, if it were possible, her features had begun to harden.

Clearing his throat, he continued, "Lady Julia has informed me, in no uncertain terms, that I committed a dreadful solecism at luncheon. I can assure you that I had not meant to interfere with your disciplining of little Pamela, and I have come to apologize." And then with a glance that would have melted four fifths of the maternal hearts of England, "Am I forgiven, Miss Gorham?"

For a moment she did not respond, and he shifted restlessly in that confounded chair.

"I accept your apology in the spirit in which it was offered. Will that be all, Sir Hillary?" With her hands still folded, she waited silently.

Sir Hillary could have, indeed he knew he should have, left well enough alone and excused himself. Clearly, the woman had no conversation and no manners and was undeserving of any more of his time. He fidgeted again, and suddenly he realized that he had begun to feel like a seven-year-old child and Miss Margaret Gorham had begun to seem like the ghost of Miss Agitha Smith. Something in Hillary Pendragon snapped, and he decided to attack that granite facade.

"Perhaps that is not *quite* all, Miss Gorham."

"Yes?"

"You must know that I am the children's guardian, and as their guardian you would only expect me to take a considerable interest in their education. I have been observing your method of education, and I find that I have some questions concerning your technique. You will, of course, be kind enough to discuss these questions with me?"

"Proceed." He waited for her to elaborate on this one-word response, but when there was no elaboration he continued.

"Quite frankly, Miss Gorham, I had supposed that such a rigid unbending approach to education as you seem to employ had become somewhat dated. In this enlightened age we understand children far better than did our fathers and grandfathers, and I would have thought that a softer, more maternal, if you will, method would be more suitable to liberating a child's mind."

He waited for her response, but as she had not moved and showed no sign of speaking he found himself, almost against his will, forced to continue.

"I should think that guiding children through life with a whistle, very much as if they were mechanical soldiers or trained dogs, would not maximize either their strength of character or their breadth of mind."

She sat still straighter in her chair. "You have formed these conclusions on the basis of a twenty-minute observation?"

"Not precisely, Miss Gorham."

"And what precisely does 'not precisely' mean?"

"I had the opportunity to observe you during luncheon today, and I have been discussing your methods with Lady Julia."

"And...?" She stared at him and waited. Sir Hillary shifted in his chair. Miss Gorham continued to wait.

"As a matter of fact, I came across you and your charges yesterday afternoon. Quite by accident, you understand."

"I understand perfectly. 'Quite by accident' you discovered

31

yourself snooping from behind a hedge and 'quite by accident' you did not choose to make your presence known."

"I beg your pardon, Miss Gorham?"

She sighed. "One of the very first lessons I attempt to teach my children is to own up like a man when one is caught. Of course, hidden as you were, I could not have recognized you. I did, however, recognize your horse." For the first time she smiled, a very thin smile. "Whatever your faults, young man, I will concede that you are an excellent judge of horseflesh."

"How very good of you to notice, Miss Gorham. But I am also commonly supposed to have some modicum of judgment in other matters as well, and I find your conduct with regard to the children decidedly harsh."

"Then you have only to discharge me."

"Is that the only alternative? Do you mean, Miss Gorham, that you will accept no criticism of your methods? Do you imagine that you yourself are totally without flaw or blemish?"

"That is entirely beside the point. I have charge of these three children, and in discharging my duties toward them I have principles which I will not compromise. These particular children require discipline. When I arrived at Pemmfield the children were completely out of control and the household was in a state of chaos. Your wards were well on their way toward becoming not only useless, frivolous, spoiled products of the aristocracy but also little monsters without even the redeeming virtue of charm. Do you wish Richard and Thomas to grow into undisciplined wastrels or Pamela to become a mindless cloying ninny?"

"Of course not. And surely you exaggerate. Pamela, in particular, is a charming child and bids well to becoming as charming a woman as is her mother."

"Nonsense. Pamela is a very pretty child, and she *can* be charming, but she does not, as yet, have one ounce of the common sense and kindness which render her mother such an attractive woman. I have come to think that the Lady Julia's of this world have paid very dearly for being raised as brainless bits of fluff, but Lady Julia herself is a very *likable* bit of fluff and Pamela is not. In any case, I see no point in continuing this conversation. I am quite willing to seek employment elsewhere."

Ignoring the last comment, Hillary continued, "Perhaps the children were somewhat wild, but surely their character could have been improved more readily by a modicum of affection rather than by the lock-step regimentation of a sergeant major.

The Pemmrington children are not trained seals."

"Those children are already surrounded, almost drowned, in affection. They have affection from servants, from nurses, from a doting mother, and, on those rare occasions when he comes to visit, from a pliable guardian. The Pemmrington children need some steel in their lives, and I intend to give it to them." Miss Gorham rose from her chair and turned toward the window, at least in part to hide the twinkle in her eye, as she continued, "Do you suppose that Admiral Lord Nelson could have won the battle of Trafalgar if his officers had all been self-satisfied little brats?"

In control of herself again, she turned and stood towering over him. Under normal circumstances, Sir Hillary would have himself stood, but she looked to be so much *his* governess that he remained seated in that damned silly chair and waited for her to continue.

Again she smiled that tight little governess smile. The smile of Miss Agitha Smith in triumph. "Come, come, young man. You *must* understand that I have had a great deal of experience in the care and education of children and that you have had almost no experience of that sort. I am quite certain that as you grow older and have devoted some time to the consideration of these matters, you will come to agree with me at least insofar as the Pemmrington children are concerned. If I were to leave Pemmfield prematurely I am convinced these children would suffer a loss, but *I* am not their guardian. Consider the problems, continue your observations, and we will discuss this matter again."

Nodding, she dismissed him. As Sir Hillary rose from the chair to make the ritual farewell he was surprised to find that Miss Gorham was actually a rather smallish woman who scarcely reached his shoulder. Being eager to escape, Hillary did not dwell on this oddity until he was on the other side of the door, where he breathed a great sigh of relief, uncrinched his legs, and loosened his collar.

Retreating to the library, Hillary Pendragon fortified himself with a generous quantity of brandy before seeking Lady Julia to explain that while Miss Gorham was not completely mollified, he anticipated no problems with her that could not be amicably resolved.

Gazing up at him from under her thick lashes, Julia Pemmrington smiled ruefully. "Oh, poor Hillary, you tried to turn Miss Gorham up sweet and it didn't work, did it? I should have warned you that she is *not* that kind of woman, but I don't suppose you would have believed me."

"My dearest Julia, she is not *any* kind of a woman at all. She is a little Napoleon in petticoats. If you must have selected someone quite so *gothic* for your children at the very least you might have chosen someone younger."

"Younger! Miss Gorham is only twenty-four—I could hardly have entrusted my little dears to anyone younger, could I?.... Hillary, you know you have begun looking a trifle green."

"Twenty-four! She looks sixty. And she called me 'young man.' No, Julia, don't you dare to laugh. Do you realize I have been bested by a woman half my size and six years my junior?"

Later that evening, Margaret Gorham took a few moments to pen a letter.

My dearest Woody,

This afternoon I met and bested *the* Hillary Pendragon. He *is* very attractive if one's taste runs to tall virile knuckleheads. He sat in my classroom and, while making token assertion of adulthood, was as easy to manage as any other charming but somewhat wayward child. With the exception of his judgment in horses, Sir Hillary seems to be of only very modest intelligence. He has, I think, survived all these years off a stock of charm and has never had any need to develop what native wit he may have been blessed with.

I have decided that Sir Hillary *cannot* be my villain. He does not have the breadth of intelligence or the spark of power. But he is very pleasant, very tall, and very attractive—a smiling simpleton. He shall make an ideal hero.

Love,

Pegasus

P.S. We are now eagerly anticipating the arrival of the Campbell sisters—Gwendolyn and Alicia. The older I am assured is not only a diamond of the first water but is also "for a woman" *très bright!* The younger, Alicia, is universally ac-

34

claimed to be very pretty and very sweet—she
will, I think, be my heroine.

Chapter 4

Whether consciously or unconsciously, the next day Sir Hillary avoided Pemmfield. In the morning he attended to some business in the village, and in the afternoon he decided to collect his thoughts while rusticating in Colonel Dillingham's extensive gardens.

The scenery in the gardens was indeed restful. In addition to masses of brightly colored fragrant blooms, Sir Hillary was confronted by a perfectly charming human tableau. The two Dillingham children and their governess sat reading in the shade of an ancient oak tree. As Sir Hillary found himself a place on the grass, the governess looked up at him shyly and then, quickly looking down again and coloring, she continued to read. She was, Sir Hillary decided, a thoroughly delectable little female— blond, soft, and with a certain pleasing nervous compliance. The two children, in contrast, did not look near so well. Anthony Dillingham's children—Sarah and Luke—were always a rather sorry-looking pair. They were both bright, emaciated, exceedingly nervous children. Hillary suspected that his cousin Anthony was not always a kind father, and in their pinched little faces Sarah and Luke had the look of children who had learned to fear and distrust all adults. To compensate for the pain in their lives they had created a wonder world of their own which seemed, at times, to be their only real habitation. And thus, although they were always perfecly behaved in the presence of their seniors, they were nevertheless also always careful to exclude those same adults from any and all significant communication. Few grown-ups had ever been able to break through their wall of fearful reserve, and Sir Hillary was justly proud that he was one or their few friends.

Today, when he arrived, they had not seemed frightened so much as bored— which was readily understandable since the reading was from a collection of dreadful sermons. Despite their boredom, Miss Porter continued reading in a soft voice for a quarter of an hour, until she was interrupted by the arrival of a footman who had come to relay a request from Mister Anthony. Miss Porter was required in the house. The governess bobbed demurely in the direction of Sir Hillary, excused herself, and scurried away.

Once she had turned the corner toward the house the children lighted up and ran to Sir Hillary, seating themselves beside him in the grass.

"Oh, Uncle Hillary, you have finally come to see us. We knew you would, did we not, Luke?"

"Yes, we watched you from above the stairs last night. We saw you as you arrived."

"But we were disappointed," Sarah continued.

"Disappointed, moppet?" Hillary grinned.

"To be sure, we had expected to see your uniform. Why don't you ever wear your colors, Uncle Hillary?"

"Yes, we so wished to see precisely how you look when you are fighting Boney," Luke explained. "It is very important to be able to picture you when one reads about your battles."

Sir Hillary chuckled and ruffled each little head in turn. "Fighting Boney I am more likely than not to be dressed in mud-spattered buckskins. I was never much of a uniform-type soldier, you know. I'm afraid you would be sorely disappointed."

"Pooh! You are the only soldier we ever talk to, and everyone knows that Sir Hillary Pendragon is perfect." Sarah laughed.

Sir Hillary was taken aback. Not by the compliment, which he had learned to expect, but by the sound of Sarah's laughter. Hillary had always associated her with a sort of nervousness that precluded laughter. He looked at the both of them carefully and saw that while they were still eager for his attention, they no longer seemed virtually *starved* for affection. It was a change for the better, and he drew the obvious conclusion—Miss Porter must be responsible for the improvement.

"I believe you have heard all the gossip and are, like almost everyone else, overestimating your Uncle Hillary. But even if I have forgotten my uniform I have not forgotten to bring you a half-dozen books and some bonbons from town. How are you doing for bonbons, brats?"

They grinned—both in anticipation of the gifts and because he had called them brats. They loved to be referred to as scamps or brats—perhaps because they were such perfectly well-behaved children.

"Well, we will forgive you then if you remember to bring your uniform next time," Sarah said, still grinning.

"And if we can have the books and bonbons today," Luke added.

"Good. I am vastly relieved. I should hate to be in your bad graces."

They chuckled again, and the three of them sat silently for a few minutes looking out over the garden.

"Incidentally, you have a pleasant new governess, don't you, brats?"

Almost instantly he realized he had destroyed the amicable silence or something equally as fragile.

"Yes," Luke answered. "She is very pretty."

"Pretty *and* sweet. She looks to be just exactly the sort of governess I would want."

Her eyes screwed up a bit, Sarah looked at him slowly before answering, "Yes, I suppose most gentlemen would like a governess like Miss Porter."

Sir Hillary chose to ignore the hint of sarcasm in her voice and continued, "Well, I happen to think you have done very well for yourselves—very well indeed. Your Pemmrington cousins have been fortunate enought to acquire a Gorgon for a governess—Robespierre and Napoleon rolled up into one."

The children had moved away from him slowly, and their faces, eager and open a few moments ago, had resumed their habitual opaque expression. Luke stood, and, drawing himself up very straight, he held out his hand for his sister.

Sarah hesitated, not being willing herself to abandon an old and valued friend quite so easily. "Uncle Hillary, how can *you* be such a knucklehead?—I would have expected more of you."

Hillary reflected on how quickly his perfection became tarnished and was about to laugh off the incident until he looked again at Luke and realized, with a shock, that had the child been old enough, he would now be requiring his own uncle to select seconds. Hillary Pendragon was a perceptive man, and he understood that he had made an awful, perhaps a fatal, mistake in dealing with Sarah and Luke. Retracing his steps as best he could he began again.

"Luke, Sarah, I have only just come into Devonshire, and perhaps I am judging things too quickly." And in dead seriousness he continued, "If I have offended you, I offer you both my most profound apologies."

The children conferred silently together for a few moments, and then they nodded, and, turning back toward Sir Hillary, Sarah began, "Uncle Hillary, we have a great secret. And if you will only take a solemn oath not to repeat any of it we will share our secret with you."

Hillary was offended. "But surely you realize that I am no talebearer."

"Yes, but this is a particularly *important* secret," Sarah persisted.

"Very well then, children, I agree," and Hillary Pendragon found himself taking a solemn oath accompanied by all the formality and ritual with which children endow such procedures.

"And now that you two scamps have me about to expire from curiosity, out with it."

They burst into speech, Luke first. "You have, of course, been judging by mere appearance, and so you will be very surprised, but we have at last found a friend who understands us."

"*I* understand you."

"Oh, you *are* grand, Uncle Hillary, and you understand a *great* deal, but you do not understand about our work and our dreams and our own private wonder world. Miss Gorham understands all of that," Sarah announced breathlessly.

"Miss Gorham!"

"Yes, we run away from here and meet with her very secretly, and she is the most gentle, the most loving, the most noble person we have ever met. I can assure you she is," Sarah continued.

"And Miss Gorham would never whip us or read us silly sermons," Luke added.

They seemed almost too excited, and Hillary answered in a very calm voice, "She whips the Pemmrington children, Luke. You cannot deny it."

Sarah bit her underlip and tried to explain. "She punishes them, and that is quite different. They *deserve* it, you see. Miss Gorham never whips just to be whipping or because she is in a bad temper with the world or because someone else has been pushing her about. And she never whips as if she enjoys it. There is a big difference, you see, but it is ever so hard to explain. Miss Gorham *acts* angry when she is disciplining the cousins, but you see she is never really angry,

38

like Papa, for example. In Miss Gorham's case it is *contrived,* so to speak. And she usually does not whip if she can think of some better punishment. Something that will teach one why one is wrong."

"Miss Porter would ignore us if she could. Her business here is placating Papa. And she does whip us too, you know," Luke added.

"Perhaps she is *punishing* you, as Miss Gorham does the cousins?" Sir Hillary asked.

"No, you have it all wrong. Punishing is because you are guilty, and then she would be a judge, but judges are not supposed to enjoy punishing. I can see it in Miss Porter's eyes—she enjoys hurting us."

"She hurts us with Papa there because he wants her to. He likes to watch," Luke said.

Hillary wished to say that they were exaggerating as children do, but he suspected that their description of Anthony's behavior might quite probably be accurate. Meanwhile the children continued.

"You know, if Papa suggested to Miss Gorham that she should whip us, she would turn on him and beat *him* to flinders," Sarah said proudly.

"Miss Gorham is not afraid of anyone, and that is perhaps why Father does not like her," Luke explained.

"And she reads to us from such wonderful books. We used to think that the novels by Miss Radcliffe and Madame de la Coeur— the novels we sneaked out of Miss Porter's room— were grand, but Miss Gorham has explained that those novels were all claptrap. Miss Gorham reads to us from Keats and from Homer and from Shakespeare."

"And not to forget Swift, and Fielding, and those fellows, Sarah. Tell Uncle Hillary about them."

"There are so many really splendid books, Sir Hillary. And Miss Gorham *never* laughs at us or at our make-believe. She helps us at make-believe."

Luke added reverently, "She is the most beautiful lady we have ever met."

Sir Hillary did not know how to respond to this flood of information, and fortunately he was spared the necessity of any precipitate action by the arrival of Miss Porter, who had come to herd the children in to their dinner.

Hillary Pendragon remained in the garden, perplexed. Hillary accounted himself a very good judge of character, and

39

once a judgment was formed in his mind he was very reluctant to abandon it. It would be difficult to modify his opinion of Margaret Gorham.

The next morning, as Sir Hillary prepared to start for Pemmfield, the Dillingham children arrived at his door and, despite the fact that it was wide open, hesitated and then knocked tentatively.

"Good morning, brats. Come in, make yourselves comfortable." And saying this, he turned back to his chest and uncovered the gifts he had brought for Sarah and Luke.

"I had meant to get these to you yesterday. But you seemed to have disappeared directly after dinner."

"Indeed we did. We sneaked away."

"And Miss Porter did not notice."

"She was with Father," Luke said sagely, thus thoroughly explaining the matter.

"Thank you, Uncle Hillary." Sarah took the gifts from his hands. "Be certain we will hide these well. They are our very favorite bonbons, and you know we will ration them out."

"I expect they will last for weeks," Luke assured him.

Sarah had come toward him holding another package in her hand.

"What is this, Sarah?"

"Hush, it is a secret. Can you take it to Miss Gorham? We do not think we will be able to make it out today."

"I told Sarah that you might not like delivering secrets, Uncle Hillary."

Ruffling Luke's hair, Sir Hillary pocketed the package. "But child, delivering secrets is one of my professions. That is a lot of what I do for Wellington, you know, and I think I would much rather deliver secrets for you than for Wellington." And then looking out the open window he grinned. "Besides, it is such a beautiful day, is it not?"

"Oh yes," Sarah said, understanding immediately. "It is best to deliver secrets on a beautiful day."

"Precisely. Now off you go, scamps, before we are discovered."

Later that morning, after a few very trying hours in the library with Mr. Duffy, Sir Hillary reminded himself of the package. He had been asking Mr. Duffy a great many questions, and he had not received many satisfactory answers. Something was wrong, and, as he remembered the package, he remembered also that Miss Gorham had refused to handle

40

the management of the estate. Perhaps Miss Gorham had some answers. He left the library in search of the governess.

Margaret Gorham was standing and watching her charges make their way to the stables. She had, wisely, refrained from taking any part in their study of the equestrian arts, but she would, she thought, follow along later to see that the children were not unduly abusing either their horses or their instructors. Miss Gorham had learned that once children achieved a reputation as tyrants, almost all adults seem to wither away before them, thus virtually assuring that the reputation would in time become fact. Lost in thoughts of this sort, Margaret did not notice Sir Hillary approaching.

He coughed softly. "Am I disturbing you, Miss Gorham?"

She caught herself up in an instant. "No, of course not, Sir Hillary. May I be of assistance to you?"

She folded her hands and waited for his reply.

He did not reply directly but merely said, "I am walking toward the stables. Will you join me?" He waited for her nod before beginning, and they had gone several yards before he spoke.

"First, Miss Gorham, I'm afraid I have become something of a go-between for your little Dillingham friends. They have sent you a package." Margaret examined him carefully for any sign of duplicity while he forced himself to tolerate the examination.

Nodding again, Miss Gorham took the package, and they both resumed their walk. Facing forward, Sir Hillary noticed himself striding as he would normally, and he was a bit surprised to see that Miss Gorham was unobtrusively matching each of his two paces with three of her own. After his experience in the schoolroom he still found it almost impossible to accept the fact that she was not a towering woman. Resisting temptation to continue at his own pace, he forced himself to slow down to accomodate the lady.

Clearing his throat and bracing himself, he began to speak. "I suspect I have been something of a fool, Miss Gorham. Do you think we might manage to start again?" She looked and saw that he was not smiling and that in fact he seemed to make no effort to exercise his very considerable charm.

"Yes, of course, Sir Hillary."

"Yes we may start again, or yes I have been a fool?"

Margaret was quite suddenly tempted to smile herself, but, with considerable effort on her part, she maintained the rigid manner of a governess. "Both," she answered in a very level voice.

"I rather thought so." And they walked on in silence.

"I had meant to ask your advice on some matters, Miss Gorham, if you do not feel that I am intruding."

"What matters, Sir Hillary?"

"Lady Julia is quite eager for you to assume some of her responsibilities with regard to the management of the estate. She has explained that you managed the Twining lands while you were with them."

"Yes, I did."

"Might I ask what are your reservations in this case?"

"I do not know that I can or should answer that question, Sir Hillary."

"Then I will rephrase it in a less general way. I have been working with Mr. Duffy for the better part of a week, and I have come to feel that there is something very wrong at Pemmfield—perhaps in the entire neighborhood. Do you know anything about it?"

"I *know* nothing, and it would perhaps be grossly unjust for me to burden you with my opinions."

"What is unjust is to allow a situation to continue where Lady Julia and, in all likelihood, the families that depend on Pemmfield are being abused. Their welfare is my responsibility, and while I realize that you may think I take those responsibilities lightly I can assure you that I mean to get at the bottom of this matter, and I would appreciate any help I receive."

She hesitated, and he felt, for a moment, that she did not disapprove of him. "Yes, Sir Hillary, there is something almost desperately wrong, but everyone is very closed about it. I cannot know what is afoot, but I do know that many improvements charged to the estate were not made and that the tenants involved are very reluctant to draw attention to the fact that they were short-changed."

"Yes, I suspected as much. The accounts did not look plausible."

"You might call in at the home farm and speak to Mr. Fulton about the common pasturage, and while you are at it you might examine the roof at the Bateses' home and the state of the young Williamses' cottage. I think the Williamses are in particular need of help."

"Thank you, Miss Gorham."

42

"You do understand that these people are not likely to talk freely to you, Sir Hillary."

"I am a patient man, Miss Gorham. Which is fortunate, since I have no doubt that it will take time to get at the truth."

She nodded again in some sort of dismissal, and while Miss Gorham made her way into the stables, Sir Hillary continued south in the direction of the home farm.

The Fultons had always managed the farm well, and with this in mind Hillary stopped at a fence to admire the rolling fields and the carefully tended garden. There was a familiar sound of hooves to his right, and Hillary turned to notice a small stallion in the pasture adjacent to the cottage. In that setting the horse seemed a total anomaly. The animal had begun to run, and it moved with a grace totally alien to any farm horse in history. In fact, on closer examination, Hillary noticed that it could not be a gentleman's horse either. The animal seemed almost wild. Well, he thought, it will be a good lady's mount when it is gelded and broken. But it was surely a pity to break such a magnificent animal. Still, a horse running wild was of no use to anyone. Slowly and with some reluctance, Hillary Pendragon turned from the pasture and made his way toward the cottage.

Mrs. Fulton welcomed him with a mug of cocoa and some treats from the oven while she sent her youngest son out in search of his father. The youngster, about ten, bowed to Sir Hillary and went tearing out of the house to return within a quarter of an hour with his father and his eighteen-year-old brother.

"Good afternoon, Fulton. I have come to see how you are doing." And so Sir Hillary began the infinitely delicate process of drawing the farmer into his confidence. He refrained from asking any direct questions so as not to strain that confidence, but an hour later, after having discussed the weather, the crops, and the status of the Peninsular Wars, Sir Hillary had come into command of several interesting facts about the bailiff. The tenants' rights to the common pasturage were not being scrupulously honored, but on the other hand Mr. Duffy seemed to be so inordinately feared that even Mr. Fulton could not be brought to make a veiled accusation.

After again thanking Mrs. Fulton for her excellent pastries, Sir Hillary took his leave. He was accompanied to the gate by the eldest son, and as they were passing the pasture Sir Hillary asked about the horse.

"That's a good horse you have there, Tim. Is is yours?"

The boy had stiffened when Sir Hillary stopped to question him and then seemed relieved that the question was merely about the animal.

"No, sir, 'taint our horse. Fact is I sometimes think that he ain't no horse atall maybe it's people or t'other way around."

"Then you are boarding the animal?"

"Aye."

"You might mention to the owner that I would be interested in purchasing the mount. He is, of course, too slight for me but would make an excellent lady's mount when broken."

There was a ghost of a smile in the young man's respectful response. "Beggin' your pardon, sir, but I don't think the owner would sell. Don't want the animal broken, you see."

"Good Lord, you don't mean it is always allowed to run free. Will it never be ridden?"

The boy's face had closed. "Him *is* ridden, sir. And I'll tell the owner what you said." Bowing low, Tim opened the gate for Sir Hillary to pass through.

Hillary Pendragon spent the balance of the afternoon visiting other farms and discovering, as he had feared, that the charges in the books were seldom reflected by improvements in the farms. In particular, the Bateses' roof had not been repaired and the Williamses were still in need of a cow, although their young child seemed on the verge of starvation. After sending young Williams out with the money for a milk cow, Sir Hillary excused himself and returned very slowly to the manor house. Secluded in the library, he spent the next few hours reexamining the books and deciding on his next course of action with respect to Mr. Duffy. And then, very quietly, he left Pemmfield so as to avoid the expected arrival of the Campbell sisters. Hillary Pendragon needed time to think, and to pay the necessary court to Gwendolyn Campbell definitely would interfere with that process.

Hillary mounted his horse, but did not return to Dillingham Hall. Instead he spent most of the night riding about the moors and the crests of the hills overlooking the sea. He had become convinced that the problems at Pemmfield were not simply limited to the petty and cruel embezzlement he had so far uncovered. The air was thick with suppressed fear and suspicion, and thus far Sir Hillary Pendragon had succeeded in uncovering only the tip of an iceberg.

Chapter 5

The Campbell sisters had arrived very late at night, and so it was with particular interest that Miss Gorham came into the breakfast room the next morning.

There was only one other person in the room—a very young lady. Margaret estimated her age at somewhere in the vicinity of eighteen, and as she was pretty rather than beautiful, and blond rather than red-haired, Miss Gorham concluded that this must be the younger of the two sisters—the gentle Alicia. Margaret took her seat and smiled at her prospective heroine.

"You must be Miss Gorham. I am Alicia Campbell. I do not mean to be forward in introducing myself, but I cannot think it would be sensible for us to continue through breakfast with no conversation." Having quickly gotten through the introductions and the apology, Miss Alicia Campbell colored and looked down shyly.

As there were no men present, it appeared to Margaret that the child's maidenly reserve was not contrived but truly a part of her nature.

"I am very pleased to meet you, Miss Campbell. And how was your journey into Devonshire?"

"I thought it was grand. This time of year the scent in the air and the colors in the field are so very beautiful."

As she spoke Margaret noticed her open countenance and pleasant soft blue eyes.

Julia had come into the room, and, trilling a welcome to the younger women, she selected the meagerest of breakfasts from the sideboard.

"Good morning Miss Gorham. Good morning, Alicia. How very pleasant it is to have company, don't you think?"

"It is so good to be here. Do you realize, Cousin Julia, that

I have never been into Devonshire before? And it is such splendid country."

Margaret smiled at Alicia Campbell. "Yes, Miss Campbell, it is a beautiful part of England, particularly in the spring and summer."

"Pooh, the two of you are hopelessly rustic. Daffodils be demned, *I* shall always prefer the bustle of London." Julia sipped her chocolate a moment before adding, "By the by, Alicia, how is your sister this morning?"

"Gwen, oh yes. Well, she did have something of a migraine, but I think your medicine will help, Cousin Julia, and she will be perfection as always in a few hours."

"I expect Gwen was not near so impressed with a two-day carriage ride and our beautiful countryside as you were, Alicia."

"Gwen has had a great deal more experience. She is *always* going off to very exciting places, and I think that is why the traveling has grown somewhat tedious."

Margaret grew more and more curious. "If Miss Campbell is ill this morning, perhaps I can help. I have had, in my professional work, extensive experience with migraines."

"Oh no! But thank you. The migraine, you see, was last night. It is just that Gwen does not like to be disturbed in the morning; she is not an early riser and is never at her best before breakfast."

Lady Julia understood. "Then I will have her chocolate sent up to her at eleven, and meanwhile we will have a pleasant coze, you and I. I know you will have a perfectly splendid visit, Alicia."

"Oh yes, I am quite certain I will." And then her face flamed and she lowered her eyes quickly. The girl, Margaret thought, has the look of someone in love. I wonder with whom. She is much too pleasant for the Dillinghams and I think a trifle simple for Sir Hillary, who in any case seems almost to be plighted to the sleeping beauty with the migraine.

Having also noticed Alicia's discomfort, Lady Julia turned the conversation to the subject of the dinner that evening, when the entire Dillingham ménage, together with Sir Hillary, was scheduled to descend on Pemmfield.

"Now I must be finishing my breakfast. I declare there is so much worry to a dinner when my Aunt Dillingham is invited. I shall be mortified if cook prepares something *too* French."

Margaret smiled openly. "I believe we have cook totally

aware of the dangers. And you must know that all the other particulars have already been attended to. Perhaps you and Miss Alicia will gather the flowers for the decorations while the morning is still cool and the children are having their lessons."

"Yes, as always, Miss Gorham, you are quite right. Come into the garden, Alicia, and we will have our coze."

Miss Gorham watched them leave and made her way to the schoolroom.

Margaret did not meet Gwendolyn until they had all assembled in the blue saloon to welcome the Dillinghams. There was scarcely time for lengthy discussion, but again Margaret was amazed at the gracefulness of Julia's introduction and explanations, especially as they pertained to the governess's presence at dinner.

Miss Gorham had only a few moments to admire and to study the ravishing Miss Campbell before the Dillinghams were announced and Lady Augusta, followed by her husband and younger son, sailed into the room. With only a nod to her hostess, Lady Augusta, an awesome vision in chartreuse taffeta, made directly for Gwendolyn Campbell.

"My dearest Gwendolyn. I should have known you anywhere, anywhere at all. You are so like your mother, don't you know? You have her fine red hair and splendid features. We were so distracted to hear of her untimely death. I understand she succumbed after a protracted painful sort of disease. So disagreeable, don't you think, for a woman scarcely in her prime? As I had told her countless times while we were girls together"—an exaggeration, since Augusta was at the least ten years the senior of the late Mrs. Campbell—"'Elizabeth,' I would say, 'you must not eat eggs—eggs are very bad for the digestion.' If only she had listened."

Miss Campbell had managed half the eccentric old ladies in the ton and did not so much as blink an eyelash. "She did, you know. Mother never ate eggs." Gwendolyn continued smoothly, "Her abstinence seems, however, to have had no beneficial effect on the progress of her disease."

Unabashed, Augusta Dillingham said, "Oh, but I am certain it did. I am convinced she would have died much more swiftly had she eaten eggs," and then, with barely a break, "Ah, here are the stragglers—my son Anthony and my nephew Sir Hillary Pendragon. I believe you may know them both. Are they not two of the handsomest men in England?"

"Indubitably," Gwendolyn said as she looked up into Sir Hillary's gray eyes and returned him a smile which illuminated her own Titianesque beauty.

Augusta peered about her. "Julia should be here to make the introductions. I declare that woman does not seem to be capable of managing anything. There you are, Julia. Do come here this instant."

Lady Julia arrived and made the introductions, although it was quite clear that Gwendolyn required no introduction to Sir Hillary or to the Dillingham sons. While Gwendolyn continued to smile up into Hillary Pendragon's eyes, Lady Augusta launched into merciless attack on Lady Julia's ability to manage a dinner in such a way as not to poison half the delicate digestions of the Dillingham family.

Julia cast a mute look of entreaty in the direction of the governess, and Miss Gorham, rising slowly out of her chair in the corner, moved to intervene and distract Lady Augusta before the evening was hopelessly ruined.

"Lady Augusta, I do not mean to interrupt, but I have been most anxious to ask your opinion of a rash which young Richard seems to have acquired."

"A rash, did you say?"

"Yes, a rather nasty sort of rash, and we are all in a quandary about what to do. I should like your advice on the possible treatment of the infection."

Having launched Lady Augusta on the subject of allergies, infections, and plagues, Miss Gorham was able to relieve the pressure on the other members of the party while simultaneously remaining quite observant herself.

Gwen had moved cautiously away from Sir Anthony and laid a hand on Sir Hillary's arm. She led him away from the others, and they were speaking privately.

"It is good to see you again, Hillary. I have missed you."

"Of course, my dear. I have missed you as well. Let me see, it has been almost a week."

She chuckled. "A week can be a *very* long time. But now I have found you, have I not?"

"And my Cousin Anthony as well."

"Ah, yes, Anthony, the second-handsomest man in all of England. Is Lady Augusta always so outspoken? Thank goodness for the brown little governess."

"My aunt, dear Gwendolyn, is an original."

"Now I have got your back up, and I did not mean to."

They were interrupted by the call to dinner, and Sir Hillary offered Gwendolyn the arm she had already appropriated.

Gwendolyn was seated between Sir Anthony and Sir Hillary, thus advancing the fond hopes of both Lady Augusta and Lady Julia. Margaret noted that Anthony was regarding the prize with something more than his usual glance of predatory lust and was probably captivated not only by her beauty but also by her anticipated fortune. Meanwhile Claude was busily conversing with both Lady Julia and Alicia Campbell. Margaret had never seen him so voluble. *He* was enjoying the evening. Alicia Campbell seemed a trifle perplexed—or was it withdrawn? In any case, it seemed certain that the light of her life was not seated at the table that evening.

"Hillary," Gwendolyn was saying, her voice carrying clearly, "I have just heard of your infamous duel with Marchpane. I wonder, is your family familiar with the particulars?"

The colonel, temporarily coming out of his wineglass, asked, "What is this? What sort of dueling have you been up to, my boy?"

Augusta spoke from the other end of the table. "A duel, Hillary! I must say you are leading a very *dangerous* existence. If I had been your mother I should never have allowed you to pursue such a *ruinous* course."

"Fortunately you are my aunt. And it was not a very dangerous duel."

"No indeed," Julia added. "Hillary says that Marchpane was so far gone that he could not remain standing and fell forward in a drunken faint at the count of ten."

"Surely it would have been more romantic to have winged him." Gwen sighed.

"My little bloodthirsty Gwen, I cannot think it at all romantic to wound a poor old fellow engaged in the effort to protect his wife's honor."

"Particularly," Anthony added, "when our Hillary was not at all interested in the charms of the wife."

Alicia had colored up again and was staring at her plate when her sister glanced at her. "Anthony, I believe we may have offended the maidenly sensibilities of my shy sister."

"No, no, I am not offended, Gwen. We all knew of the duel, although I had not expected it to be discussed quite so openly."

"My poor little sister. But be assured that your confusion is entirely charming, is it not, Anthony?"

"She is your sister and could be naught but charming, Gwendolyn. And Alicia has made a good point, you know.

Miss Gorham, at the least, seems disapproving of such openness at the dinner table. I'm afraid my Cousin Hillary's pursuits are often a trifle too colored for such a proper governess."

"Mr. Dillingham, I appreciate your concern, but I can assure you that I do not, by my presence, wish to restrict the conversation at the table. I should not think of intruding my own values on the gathering of your family, nor is my propriety deeply offended by the recitation of an occasional quaint anecdote."

Julia gurgled, "I believe Miss Gorham is telling us that we may all proceed to be quite as wicked as we wish. She will not take the cane to us."

"And *I* agree with Miss Gorham and with Miss Alicia Campbell," Lady Augusta boomed. "I cannot approve of loose conduct at the table."

The dinner was completed in relative silence except for the flow of pleasant conversation maintained by Lady Julia and Claude Dillingham. Margaret saw Miss Gwendolyn direct several excessively melting looks at Sir Hillary. But this was a very minor sort of transgression and Margaret was genuinely disappointed that the dinner would provide no more colorful incidents she could store up for use in her novels.

Eventually the dinner was over, the gentlemen were left to their port, and the ladies had assembled in the blue saloon. Lady Augusta seemed still to be captivated by the subject of Richard's rash, and although the lady had a hypochondriac's fear of infection she had worked herself into such a pitch of involvement that she insisted on waking her grandnephew to examine his condition. Margaret Gorham could not immediately agree to this scheme but was eventually reconciled to the notion that the examination, in putting an end to the discussion, might be the lesser of two evils.

Miss Gorham and Lady Augusta excused themselves from the room and went up the stairs to waken Richard from his deep and peaceful sleep so that he could be picked and pulled at until his great-aunt was convinced that she had determined the full extent of the plague.

Without bothering to lower her voice, Lady Augusta began her diagnosis.

"I have seen it before. I know what it is, Miss Gorham. *I* understand these things."

Young Richard, with Margaret seated beside him, waited while Lady Augusta drew herself up. "There is no shadow of a doubt in my mind. Young Richard has contracted the ring-worm."

Margaret had placed a calm hand on the boy's shoulder, at least in part to silence him. "Ringworm! But that is very unlikely. You must know that Richard does not take to either dogs or cats."

"Miss Gorham, do you doubt my judgment? I tell you Richard has been into some sort of mischief and has gotten himself a head full of ringworm. But if you do not believe me, go and fetch Hillary. He has traveled all over the world and he has become acquainted with all sorts of very exotic diseases. Hillary will confirm me in my diagnosis."

Hiding a smile, Miss Gorham returned to the blue saloon to "fetch" Sir Hillary, and she found him smiling fondly into the eyes of Miss Gwendolyn Campbell. They made a stunning couple and Margaret was most reluctant to interrupt the tête-à-tête, but she forced herself to cough discreetly and wait.

Gwendolyn was the first to notice Miss Gorham's existence, and tearing her turquoise eyes from Sir Hillary she turned to the governess with something less than sweetness in her expression. "Yes, Miss Gorham, you wished something?"

"Lady Augusta has requested Sir Hillary's presence in the nursery. She wishes him to examine young Richard's rash."

"Certainly it can wait." Gwendolyn was pouting.

Hillary patted Gwendolyn caressingly on the shoulder and turned to Miss Gorham. "My aunt asked you to fetch me, did she, Miss Gorham?"

"Those were her precise words, Sir Hillary."

"Well, I delay only at my own peril. Shall we get it over with, Miss Gorham?" And bowing low to Miss Campbell he followed Margaret out of the room.

They were halfway up the stairs before he began to speak. "Do you suppose it is dreadfully contagious? Will my aunt have us all placed in quarantine?"

With difficulty Margaret suppressed a smile. "I do not think that levity is an entirely appropriate response to the situation. Your aunt is convinced that the child has ring-worm, and I am equally convinced that he does not have ringworm."

"And you, Miss Gorham, are graciously offering me the alternative of antagonizing either my aunt or yourself. I begin to believe that Sir Hillary, and not Master Richard, will be the true victim of this disease. I would not give myself odds against either of you two ladies."

"Nonsense. I have great faith that you will be able to charm your aunt into accepting the obvious."

"I had better be able to charm my aunt, hadn't I? Charm is wasted on you, is it not?"

"Thank you."

Sir Hillary, who had not been aware that he had been advancing a compliment, remained silent until they reached the nursery.

They arrived to find Lady Augusta sitting in the light of a single candle staring grimly at the hapless Richard.

"I have come, my dearest Aunt Augusta, to humbly offer you my services. What is the problem?"

"It is young Richard here. He has been up to all sorts of mischief, as usual. I declare I don't know how Julia can let them all run about so. Richard has gotten into something and contracted ringworm, and soon the whole household will be infested. Come, Hillary, and have a look for yourself."

Sir Hillary held the candle and examined Richard's head with a great show of care for several very long minutes. "Are you quite convinced it is ringworm, my dear aunt?"

"It is sure to be either ringworm or some sort of exotic disease that I feel certain *you* will be able to recognize from your travels. What is your opinion, Hillary?"

Hillary rubbed his chin and studied the matter silently for several moments, during which time he managed to smuggle the child a very conspiratorial wink accompanied by a comforting grin. "No, Augusta, I do not *think* it can be ringworm. I have seen a rash like this only once before—in the Sultan's harem in Tunisia when one of the most favored wives brought her child to me. By the by, I shall tell you about the Sultan's harem in in Tunisia sometime. The conditions there were deplorable. In any case, the young woman brought me her infant and told me of his disease. I believe our Richard is suffering from the same ailment—a rare form of childhood leprosy."

"Leprosy, did you say leprosy?" Augusta asked, stunned for the moment until she began to examine the fascinating clinical possibilities.

Miss Gorham spoke in a very level voice. "And what, Sir Hillary, do you recommend for the treatment of childhood leprosy—soap and water?"

"Only in moderation, Miss Gorham, only in moderation."

And then, ruffling Richard's hair, he continued, "Almost all children recover in a day or two."

As Lady Augusta had already sailed from the room she was not present to hear the optimistic prognosis.

"Oh, fudge, Uncle Hillary. Did you *have* to tell Aunt Augusta such a plumper? Now she has run down to inform all of Devonshire that Richard Pemmrington is a leper."

"True, and I expect she will then abandon the rest of us and take the carriage. We shall all have to walk back to Dillingham Hall."

"What a coil it has become, Uncle Hillary."

Miss Gorham spoke quietly. "Hush, Richard. Not to worry. I am certain your Uncle Hillary will be able to reassure Lady Augusta. No one will think you a leper."

"You will protect me, won't you, Miss Gorham? It is only a very little sort of rash, after all."

"It is scarcely a rash at all, and, Master Richard, you have my apology. I was seeking only to distract your great-aunt when I introduced your rash into the conversation. I did not anticipate such very nasty complications."

Hillary was taken aback both by the apology and the tone in which it was delivered, but young Richard seemed to take both perfectly in stride. "Oh, no need for you to feel badly, Miss Gorham. None of us can ever anticipate what Aunt Augusta is likely to do, and we have been living with her forever, have we not, Uncle Hillary?"

"At least that long, Richard." His uncle smiled.

Miss Gorham was fluffing up the pillows when the child, who had begun to fret, spoke again. "The thing is, though, that I think leprosy is rather close to the truth."

"Good God, why?" his uncle asked.

"It's because of my sins, you see. I read in the Bible that God punished people for their sins by making them lepers. You do know, Miss Gorham, why I have this plaguey thing?"

Margaret had stopped and looked at young Richard very slowly. "No, I don't know, Richard. Why don't you tell me?"

She had loosed a torrent. "I have this rash—I expect it will never go away—because of how very cruel I was to Jamey Tate. I know now how wrong I was. Mrs. Tate works so hard to keep him, and he is not a bad sort of boy, only different, you know. He has a wonderful way with animals. But Jamey is always so frightened because people call him names and throw things at him, and if I were Jamey I would be terrified as well. And I was as bad as all the rest of them. God has punished me with this rash, don't you see."

Margaret Gorham took the child by his shoulders and looked into his eyes before speaking. "You know I would not lie to you, Richard."

"Of course, Miss Gorham."

"Then here is the truth, as I see it. You have seen that you did something that was less than noble, and you have made a restitution. If you wish to make up for being cruel to Jamey, all you need to do is make a particular effort to be kind to him and to be kind to all the other Jamey Tates of this world. I think that Jamey has already forgiven you. Hasn't he?"

Richard nodded. "Jamey has, but will God?"

"I'm quite certain that in a situation such as this, God will forgive you as well. And besides, Richard, my dear child, if we were all to get rashes to mark us for our sins, we would all of us begin to look like strawberries in waistcoats. Rest easy, Richard, the rash will pass."

"If you say so, Miss Gorham." The child still seemed doubtful.

"Yes, and I say so as well, Dick, and I have had all sorts of experiences with exotic tropical diseases," Sir Hillary said, touseling him. "Now do you think you will be able to get back to sleep, or shall we send nurse up with some milk?"

"I am *not* a baby, Uncle Hillary."

"No, of course not, you are my Richard the Lion-Hearted. I could not want a better ward, but you know Miss Gorham and I have to go down and mend the damage I have wrought before Lady Augusta pronounces all of Pemmfield a leper colony."

Margaret tucked young Richard into his blankets and then preceded Sir Hillary through the door.

He caught up with her and began to speak. "You have my thanks, Miss Gorham. I am coming to understand why Lady Julia places such faith in your abilities with the children."

"You exaggerate, Sir Hillary. It was you who finally turned his mind from the problem."

"Yes—the nurse-and-warm-milk gambit always takes the trick, don't you think?"

"Almost invariably."

"I shall also, while I'm at it, thank you for the help you rendered me yesterday. I have dismissed Duffy and have be-

54

gun remedying the worst of it. Have you any suggestions for a replacement as bailiff?"

She stopped and hesitated before answering. "William Paul's oldest son is rather bookish and very competent. I believe he might make an excellent bailiff."

"What, is John Paul back from the wars?"

"Just since I have arrived. He was wounded and discharged."

"I've never met the boy, but the Pauls are a good family."

She hesitated and looked up at him quizzically. "Did you not know that his father, William Paul, has been transported for poaching?"

"William Paul transported! He was Scott's most honest tenant."

"So Lady Julia assured me. I had just arrived and did not feel competent to intervene, but Lady Julia went to the authorities and pleaded in his behalf."

"And?"

"And they would not listen. . . . She wrote to you about the matter, did she not?"

"Yes, I recall it now. She wrote that one of her tenants was being transported for poaching, but she did not mention the name. I can assure you, had she explained that it was William Paul, I would have come into Devonshire to investigate."

"Then you will not be holding the son accountable for the sins of the father."

"I shall, of course, have to ascertain that the son is not so very bitter as to preclude his acting as bailiff. But I will, at the same time, investigate the whole matter. I cannot think William Paul could have so disintegrated since I saw him last to warrent being transported."

And then, after another few moments lost in thought, he asked, "Will you be willing to work with Mr. Paul and take over some of Lady Julia's responsibilities in the management of the estate?"

For the first time she glanced away from him. "I should be happy to do so, so long as I remain at Pemmfield, Sir Hillary. But I would be less than honest if I did not explain that I am unlikely to stay here long."

"I see. What have I done to offend you now?"

He looked so artificially woebegone that she was sorely tempted to chuckle, but again she restrained herself. "I can assure you, Sir Hillary, that it is nothing anyone has done.

I have a professional history of not remaining at any post for more than six or eight months."

"Miss Gorham, I would never have taken you for a *flighty* person."

Ignoring his sally, she continued, "I am a person of some talent, Sir Hillary. And my particular forte is organization. Once a household is organized and running efficiently, I tend to seek other positions where my talents will be more fully exploited." She had turned and was not looking at him at all.

"But then there is a chance you will stay at Pemmfield."

"A very small chance," and, biting her lip, she continued, "You see, I have recently come into a modest income of sorts and I am considering retiring entirely from the profession of governess."

Hillary, sensing that, for some cause or other, Miss Gorham was finally in less than perfect command of herself, continued, "Well, I think you ought to give us a chance, Miss Gorham."

"Yes, I might stay, but you see, it would contradict the patterns of years."

Hillary grinned. "And it has been so *many* years, Miss Gorham, that I suppose we must bow to your very *mature* judgment in these matters."

The point was not lost on Margaret, and she rallied, answering with her hands firmly folded before her and her eyes meeting Sir Hillary's, "True, Sir Hillary. I was most fortunate to have achieved an early and solid maturity of character."

"And you are implying, Miss Gorham—I believe I have learned to read your character—that I have not achieved the same maturity of character."

She remained silent, and he continued, "But surely I can claim *some* maturity for my years. Might I remind you, Miss Gorham, that it is not the act of a very young man to be a trusted assistant for Wellington himself, nor is it the act of a very young man to engage in duels with a marksman of Marchpane's skill."

She smiled smugly. "Perhaps that is so, Sir Hillary. But surely it is the act of a very young man to *boast* of such things," and, turning to hide the twinkle of triumph in her eyes, Margaret continued down the hall.

Lost in pleasant thoughts, she found herself suddenly almost colliding with something, and looked up to find her way barred by Anthony Dillingham.

"Ah, Miss Gorham. I have come in search of the child leper.

And, by the by, where have you sequestered my Cousin Hillary?"

"If you proceed down this hallway, Mr. Dillingham, you will encounter both. But I pray you do not wake the child."

"Oh, but I am not at all certain I wish to proceed now, my dear Miss Gorham." His breath, Margaret noticed, reeked of alcohol.

She stared straight at him, her eyes barely veiling her contempt. "I am waiting, Mr. Dillingham, for you to stand aside."

"You know, somewhere I have got the notion that you do not like me, Miss Gorham. I can assure you that it would be to your advantage to overcome those feelings."

Sir Hillary had arrived to hear this last. "Come along, Anthony. We have got to dispel these rumors of childhood leprosy."

With something less than grace, Anthony joined Sir Hillary, and they continued down toward the saloon while Margaret turned toward her own rooms.

"Selfish Cousin Hillary. You had the bitchy little governess all to yourself. Must share, you know. I'll offer to share *my* governess."

Hillary placed a hand on his cousin's shoulder. "My dear Cousin Anthony, pray mind your tongue. I should hate to have to face another duel until you are quite sober. Now let us return to the blue saloon, where we can both flirt with the fair Gwendolyn."

Chapter 6

The next morning, while Margaret was engaged in her duties as governess, the other ladies had assembled in the small drawing room and were entertaining Sir Hillary and Mr. Anthony Dillingham. Both those gentlemen made their appearance precisely at eleven—the one, Sir Hillary, to visit and to continue his work on the accounts, and the other, Mr.

Dillingham, to visit and to further his acquaintance with Miss Gwendolyn Campbell.

The light sound of Lady Julia's laughter filled the room. "Hillary, you should not have, you really should not have begun that farradiddle on childhood leprosy," she scolded while continuing to chuckle. "We shall *never* hear the end of it."

"Au contraire, my dear Julia. I have spent the entire morning in a state of abject repentance prostrate at the feet of our Aunt Augusta. I have apologized and debased myself to such an extent that, I might add, I am totally exhausted by my efforts."

"To be sure you are, Hillary." Gwendolyn smiled. "And of course, Lady Augusta, being a member of the weaker sex, could not resist your blandishments and she has granted you a pardon. Hillary, you are quite incorrigible!" And placing her hand on his arm, drew him slightly away from the others.

"Am I, Gwendolyn?" he asked.

"Quite incorrigible."

"Nonsense. I merely play my part. Most ladies of my acquaintance *choose* to be offended simply for the joy of granting such pardons. It is something of a mockery, is it not, Gwendolyn?"

"All of life is a mockery, Hillary. We play, as much as possible, by the rules and hope to win."

"Perhaps, Gwendolyn, but have pity for me at least, for I am as much a victim of the situation, perhaps more so, than any of those very forgiving ladies," he answered quite seriously.

"Now you *are* being very silly, dearest Hillary. Are you expecting the world to sympathize with the plight of poor Prince Charming?"

"But I am not Prince Charming, am I? That prince, if I remember correctly, had only to kiss a single princess once, while it seems that I am destined to repeat the role for a lifetime."

Gwendolyn Campbell ran a finger along his arm. "Ah, but from choice, Hillary, from choice. How many of us, myself included, would relieve you of the role of suitor and confer on you the role of husband?"

"And then, of course, Gwendolyn, I should not need to charm you—my money would provide charms sufficient. No, I prefer liberty even when it grows tiresome." He very gently freed himself.

"To a woman with a fortune of her own, your wealth is not your single greatest asset, you know. And *I*, as your wife, would never attempt to curtail your liberty."

"No, Gwendolyn, I don't believe you would," he said, looking down at her good-naturedly. "And here I have begun to fancy a wife who would murder me if I so much as looked at another woman." And then, with his usual disarming grace which nevertheless put an end to the conversation, "Come, let us rejoin the others, or we will be accused of being dreadfully exclusive."

Lady Julia and Alicia, with Anthony's unenthusiastic help, were discussing plans for the entertainment of the houseparty. "You must know, Hillary, that Gwendolyn is accustomed to a great deal of excitement, and I believe the country may become dull for her. It has certainly become dull for me, and it is my home. You and Anthony are enjoined to entertain us."

"But I have come into Devonshire to work, Julia."

"And we shall not need a *great* deal of entertainment, Cousin Julia. My sister Alicia has plans for occupying herself picking cucumbers or some such thing. So droll, is it not?"

"No, no, we cannot pick cucumbers! At least not as yet, Gwen. They have not even set fruit yet," Alicia answered without any hint of the sarcasm which dripped from her sister's lips.

Gwendolyn laughed at her. "Behold before you a damsel London born and bred. My dearest sister, wherever did you learn so much about cucumbers?"

Alicia looked down, confused. "You know, Gwen, I have always loved the country. I believe I should *prefer* to live in the country."

Before Gwendolyn could answer, Sir Hillary, with his natural chivalry toward any woman in distress, intervened. "Of course you should. *Everyone* would like to live in the country sometimes. How often I feel confined in London."

Alicia looked up eagerly. "Then you *do* understand. Thank you, Sir Hillary. Gwendolyn prefers a life of activity and sophistication, but I'm afraid I'm not very bright and I don't have a fortune and of course I'm not beautiful. I'm afraid that all and all I'm not very ambitious either." Hillary looked for coyness in her glance and saw none.

"Nor should you be ambitious, my dear," Julia said wisely. "Silly women usually do very well for themselves. I know because I am myself excessively silly but I have always found someone to take care of me. There was my dear papa and then dear Scott, and when I lost Scott, Hillary came to manage my affairs. And now I have found great support in Miss Gorham." She sighed. "Had I not lost my Scott I would have had the best of lives.... On the other hand, I don't believe I could have managed at all if I had been blessed with brilliance, beauty, *and* a fortune. It must be quite *exhausting*, Gwendolyn."

"I shall contrive, Julia. But tell me, do you seriously compare Miss Gorham, a mere governess, to Sir Scott and Sir Hillary?"

Anthony, who had remained relatively silent, smiled. "And Miss Gorham is not merely a governess, she is a dour Friday-faced governess—the worst sort."

Julia took a moment to answer. "Hillary agrees with both of you, but I think you are wrong. Miss Gorham is not very expressive, to be sure, but she *is* dependable and in her own way, very kind. She has been most helpful, of course, but she is also a very good listener, and when I am terribly discouraged Miss Gorham always has wise words of encouragement."

Anthony countered, "And you, dear Julia, are a great innocent. Margaret Gorham is a martinet—a dictator—a woman totally immune to any opinion save her own."

"But you do not understand her well, Anthony. Nor do you, Gwen," Lady Julia persisted. "It *cannot* be pleasant for a gentlewoman to be forced into a situation so very near servitude."

"True, Julia," Gwendolyn said. "Still, *I* would in your place find it very depressing to have a dried-up prune of a woman wandering about the place. Your Miss Gorham gives me the chill. Such rigidity of character seems almost unnatural."

Hillary, who was finding the conversation decidedly unpleasant, intervened to make an end. "Margaret Gorham is from Yorkshire, and, given the climate in Yorkshire, I think that such sternness of character is entirely natural and even appropriate."

Everyone chuckled except Alicia, who seemed suddenly caught up in thought. "Is Margaret Gorham from Yorkshire?"

"I have just said as much, my child." Hillary smiled.

"Oh, she must be *another* Margaret Gorham." Although the others were ignoring her, she saw the confusion in Sir Hillary's eyes and continued, "You see, I have a friend from Yorkshire who grew up with a Margaret Gorham, but it cannot be the same one." As they were both at that moment asked for their opinion of an excursion into Exeter, the subject of Margaret Gorham was finally laid to rest.

After leaving Anthony to the ladies and completing some work in the library, Sir Hillary set out in search of Mr. Paul's oldest son. He had never actually met the boy, but he did not anticipate any difficulty in arranging a meeting. In this, Sir Hillary was quite mistaken.

No sooner had he opened the gate to the very shabby cottage than Mrs. Paul met him and barred his way with a combination of blinding hostility and ashen-faced fear. No one was going to talk to her son John. John knew nothing. They had already taken her husband, wasn't that enough?

Hillary, who had had a great deal of experience with genuine hysteria in the war, recognized the symptoms and realized that it would be quite futile to try to convince the woman to cooperate. Soothing her as best he could, he excused himself and returned to the manor house, where he mentioned Mr. Paul, very casually, to Julia over tea.

"You know it was quite queer, that whole thing, Hillary. I remember Mr. Paul as being a very good man. Scott used to say that next to Mr. Fulton he was the best man at Pemmfield, and he was perhaps the most honest. I think that the colonel was being excessive in transporting him, and in fact Miss Gorham and I went over to speak to him about the whole matter. But he pooh-poohed us, as men are wont to do women, and we were able to accomplish nothing."

The next morning while the children were at the stables, Hillary sought out Margaret Gorham.

"I have decided, Miss Gorham, not to involve you in the management of the estate."

"Why?" she asked.

"I made an attempt yesterday to meet with John Paul. His mother's almost hysterical reaction has convinced me that the unraveling of the mystery at Pemmfield may not only be difficult but also dangerous."

Miss Gorham did not seem either surprised or nonplussed by the harshness of his remarks. She sat pensively for a few moments, her face the mask it had almost always been in his presence.

"No, Sir Hillary, it is not a happy community. And the two natural leaders of the community have been silenced, have they not? Mr. Paul has been transported and Mr. Fulton has withdrawn almost entirely from day-to-day intercourse with the manor house."

"Does John Paul know the cause of the fearfulness?"

"I have spent some time with John Paul. They don't quite trust him, you know, because he is bookish and his education has set him apart, but he is not a coward and I believe he knows and can learn a great deal more than we."

"How old is he?"

"I don't know. I believe he is in his early twenties. He comes to lecture the children on botany from time to time. Perhaps I can arrange a meeting for you with Mr. Paul."

"I should prefer it if you didn't. I repeat myself, but I must be quite certain you will not become directly involved in this investigation. It is not woman's work. I thank you for your assistance heretofore, but until this matter is resolved, it will be my responsibility and my responsibility alone. Do I make myself clear, Miss Gorham?"

"You have made yourself quite clear, Sir Hillary." Margaret Gorham drew herself up to her full height, and there was a glimmer of hostility in her eyes as she swept from the room.

In something of an evil humor, Sir Hillary left Pemmfield and made his way into the village, where he stopped at the local inn to have a light luncheon and to gather some additional information. He returned to Dillingham Hall early in the afternoon and had just sequestered himself in the library when he saw a familiar and very welcome figure on horseback coming up the drive. Sir Hillary left the library, and met his young friend Robert Mansfield coming up the stairs to the main entrance.

"Damned if you aren't a sight for sore eyes, Robbie my boy—a civilized face in the wilderness."

"Lord, I've been accused of a great many things, Hil, but never before has anyone thought to call me civilized. Devonshire must be a very strange place." The younger man looked up with a species of worship in his eyes, and Hillary returned a look of great affection. They had between them managed a number of very daring situations, and having worked together for over a year, largely behind enemy lines, they had forged a kind of closeness rarely experienced between men in peacetime. In fact, before Robert Mansfield's advent, Sir Hillary had preferred to work alone, but this staid, russet-haired, relatively pedestrian product of Yorkshire had, from the beginning, been able to play a quiet but perfect second to Sir Hillary Pendragon.

Half an hour later both men were settled in the minuscule library with the door shut firm and a bottle of brandy between them. After a dilatory sort of exchange of pleasantries Hillary looked up and locked eyes with Mr. Mansfield "You must know that I dote on your company, Robbie—truly I do—but I have been wondering this past week or two why you decided to follow me into Devonshire."

Hillary was more than a little surprised by the younger man's obvious confusion.

"By God, it isn't a woman, is it, Robbie?"

"It's not what you think, Hillary. It's *serious*, you see."

"You are in love? Not another suitor for the fair Gwendolyn?"

"Gwendolyn! Good God no. She is not my type at all. More your sort if it comes to that—and I tell you quite honestly that I hope it will not, because, despite everything, I do not like Gwendolyn above half. She is not always kind to Alicia, you know."

"*Alicia!* Of course, and it *is* perfect. I wish you happy. So you are her secret love."

"Yes, and I'm afraid it will remain a secret. Alicia has no fortune, of course, and although her mother's family was very old, there is not all that much on the father's side. Still, I do not think they will let her settle on a mere Yorkshire squire. It will reflect badly on the family, don't you see, and it might put a shadow on the fair Gwendolyn's ambitions."

"Do you know all this or is it merely speculation?"

"I know that I have been introduced to the father three times and he has yet to acknowledge my existence when we pass in the street. I know that Alicia dares not speak of our courtship, and we have been reduced to stratagems of meeting by coincidence in Devonshire. I tell you, Hillary, it is not how I would wish to behave, but I *cannot, I will not,* give her up."

"Nor should you. The girl has been mooning about like a lovesick calf since her arrival. And I don't believe your suit is hopeless. Although Mr. Campbell is proud, he *can* be influenced. Your income is quite decent and you are sincerely attached. Campbell can be brought to see reason. Leave the planning of the thing to me!"

"Haven't I always? But if you can pull this off for me, Hil, I swear I shall be eternally in your debt."

"Please, Robbie, I can't *bear* grandiloquence. Come, it is

63

already late in the afternoon. Let us get back to Pemmfield and make your presence known before the delightful Alicia goes into a hopeless decline."

It seemed a replay of Hillary's arrival the week before, and, with some second sense for not repeating the ignominious, he insisted they dismount first at the stable. He was a few feet behind Robert as that young man rounded the hedge to the house. As he somehow knew he would, Sir Hillary heard the now familiar whistle, and he was not surprised when Robert Mansfield suddenly stopped. But Sir Hillary was totally unprepared for what followed.

Robbie yanked the hat from his head and waved it in the air, yelling, "Pegasus—Pegasus Gorham!"

Sir Hillary rounded the hedge and saw the governess turn quickly as the children entered the house, and then she lifted her skirts and ran straight at Mr. Mansfield, to be swept up in his arms and lifted high into the air. They were both laughing as he set her down.

"Imagine discovering you in Devonshire, Pegasus. It must be my lucky star. But whatever are *you* doing as a governess—and in brown bombazine at that? It is not at all in character, don't you know."

Still laughing, she replied, "Well, no, Robbie my lad, but don't *you* go exposing me. I have become a very *sober* woman."

"Gammon, if they knew what a wild creature you are they would cast you out upon the moors without a character."

"Very likely, but then it is all the more important that we do not let on. My employers are very pedestrian people."

"They must be idiots if they think for a moment that Pegasus Gorham is a fitting governess." He turned. "Oh, incidentally, may I introduce my very good friend Sir Hillary Pendragon."

She turned and saw him. There was a moment of surprise, and then the governess mask was firmly in place. "Thank you, we have met." She sent a curious look at Robert, wondering, Sir Hillary supposed, what had become of that young man's judgment.

Hillary, not to be accused again of spying, allowed them to believe he had just arrived, and, after making a bow to Miss Gorham, he excused both himself and Robert Mansfield. "I'm certain Miss Gorham will excuse you, Robert, so that you may pay your respects to the Campbell sisters. I noticed

64

Alicia is in the rose garden, and I suppose we might go there to meet her."

"Rather," said Robert, grinning.

The meeting with Alicia went smoothly, and Hillary arranged to allow the couple a few minutes alone before they returned to the house, where Gwendolyn and Lady Julia were occupied with their needlework. Julia took an immediate liking to young Mansfield, and displaying rather more intuitive sense than Sir Hillary would have given her credit for, she set out to draw the young man out, thus forcing Gwendolyn, who had barely remembered him from London, to take some notice of the squire from Yorkshire and to acknowledge him as a gentleman.

Rather than overstay their welcome or elicit alarm from Gwendolyn, the gentlemen left after three quarters of an hour—the younger one very pleased with himself and the older one strangely puzzled. Sir Hillary would have himself introduced the subject of Miss Gorham, but fortunately Mr. Mansfield did so as soon as he was out the gate.

"You know, I feel like a dog, being so happy and poor Pegasus a governess. I never thought it would come to this. Even after the captain died I had thought they would muddle through. But Pegasus always took too much upon herself, and I see Phillip has gotten his stay at Oxford and the girls their portion because Pegasus did without—being Pegasus she probably sent money home. It is a great pity to see her a slave for wages."

"Believe me, Miss Gorham is no slave in that house. More like a slave driver than slave. I take it, Robbie, that Miss Gorham is a friend of your youth."

"Oh, Lord, yes, indeed she is. We grew up together. Shared the same governess when we were little—being of an age, so to speak. Although Miss Woodruff always did prefer Pegasus despite her wildness. Our Pegasus has a brilliant mind, you know, as well as being up to anything." And he sat back musing. "If I hadn't promised to keep mum I could tell you of the most awful scrapes we managed to get ourselves into. There were five of them and three of us, although her little sisters were too small for sport. But our Pegasus was *always* the leader."

"That she retains. A marked capacity for leadership."

"Oh, I don't mean that she was a sergeant major. Pegasus was quite strict in her own way and always very responsible, but she was never stiff-rumped. In fact, in the village she used to be called the young lady heathen. And she was a sort of heathen, you know. Miss Margaret Gorham seemed almost a stranger today, but I'll lay you odds, Hil, that our Pegasus gets off for an hour or two each day and reverts to type."

"Are you implying, Mr. Mansfield, that our staid, strict little governess has a secret life?"

"Don't you laugh at her, Hillary. It isn't fair. You have always had everything, and you cannot possibly understand Pegasus Gorham. You know, she was once determined to go off in disguise and fight Boney. She could have, too. She was braver than all the rest of us rolled up into one. I have seen her, scarcely fourteen herself, climb through spiked fences and pass fierce dogs only in order to bring a little food to her friends at the orphanage. The foundling home near our village was a disgrace, and no one would help improve the miserable conditions. I took food as well, but I would never have known what else to do."

"And Miss Gorham did more?"

"I should say she did. The children were all starving, and when one of her friends died, Pegasus was quite prepared to assassinate the administrator. We convinced her to exercise some restraint, and so she did, in a way."

"In a way?"

"Yes, in a way. She ruined the man, you know. Pegasus wrote letters to the *Yorkshire Times* over the preposterous name of the Reverend James Higby the Third. And, in the guise of a concerned clergyman, she gave them all the brutal details in very compelling prose. She had half of Yorkshire in tears before the administrator was dismissed in absolute disgrace, and I can tell you the situation improved vastly after that. My own father took an interest in the running of the place. Strange thing is that only a handful of us ever knew who the Reverend James Higby was."

"Yes, I will admit, Robbie, that Miss Gorham is a very virtuous and a very determined woman, but, in truth, I find it difficult to think pleasantly of a woman who quite so clearly detests me."

"You've set her back up, have you, Hil? It must have been your infernal charm. Undoubtedly she believes you to be a silly fop—one of the sort that our Pegasus learned to chew up and spit out before she was six years old. Curious, but I believe she would have liked you had she met you as I did, in the field. You have a kind of recklessness in common. But you both have cultivated such different faces for public consumption."

"Now, I recall that you *did* tell me about a Pegasus, but of course I always supposed you were describing a boy."

"Tomboy, more like."

"Well, I cannot help thinking of her more as a holy terror, but I am prejudiced *I* did not plight my troth as a child."

"Nor did I. I never thought to marry Pegasus—gracious no. Much as I love her, I always knew that to marry Pegasus would be like courting a whirlwind." And then after a few moments he continued, "Incidentally, she gave me this packet to give to the Dillingham children."

Sir Hillary patted him on the back. "I think, Robbie, I should be jealous. You have just replaced me as a go-between."

"Our Pegasus is still feeding the orphans, is she?"

Chapter 7

Robert Mansfield ran the gauntlet of the Dillinghams at dinner that evening. Within moments of the serving of the first course, Lady Augusta had ascertained his status in Yorkshire, the family history for the last two hundred years, and the number of sheep, cows, and tenants his father kept. It was only then that Mrs. Dillingham decided that, although not exalted, Mr. Mansfield was more than respectable and as a friend of her dear nephew's ought to be offered the hospitality of her home. "Hillary will assure you, Mr. Mansfield, that we do not stand on ceremony at Dillingham Hall. We are very comfortable and informal, are we not, Hillary?"

"To be sure, Aunt Augusta."

"Are you married, Mr. Mansfield, or are you contemplating marriage?" Augusta continued relentlessly. Robert was hesitating, and before Hillary could effect a rescue, Claude guided the conversation into less sensitive terrain.

"Do you care for my new coat, Hillary? I have been assured that lavender is all the rage."

Hillary grinned with something like understanding in his eyes. "As always, Claude, I am flabbergasted and humbled in the face of such sartorial splendor."

Robert smiled at Claude. "Do not take offense, Mr. Dillingham. Despite his reputation as a leader of the ton, our Sir Hillary is a very slow top when it comes to fashion. He is always roasting me when I dress with the least bit of imagination."

Hillary sighed. "*Imagination*—is that what you call it, Robbie? Somehow *I* would have described your penchant for color in some other way."

Robert was not to be intimidated, "Of course you would, Hil; and you do, regularly and graphically. Simply because you yourself are a great hulk of a man and so must dress with the utmost of sobriety, you get all high in the instep whenever any of the rest of us fellows displays a modicum of flair."

"Robbie Mansfield, the last time I looked you were all of three inches less well endowed than I am, and, believe me, that does not make you any the less laughable all decked out to look like a peony in bloom."

"Yes, Hillary, but your friend Robert does have the right of it. It is all very well for you big tall military gentlemen to dress very conservatively—although thank goodness Mr. Mansfield does not restrict himself to the drab colors you seem to favor. Still, it is quite another matter for a gentleman such as myself. *I* do not have very many inches in any direction. Nature has not granted me an imposing physique, and so, instead of stature, I must settle for color and cut."

"But my dear Claude, stature is not a function of size." Hillary was speaking almost seriously. "Nor are all gentlemen in the military great hulks as I am. Bonaparte himself is about your own height, and he runs to fat. Yet he has managed to acquit himself rather well in the battlefield, don't you think?"

Claude considered this for a moment before answering. "True, and I think he has done so well at least in part because he is small. Small men *must* assert themselves—nature is not kind to her runts, don't you know. I suppose I might, if I wished, set out to conquer worlds and mold civilizations, but I think my preoccupation with neckcloths and waistcoats is a deal less dangerous and infinitely less harmful to the rest of humanity. Besides," he added, looking in his mother's

68

direction, "Mama would not ever have allowed either of us to go off to war—too wild, you know."

Anthony had just arrived late for dinner, and, in an obviously nasty humor, he nodded in acknowledgment of their introductions and joined the conversation. "What is too wild, my brave little brother, or need I ask? Just yesterday you were attempting to convince me that any activity which might so much as wrinkle a neckcloth was not befitting a gentleman."

"Did I say that, Anthony? Well, I suppose I was referring only to those of us who are members of the brotherhood of dandies. I did not mean to reflect on other gentlemen."

Hillary turned to Anthony and explained, "We have been speaking of the military life, Anthony."

"Ah, were you now. Let me not deflect you, Cousin Hillary. It it not often we have the privilege of entertaining a bona fide hero of our nation. Tell me, were you offering my little Claude a pair of colors? I cannot think they would suit him, you know. He would jump like a rabbit at the first sound of battle."

Hillary set down his cup. Though he had no intention of creating a scene he felt he should respond to Anthony's disagreeable remark. "I, on the other hand, who have had somewhat more experience in these matters, think Claude would acquit himself rather well as a fighting man. But the question is academic, is it not, since my Aunt Augusta is not likely to approve of the venture."

"No, she would not. When I was much younger I suggested a military career for myself, and my charming mother would have none of it. My mother, you see, persists in thinking of me, her firstborn, as a tender, refined, gentle sort of chap. It goes without saying that she thinks of Claude as—"

"Claude," Robert interrupted, "are there any good tailors in Devonshire, or are you reduced to traveling to London for a decent waistcoat?"

"I make do with the locals—by and large. I have a small income and an allowance from Mama, but it does not run to extended visits to the capital. I suppose I do not manage my resources as well as Anthony here—he is *never* short of funds, you know. Anthony is a positive *genius* with money. My brother is the only man I know who has amassed a fortune at the gaming tables—and most of it within the last year."

"Yes, little brother, I *am* a cunning gambler. But enough of this." And turning to Sir Hillary he asked, "Rumor has it that you have given Duffy his marching orders. Have you really given him notice."

"Yes, I have."

"I do not mean to intrude, Hillary, but might I ask what prompted your decision?"

Hillary hesitated several moments—just long enough for Anthony to realize that he resented the question. "I found his services unsatisfactory. I believe I have cause."

Anthony raised an eyebrow. "Duffy is a good man. I do not believe you will find a better man available in the neighborhood. I think it unfortunate if you have given him notice simply because of malicious gossip from the tenants."

Claude was removing a speck of lint from his coat when he spoke. "Well, I never liked the fellow myself. I always thought he had beady little snake eyes."

The colonel coughed, and the table fell silent. "Hillary, you *may* have been justified." Reginald had just emptied his fifth glass of the evening, "Of late there has been bad management—very bad management—at Pemmfield. So much poaching, for example—just last month I had to transport that fellow Paul."

"You sent William Paul off to Australia for poaching?"

"No, no, of course not. I would never, as a magistrate, have sent a father of four off merely for bagging a rabbit, and certainly not in these troubled times. But the man had taken a sudden turn for the bad in the last year or two. Anthony, who has become a great aid to me, looked into the matter himself. He found that William Paul had acquired a history of malicious mischief and skulduggery. The man has even been accused of an act of arson which resulted in two deaths— although nothing could be proved. Men such as that are not found on well-run estates, are they?"

Anthony was refilling his father's glass. "No, of course they are not, Father, but you take these things too seriously. Do not, I pray you, become overwrought. My father, you know, is one of the most conscientious magistrates and respected landholders in Devonshire. I believe Colonel Dillingham enjoys farming quite as much as he ever did the military."

The conversation was thus returned to the subject of the wars, where it was to remain throughout the balance of dinner and the hour spent over port.

Early the next morning, Robert asked Sir Hillary's assistance in delivering the package to the Dillingham children.

With a great deal of ceremony the two of them advanced into the schoolroom, and then, with an innocent-seeming smile, Sir Hillary dismissed the governess.

"We have brought a package for you brats," Hillary said, his eyes alight with mischief.

"A moment, Uncle Hillary," Luke whispered. "We must first take precautions." And the two of them, Luke and Sarah, peeped out into the hall to see that no one was in sight.

The formalities completed, Robert Mansfield spoke. "Miss Gorham gave this to me and asked that I place it directly into your hands, Miss Sarah. Knowing Miss Gorham, I can imagine that it is a very important package."

"How well do you know Miss Gorham?" Luke asked with just a hint of skepticism in his voice.

"We grew up together in the woolly wilds of Yorkshire. We shared a governess and we shared all sorts of mischief. Miss Gorham, as a child, was always up to anything."

"She still is, you know. She is very good." Sarah took the package from his hands and sequestered it in the corner of the bookshelves behind a series of primers.

Hillary hesitated and then spoke quietly. "You know, you *need* not tell me, children, what is in the package, but I am become very curious."

"I don't know that you would approve, Uncle Hillary." Sarah was twisting her hands in indecision.

"Of course he would approve. Your Uncle Hillary is not some old stick in the mud," Robert said.

"Do *you* know what is in the package, Mr. Mansfield?"

"Well, I think I may have guessed. You see, Sir Hillary and I have spent some time learning how to guess what is in secret packages, and I have the advantage because I do know Miss Gorham very well." Taking a child on each knee he continued, "It was too heavy and regular in shape to be anything to eat except perhaps a box of bonbons, but, as strict as Miss Gorham is, I did not think she would be going to such fuss and bother over something as insignificant as bonbons."

"Indeed she would not, Mr. Mansfield," Luke assured him.

"So, I thought to myself that your package must contain a book, but, as I couldn't feel the *spine* of the book, I was forced to conclude that it was a sheaf of papers and not a book at all. Am I right?"

Sarah was very impressed, "Mr. Mansfield, you are brilliant. I don't wonder you are an agent extraordinaire for Wellington."

"Thank you, Sarah, but remember, I have had a great deal of experience. There is one issue I have yet to resolve, and you could help me if you would. Who wrote on those papers, yourselves or Miss Gorham?"

Sarah set out to explain. "We did. It is not a book precisely. It is our very own secret world. We have been writing on it for months, and there has never been anyone to share our world, and now Miss Gorham has come and she understands and she even makes very good suggestions about what color dragon fire is and how a knight in shining armor might dress when he is not in shining armor. She understands such things, you see."

"Of course she understands such things. Our Pegasus was always a scribbler, and when she was your age she was writing up her own secret worlds. It was not all clear sailing, though. That penchant for scribbling landed her in the suds at least once."

"What happened? Did her father catch her and whip her?" Luke asked quietly.

"No, the captain would never have done that. The thing was that Pegasus gave her dragons and ladies and knights *real* names, and this very mealy-mouthed nasty boy named Tommy Hendricks got hold of a few pages she had written about Mrs. Treakle, and circulated those pages in church one Sunday. Mrs. Treakle was the most starched-up old puss in our neighborhood, and so, naturally, Pegasus was in deep trouble. The captain was abroad at the time but I have never seen Mrs. Gorham half so angry as she was that Sunday. It was bread and water for a week for poor Pegasus, and she was confined to her bedroom for the duration."

"It could have been much worse." Luke nodded sagely.

"Well, I suppose it could have been worse at that, but I was very young and I didn't much like Mrs. Treakle—no one did—and so I thought it was dreadfully unfair. I meant to do something about it, too. First I searched out Tommy Hendricks and, after I had beaten that little nark to a pulp, I gathered together a big basket of pastries and one exquisite plum pudding and climbed up in the middle of the night to Pegasus's window."

"That was very brave of you, Mr. Mansfield, and shows that you are worthy of Miss Gorham's friendship," Sarah assured him.

"Yes, Sarah, that is precisely what I thought myself. But Pegasus wouldn't take the pastries. She was delighted to see

72

me, of course, and was very pleased that I had milled down Tommy Hendricks, although she intended to do so herself just as soon as she was freed from her bedroom. But she would not take the pastries—not even the plum pudding." Robert's mind had wandered back across the years, and there was a half-smile on his lips, "'Robbie,' she said to me, 'I think I really ought to take my punishment as a man. It wasn't right of me to cause anyone such embarrassment and pain—even Mrs. Treakle, who would not hesitate to do so to others. But I don't want to be like Mrs. Treakle, and I solemnly swear that I will never again write anything about anyone unless I am quite certain that no one will ever know who I am writing about. Meanwhile, Robbie, I do wish you would take those pastries away, because I am *sorely* tempted.'"

"She didn't even take the plum pudding?" Luke asked in awe.

"No, she didn't. Not even the plum pudding." And then Robbie grinned. "But I did. I ate all the pudding and all the pastries just as soon as I was out of sight of the Gorham cottage."

Hillary Pendragon did not know which he found more cloying—the thought of that sickly sweet little girl or the thought of Robbie devouring all those pastries. Sir Hillary would have liked to make several acidulous comments about smugly virtuous little girls, but he restrained himself, at least in part because he knew that any criticism of Miss Gorham would not be well received by the other three occupants of the room.

Fortunately Miss Porter had come to the door and the children had fallen silent. The gentlemen stood and welcomed the lady before excusing themselves from the schoolroom. Luke darted out after them and about fifteen feet down the hallway he pulled at Sir Hillary's coatsleeve until that gentleman bent his head and Luke was able to whisper, "Uncle Hillary, give our best to Miss Gorham and tell her that we will meet her at the regular place and the regular time on Tuesday." And the boy had darted back down the hall and into the schoolroom before Miss Porter came to retrieve him.

Several hours later the two gentlemen were alone together in the blue saloon at Pemmfield. Robert appeared to be deep in the midst of letter writing while Hillary was sitting staring absentmindedly out the window. Robert laid down his pen and studied his friend for a few minutes before Hillary finally turned and met his eyes.

"Yes, Robbie?"

Robert Mansfield's eyes had narrowed into a question. "Hil, you are disturbed about something."

"Is it so obvious?"

"Perhaps not to others, but I have seen that expression of yours in Calais, in the Pyrenees, in Portugal, but I confess I had not expected to see it in Devonshire. What is ailing you, Hillary?"

"This is your holiday, Robbie, and you have your Alicia. There is no need to concern yourself in these matters."

"Then there *is* something wrong and it is not something personal. It is something to do with Pemmfield?"

"Yes, Robert."

"We have always worked *together,* Hillary."

Hillary hesitated a moment longer and then shrugged. "Let us take a turn through the gardens, Robbie."

Five minutes later the two gentlemen were apparently entirely engrossed in the study of the spring foliage when Hillary spoke. "You were quite right, you know. There is something dreadfully wrong about the goings-on at Pemmfield. And I cannot seem to get at the *root* of it."

"Do you suspect anything or anyone?"

"The bailiff, for one, is almost certainly involved, but beyond that I know only that virtually all the tenants are extraordinarily fearful. The sort of fear we have seen so often in the villages in Spain. I know also that there is something very smoky in the matter of William Paul's transportation to Australia. But I am still at the stage where I have a great many questions and very few answers. I can recognize some of the symptoms but I have no clear conception of the disease itself."

"I do not mean to intrude, Hillary, but have you thought to ask Pegasus for her opinion?"

"I have discussed the matter with Miss Gorham—in fact, she has been most helpful in pointing me in the direction of the problem. I do not know how much she knows, and she is certainly not telling me all she suspects. It is clear, however, that the matter may be quite serious, and I will not have an innocent woman blundering about where she may be hurt. I told Miss Gorham not to meddle."

"Good Lord, Hillary, do I understand you correctly? *You told Pegasus not to meddle*—in those words?"

"Yes, of course I did. You would have done the same, Robbie."

"Gammon! In Yorkshire men have been beheaded for less. What did she say to you?"

"She did not seem to take it well."

"I am amazed that she took it at all. There is no protecting Pegasus Gorham, and I, for one, would be afraid to try. Besides, she is the best of comrades to have in a difficult situation, and I do not doubt that the people here would confide in her sooner than they would in either of us." Robert stood examining the foliage for a few moments, and when he continued he was almost musing. "I should have liked to have seen Pegasus's face when you told her not to meddle. You were always very courageous, Hillary—almost to the point of folly."

"To be sure, but, of course, I could not know to what great danger I was exposing myself." They were bent examining a rose bush for several minutes before Hillary spoke again. "Do you still think you would like to join me in this venture, Robbie?"

"I should feel dashed hurt if I was left out."

Hillary nodded. "Thank you, and I can certainly use your help. In fact, my intuition tells me we may be using other members of our department as well."

"As bad as that?"

"Almost certainly.... To begin with, Robbie, I think it might be better for the both of us to abandon Dillingham Hall. We will stay, instead, at Pemmfield Manor, where we will be freer to examine the problem."

"I think that would be a capital idea, Hillary. Your Aunt Dillingham is a wonderful woman and all of that, but if we are to unravel this mystery, we ought to be smack dab in the midst of it."

"I rather thought that particular suggestion would meet your approval. And Alicia's as well. But take care not to be obvious in your attentions until I have succeeded in reconciling the powers that be."

"Of course I will be careful. We have not come this far, Alicia and I, to queer it now. I don't know about Mr. Campbell, but Gwendolyn will come around like a charm with a bit of sweet talking from you. That girl is besotted."

"She may be."

"May be! Half the girls in London are in love with you, Hillary, and it cannot be your fortune that does it—although a fortune the size of yours is never a disadvantage in the marriage mart. Two months ago I would have begged you for the secret of your success with the ladies, but now I find it oddly sufficient to have just one sweet girl in love with me. I don't know what I should do with all the others."

"Ah, you have hit upon the nub of it, Robbie my lad. I do not have that one girl, and I do not know what to do with all the others."

"Poor Sir Hillary. Still, I expect you will manage."

"I always have, have I not, Robbie? But I begin to think that you dull pedestrian monogamous fellows have the right of it. Juggling half a dozen hearts can grow vastly tedious."

"Heavy going, is it?"

"Not *heavy,* precisely, as there is not much substance in any of these hearts, but the juggling itself requires a great deal of concentration and can become quite exhausting."

At dinner that evening Gwendolyn and Julia both expressed themselves as delighted that the gentlemen would be staying at Pemmfield. Alicia was even more delighted but had the good sense to conceal her own feelings. Even Margaret Gorham smiled when the suggestion was made, although Hillary, who had been observing her carefully, thought it was not exactly a pleasant smile. Miss Gorham had the look of a cat who has swallowed the cream. The smile lasted only a moment, and then it was gone and Margaret Gorham was again very prim, very erect, and almost starkly silent. Hillary noticed that only her eyes moved and that she was, all the time, carefully observing every other person at the table. For the duration of the dessert course, Hillary entertained the wild fantasy that Margaret Mellicent Gorham was, in reality, a spy for Napoleon masquerading as the perfect governess—perfect, that is, except that there was about her absolutely no sign of the meekness characteristic of the ideal governess.

Hillary did not think of Gwendolyn Campbell at all. He merely assumed that she could be avoided while he continued his investigations at Pemmfield. He was mistaken. Miss Campbell, knowing nothing of the real reasons for Sir Hillary's change in domicile, interpreted that change as a reflection of his growing attachment to herself. And since she was not by nature a passive personality, she felt it vital that the gentleman understand that Gwendolyn Campbell was also eager to advance that attachment in any way possible.

With such an advancement in view, she happened to meet Sir Hillary as he and Mr. Mansfield were retiring to their rooms that evening. Robbie, grinning, proceeded on to his own room, thus leaving his comrade-in-arms alone and defenseless in the hands of the enemy.

Gwendolyn Campbell, a vision in shimmering green silk, moved slowly forward and stopped a full six inches from Sir Hillary. Very slowly she raised her eyes and smiled up at him.

Hillary braced himself and returned the smile. "Gwen, dearest, don't go playing with fire—you are far too young and you may be burned."

"*You* wouldn't take *advantage* of me, Hillary?"

"Quite right. I never take advantage of innocent young ladies. It's too dangerous."

"I may be worth the danger, Hillary."

"You may at that, my sweet." He smiled as he was ruffling her hair casually. "And it is *very* tempting, but I cannot let you become too involved."

"A *lady* is never *too* involved. You will not break my heart, Hillary—I'm quite grown up, you know."

She was very close and very beautiful, and so he kissed her. It was a light sort of kiss, but Hillary was very expert—far more expert than the young lady could have believed possible. Gwendolyn Campbell's savoir faire was not up to the occasion, and she was quite shaken when he stepped away from her.

"Think again, Gwendolyn, before you decide to be quite so grown up. Go to bed now, girl, and pleasant dreams." He patted her paternally on the backside and sent her to her room.

Perhaps if Hillary Pendragon had not been trained to be observant he would not, at that moment, have noticed the figure in brown bombazine move silently through the shadows. He did not see her face but Hillary could well imagine what Miss Gorham was thinking.

Before retiring, Margaret managed to spend some time on her novel, and then, almost as an afterthought, she decided to write Miss Woodruff.

My dearest Woody

We have had a delightful surprise. Robbie has arrived in Devonshire. It is good to have him here, although I wonder from time to time whether he will unwittingly destroy my character as a governess.

It seems that Robbie has been working with Sir Hillary Pendragon behind French lines, although why the two of them should make a pair I cannot understand. Robbie was always a *reasonably* good judge of character—still, I suppose that in the military these assignments are not entirely voluntary, and I confess that Sir Hillary is not *quite* as stupid as I had believed. I don't suppose anyone would have been *that* stupid.

We are not to mention it, but it seems that Robbie is in love with Alicia Campbell and she with him. It will be a perfect match. She is a lovely simple kind of girl and I was quite right to cast her as my heroine. Unfortunately, her sister, although beautiful, is neither simple nor kind—a cat in black lace more like. I don't suppose Robbie wants his attachment broadcast about until he has overcome the family's defenses. I wish him well. It will be especially lucky that they will settle in Yorkshire, as the family Campbell is almost invariably in London.

Now that the characters have been assembled, my new novel is proceeding well. Picture a bleak castle somewhere in the Orkneys. Do the Orkneys have castles as well as seaweed?—well, no matter. The heroine clinging precariously to life in the face of strange malignant threats will be Alicia; but, of course, Sir Hillary can no longer be allowed to be the hero. It would be too unfair to Robbie, and, although the names will be very different, I *could* not feel right about it. Robbie himself will make a splendid hero, and Sir Hillary will become one of the minor characters. He will be the honest respectable knucklehead—the one in the gothic novel who, despite the wild entreaties of the heroine, refuses to believe that she is in grim danger.

Sir Hillary will also become a sort of consolation prize for the feline Gwendolyn who is bent on seducing every man in the book and, most particularly, the hero.

The villain—and he will make a splendid villain—will be Anthony Dillingham, who is a thoroughly disagreeable man. And, presiding over the whole, like a giant spider, will be the evil genius of the castle—the mad old Lady Augusta.

I am working out the intricacies of the plot and thinking of you.

Pegasus

P.S. Remember, my very dearest Woody—burn this letter.

Chapter 8

It had not been a pleasant night for Sir Hillary. He had lain awake long into the morning, with his mind a jumble of half-formed suspicions only some of which seemed to have any relation at all to the problems at Pemmfield.

He still had, for example, nagging doubts about the character of Miss Margaret Gorham. She could not be the rigidly proper governess she wished to appear—even Robert conceded that much. Then what or who was she?

Thus by eight o'clock the next morning, Sir Hillary was in a mood best described as suspicious when he happened to see Miss Gorham coming across the south lawn in the company of a dark sturdy young man dressed in the casual clothes of a laborer. Hillary could see that the two of them were deep in conversation, and were it not for Miss Gorham's ramrod posture, he would even have assumed that their passage across the garden was flirtatious. There was something in the easy informality between the two that Sir Hillary Pendragon could not like.

Sir Hillary quickly made his way down into the garden and set out on a path which would, shortly, intercept that of Miss Gorham and her companion. Temporarily he lost sight of them but within three or four minutes their paths crossed and Sir Hillary greeted Miss Gorham. Hillary thought he might have surprised a look of confusion on the young lady's face, but as it was so quickly supplanted by the governess mask, he could not be certain. Motioning the young man to remain where he was, Miss Gorham, without preamble, requested a few words with Sir Hillary.

Hillary nodded his agreement and was led, very much like a child, several yards off. Margaret Gorham turned to him and beckoned him to be seated, but, pleasantly, he refused. Sir Hillary was nothing if not a quick study, and he would not repeat a situation in which she towered over him.

Standing there prim and proper and dressed in drab black, Miss Gorham did not have the look of a lady who had just been caught out in a compromising situation. Suddenly, Sir Hillary could not suppress a chuckle. There was something intrinsically ridiculous about the whole scene. *The* Sir Hillary Pendragon sequestered in a rose garden at the ungodly hour of eight in the morning with a female sergeant major cleverly disguised as a governess.

"Sir Hillary, this is *not* an occasion for levity," Miss Gorham informed him repressively.

"Do you think not, Miss Gorham? Tell me, are you accustomed to meet men in rose gardens at eight o'clock in the morning? I find the entire matter tastes a little of the ridiculous."

"When I come into a rose garden, Sir Hillary, it is to study the beauties of nature, and when I come accompanied, I do so in the anticipation of intelligent conversation."

"I see, and I humbly beg your pardon if I disturbed you and the young man in your appreciation of nature or if I interrupted you in the midst of a particularly intelligent conversation."

She glared at him. "I am here, Sir Hillary, to discuss very serious matters, and if you insist on inappropriate levity you may leave."

Hillary hesitated a few moments, half determined to turn and leave, but it was then he noticed that Miss Gorham was in deadly earnest. And so, suppressing an instinct to laugh in her face and an even stronger instinct to take her over his knee and paddle her, he settled himself in to listen.

Miss Gorham pulled herself up very tall and peered into his face intently for a moment or two before beginning. And then it was not at all what he expected. "Robert Mansfield has assured me, Sir Hillary, that you can be trusted. That, despite your casual appearance before the world, you can be *absolutely* discreet should the occasion demand."

"Do you doubt Mr. Mansfield's judgment?"

Margaret Gorham was quite serious as she replied, "I have never before had any cause to doubt Robert's judgment, but I know him to be a very kind and very trusting individual. There are lives at stake here."

"And you hesitate to entrust those lives to an empty-headed fop—am I correct?"

She did not flinch. "Yes, quite correct." Never had her resemblance to Miss Agitha Smith been so pronounced.

"Miss Gorham, if you expect me to be intimidated because you choose to assume the posture of a governess with a recalcitrant schoolboy, you will be disappointed. You have asked me a very serious question, and I will not answer it until we have some sort of understanding that we are *both* of us responsible and adult."

She looked down for a moment, and when she lifted her head she was, in a tentative sort of way, smiling. "I imagine that I am becoming quite ogrish, am I not? And just now I had not meant to be so. I'm afraid that treating the world as if it were comprised of unruly children is one of the hazards of my profession. You are quite right, of course: the question is rude enough to begin with without adding to it the insult of condescension. I am asking your opinion as a responsible adult and not as a little boy in short pants. But I still require an answer."

"Miss Gorham, I am not, nor do I claim to be, a man of *many* virtues. I can, however, be trusted to be absolutely discreet, especially when there are lives involved. I have lived in the midst of such situations for some years now, and I believe, if you will pardon my saying so, that I have far more experience at such matters than do you."

He fully expected her to bridle at this implied criticism, but she did not. In fact she became somewhat thoughtful. "Very like you do." She had looked away from him and had, almost unconsciously, begun to liberate a branch with a single rosebud from some debris which had entangled it. "To be sure, I would have preferred to have been in the fields of France or in the Peninsula, but there is no gainsaying that I have never been out of England." And then she smiled ruefully. "Robbie and I used to talk of disguising me in my brother Michael's clothes and enlisting me in the navy. But I knew, instinctively, that sooner or later I would be discovered and my mama would be mortified. I suppose I have become quite jealous of you and Robbie. Strange, the dreams of one's childhood. I, who would have given the world for a taste of adventure on the high seas, have become a governess, and Robert Mansfield, who wished only to remain in Yorkshire and breed pigs, is off to the wars...." And then, forcibly bringing herself back to the problem at hand, she turned to face Sir Hillary. "Bear with me; my mind does not usually wander so. I was about to inform you that the young man with whom I was speaking is John Paul."

"And?"

"And I should like you to talk to him. He is quite fearful, of course, and he does not know precisely what the nature of the danger is. They do not confide in him as freely as they could, because he is somewhat bookish and because he has newly returned from the wars to find his father transported. He does understand that it is a very bad situation and that at least two people have already died because of it."

"Is Duffy near the root of the problem?"

"Mr. Duffy is certainly a part of it, although his is not the guiding intelligence. There is some sort of conspiracy to intimidate all the villagers, but to what end we cannot be certain. John Paul suggests it may have something to do with the free trade—perhaps even espionage." Then, reaching out, she placed her hand on his arm in an entreaty. "Do talk to John gently. He will not know how to relate to a grand London gentleman, you know."

"Miss Gorham, your faith in me staggers the imagination. Are you suggesting I might offer the young man snuff or scrutinize him with my glass?" And so saying, Sir Hillary turned his back on her and went to where John Paul had remained standing.

Miss Gorham performed the introduction and excused herself.

Sir Hillary found himself confronting a young man somewhere between twenty and thirty who was very solid but nevertheless seemed bookish and bumbling. He appeared to be fairly intelligent but was badly frightened and, despite Sir Hillary's best efforts, somewhat in awe of the gentry. It was also clear that he adored Miss Gorham, and Sir Hillary could not ascertain the quality of this adoration—was it Robbie's hero worship or was it something quite different? As to the matters of the estate, Sir Hillary did not push to get more information. Those relationships which became rich veins of intelligence were slow to develop, and Hillary was content to bide his time. Instead, he assured the younger man that he, Sir Hillary, genuinely wished to root out the evil in the neighborhood, and that he would do his best, and his best was a great deal—to have William Paul returned to England if it was found that he had been harshly sentenced.

Trust and gratitude were reflected in the young man's eyes when he took his leave to return to the fields where his absence might, in time, be noted.

They had agreed to meet clandestinely the following evening, and, deep in thought, Sir Hillary returned to the manor house. A picture was slowly forming in Hillary Pendragon's mind, and while several of the areas were still in shadow and some of those shadows were totally without form, he began to see a pattern emerging to the events at Pemmfield—and the pattern was profoundly disturbing.

Sir Hillary spent the balance of the morning gathering information in the village, while Robert Mansfield, for his part, escorted the ladies in their carriage around the Pemmfield estates. But while Mr. Mansfield's heart was securely fastened on Miss Alicia Campbell, his eyes and mind were otherwise occupied. He stopped on occasion to ask a question or two of a tenant, and although these questions seemed to be quite innocent— almost vacuous—he had after a few hours firmly convinced himself that Sir Hillary had, if anything, understated the grimness of the situation.

Margaret Gorham spent the morning with her charges. Pamela had received a lovely doll from the Campbell sisters, and she had been determined these last few days to abandon her lessons in order to tend her new plaything—to dress it, to debate its wardrobe, and to discuss, at length, her plans for its marital felicity. It had become a dreadful chore to keep Pamela's little mind firmly fastened on the rigors of long division, and it became quite impossible when nurse produced a scrap of cloth which would make the debutante doll a splendid gown for her coming-out ball. Little Pamela was left in the care of nurse, and Miss Gorham ushered the two boys into the garden for a bit of nature study.

Thomas Pemmrington did not enjoy nature study. In fact, whenever young Thomas was out of the house or in an environment which was not completely protected by the artificialities of social restraint, he became quite fastidious and even nervous. As usual, Miss Gorham and Richard managed

83

to ignore his obvious discomfort and the three of them spent much of the morning discussing the state of nature, the war on the Peninsula as compared to the Peloponnesian wars, the new movements for extension of the franchise and reform of the Corn Laws, and even the suggested laws for the prohibition of the slave trade on the high seas. In short, the governess and her students were immersed in discussions which many young gentlemen in England were never exposed to but which were, nevertheless, in Miss Gorham's judgment, absolutely essential if these same sprigs of the aristocracy were to mature into men capable of exercising responsible authority.

Suddenly Richard jumped to his feet. "Look over there, Miss Gorham! Did you see Jamey Tate? He was peeking at us from behind the bushes."

Thomas was dusting off his sleeve for the tenth time. "You can leave him be now, Richard. Surely you have done your penance and need no longer concern yourself with the Tate boy."

Miss Gorham seemed not to have heard Thomas' comment. "Do you think that Jamey looked especially frightened just now, Richard?"

"Yes. You know, I believe he has been particularly frightened these last few days, and it is not simply that everyone calls him names and throws things. I think there is something else on his mind."

"Wait here, Master Thomas. Your brother and I will see if we can find Jamey Tate. We may be able to help him. If we have not returned in half an hour you had better go back up to the schoolroom and complete the geography lesson on your own."

A few minutes later the Tate boy had been located in the hayloft of the stable, a place where, Richard assured Miss Gorham, Jamey almost always went to hide. "And it's a capital hiding place too. He took me there only last Friday, and we spent hours playing with the baby kittens he keeps.... You can come out now Jamey. It's only Miss Gorham and I, and we are both quite safe."

A little head appeared and then a body and, finally, the whole of the elflike creature that was Jamey Tate. "You be Miss Gorham? Me mam says yer a right one. You won't be telling people where Jamey is hid, will ye?"

"No, of course not, Jamey. I would not tell a soul. May we

84

come up there and talk with you? I have not sat in a hayloft since I was a girl and I would very much like to do so again."

No other lady of Richard Pemmrington's acquaintance would have ever suggested sitting in a hayloft, but young Richard had learned never to be surprised at anything his governess might do. Moreover, since he was fast becoming convinced that Miss Gorham was the quintessential lady, he made no attempt what so ever to dissuade her from doing something so very unorthodox.

Together they climbed up into the loft, and, as young Richard was able to produce a handful of bonbons from his pockets, the three of them were within minutes thicker than thieves. Slowly the conversation came around to the subject of Mr. Duffy, and although Jamey Tate could not express himself very coherently, he seemed to know a great deal about Mr. Duffy. Margaret could understand little of it herself, but Richard, in a week or so, seemed to have mastered the art of communicating with this strange and shy young child.

"You know, Miss Gorham, Jamey has only two kinds of people. Right ones and wrong ones, so to speak. He doesn't like Mr. Duffy at all—he says Mr. Duffy is the second-worst man in the county."

"And who is the worst?" Margaret asked.

Jamey buckled up. "He won't say, Miss Gorham, but I think from what he has let drop before that I know. It seems strange, to be sure, but Jamey thinks Uncle Anthony is the very devil himself. My uncle must have beat him. He says he has seen Anthony kill things cruel-like—Jamey is very fond of animals, you know. Here, Jamey, have another bonbon. And not to worry—Miss Gorham, Sir Hillary, and I will protect you from Mr. Anthony and Mr. Duffy. Won't we, Miss Gorham?"

"We will do our best, Jamey," Margaret answered.

A few minutes later young Richard was dusting the straw off the back of Miss Gorham's gown and they were returning to the house for lunch.

"Miss Gorham, there is something dashed smoky going on around here, is there not?"

"Yes, I think there very well may be, Richard."

"Then there will be work to be done setting everything right. May I be a part of it?"

"I don't know. I don't know that I will be allowed to be a part of it. Women and children are so often excluded from anything significant."

"Why?" he asked as they were approaching the kitchen door.

"I suppose on the pretext that we are being protected. I think it is all flummery, but it is the way of the world, Richard."

"Well, if Uncle Hillary is in charge, everything will turn out for the best. He is the bravest brightest man ever, don't you know. And when I grow up I will be just like him—except I don't think I can bear to be so very pleasant to everyone as he is—always smiling to the stupidest people."

Fortunately they had arrived at the kitchen door and Miss Gorham was spared the necessity of commenting on Richard's analysis of his uncle's character.

Chapter 9

An important part of Hillary Pendragon's value to Wellington was the extraordinary interpretive power of his mind. Intuitively, he was able to piece together a complex puzzle from very few bits of information. Sir Hillary began by accumulating any number of diverse observations—a slip of the tongue, some object out of place in a room, exchanged glances between people who should not have been acquainted—these he regarded as small parts of a jigsawed whole; to be painstakingly reconstructed section by section. Not until the broad outline of the puzzle was pieced together did Sir Hillary attempt to analyze it.

Sir Hillary's methods had been successful not only because of his superior intellect but also because he had managed always to work in a mental state approaching absolute detachment. Hillary Pendragon *never* allowed himself to be irritated or swayed by emotions.

Unfortunately, in the situation at Pemmfield he found that he could not, as yet, force himself to think very clearly. How could he remain dispassionate when the welfare of these people had been, for years, his personal responsibility? In a very real sense, everyone at Pemmfield was his family. Here, he *was* emotionally involved, and almost inevitably his emotions had begun to seriously interfere with his thinking. The puzzle at Pemmfield was not coming into focus as it should. For example, in the vast jumble of odd little facts and discrepancies there was one set of anomalies which persisted in coloring his vision. He knew that there was too much which remained to be explained—too many discordant notes—in Miss Gorham's character. For example, he could find no reasonable way of accounting for seeing Mr. John Paul coming into the garden with Miss Margaret Gorham at an hour when Miss Gorham should just have been descending to the schoolroom. The two of them had been walking for some distance, and they seemed to enjoy a state of familiarity which was not only strange but somehow deeply disturbing. Of course, Miss Gorham was protective of the young man—as she seemed to be protective of almost everyone with the possible exception of Mr. Duffy and of Hillary Pendragon. But protectiveness could not, in itself, begin to account for their presence in the garden at that hour in the morning.

Without once attempting to analyze his own very emotional response to this matter, Sir Hillary decided that before he could clear his mind to consider the mystery at Pemmfield in general he would have to resolve some of the mystery surrounding Miss Gorham and, in particular, the matter of Miss Gorham's early-morning expedition.

At dinner that evening Hillary announced that he would not be spending the night at Pemmfield. This announcement appeared to be accepted without any comment, but later, when the ladies had gathered in the drawing room while the gentlemen had been left to their port, Hillary's proposed absence was discussed at length.

"Depend upon it," Julia said, her eyes twinkling, "it will be Madelaine Quincey."

Gwendolyn Campbell responded on cue, "And who, pray tell, is Madelaine Quincey?"

"Mrs. Quincey is our very own local wicked widow. She is very ravishing and equally attainable. Actually, I am rather fond of her myself. I could not, of course, burdened as I am with scruples, think to pursue her style of life, but she *is* enchanting. Hillary has always been very discriminating in his choice of women, and Madelaine Quincey can be proud to have attracted his attentions."

"Shame, shame, Cousin Julia! You have lured me into the wilds of Devonshire on a false scent."

"No, I have not, Gwen dearest. If we cannot bag you this particular fox it will not be because of Madelaine Quincey. She is no competition for you. To be sure she is a widow and very beautiful, but where Hillary finds such easy comfort he is unlikely to look for a permanent attachment. Madelaine is a woman of the world, and I suppose she will eventually remarry, because she has so very much to offer any man—but she will not marry Hillary Pendragon."

Gwendolyn's eyes had narrowed. "No, Hillary is too proud to even consider marriage to an easy widow. Still, Julia, do you think you might arrange it so that I can meet Madelaine Quincey?"

"Why ever for, Gwen?"

"I might learn something about what sort of bait our fox is fond of."

Alicia Campbell had begun to color, and, turning to Miss Gorham, she very quietly suggested a turn in the gardens. "It is not that I disapprove of this sort of conversation, Miss Gorham, it is simply that I find such worldliness very depressing."

"Yes, I know what you mean. It is something like a wisp of the shadow of death on a clear spring day." They were both speaking very quietly as Margaret continued, "But Alicia, if you do not learn to understand how the people around you think, you will never be able to assess either their worth or your own."

Gwendolyn had turned to her sister. "Alicia dear, do you have secrets or are you merely acting the part of the very delicately nurtured female in order to assuage the wrath of the righteous governess? It will not do, you know." And then to Margaret, "Alicia simply must acquire a *little* town bronze or I am afraid she will be very disappointed in life. Life is not kind to hopeless romantics. Don't you agree, Miss Gorham?"

"I have found, by and large, that life is not kind to the vast majority of mankind, nor have I discovered a *sure* means to better one's odds, but, perhaps, a cheerful disposition coupled with a firm understanding may enable one to face life's adversities better than would a veneer of cynicism."

Lady Pemmrington spoke before Gwendolyn had managed a reply, "Yes, precisely, Miss Gorham. You are always so wise." Julia was smiling thoughtfully. "Tell me. Do you think that because I am fond of Madelaine Quincey and because I do not resent her relationship with Hillary, I too am a cynic?"

"Not at all, Lady Julia. Would you still be fond of Madelaine Quincey if she had been involved with your own husband—Sir Scott?"

"Dear me no. I would have been inclined to murder her."

"And if Madelaine Quincey was involved with the husband of a friend? What would you do then?" Margaret asked.

"I don't really know what I would do. It would be so difficult to know how to proceed without hurting anyone unnecessarily.... But I do know that I would not be *fond* of Mrs. Quincey. I would probably be tempted to give her the cut direct every time the opportunity arose."

Gwendolyn laughed. "Miss Gorham, you are right again. My Cousin Julia is as hopelessly romantic as is Alicia—the sole difference being that Julia has a few more years of life under the belt. That added experience does not, in any significant way, seem to have matured her judgment in these matters. *I* should not be surprised or particularly resentful if my husband were involved with other women, and I should be very surprised if the husbands of my friends were not. But it is strange that while Sir Hillary calls on a wide assortment of Mrs. Quinceys one never hears of his name coupled with any of the high fliers favored by other members of the ton."

"Muslin company—Hillary?" Julia trilled. "Hillary is far too fastidious for such as that. Hillary Pendragon has never had to *pay* for his pleasures."

Gwendolyn Campbell turned back toward Margaret. "And what, Miss Gorham, do you think of a man who never pays for his pleasures?"

"My dear Miss Campbell, if I should ever encounter such a man I would consider him a freak of nature and counsel him to join a circus. It has been my experience that we all, men and women alike, invariably pay for our pleasures."

Gwendolyn's smile dripped sarcasm. "I bow to your superior wisdom, Miss Gorham. You would have made a splendid clergyman. But does not such excessive virtue become a trifle confining?"

Alicia, who had become vastly more courageous in the last few days, surprised everyone, herself included, by coming to the assistance of the beleaguered governess. "Gwendolyn, you are being quite unfair and cattish. Miss Gorham is not a starched-up Calvinist clergyman, and virtue is not some sort of shroud in which one is buried. Anyone would look stodgy-virtuous if their profession required them to dress in blacks and browns. Don't you think so, Julia?"

"Indeed I do. Blacks and browns are very depressing."

Margaret patted Alicia on the hand and nodded to Lady Julia before addressing Gwendolyn. "No, Miss Campbell, I do not *feel* confined. But remember you are still very young. Ask me again in twenty years whether virtue is such a terrible burden."

Fortunately, at that moment, the two gentlemen joined them and the conversation turned to less sensitive subjects. Sir Hillary did encounter several particularly arch looks from Miss Campbell, but he ignored them. Hillary was no fool and he knew how his announcement would, of necessity, be interpreted. In fact he had called on Mrs. Quincey only once since his arrival in Devonshire, and he had found that one visit depressingly flat. Hillary had, however, never suffered from his reputation as a rake, and he had always been quite content to let the world think what it would of his libertine propensities. And so he simply ignored Miss Campbell's arch looks and even found himself taking a certain sort of perverse pleasure in the veiled contempt he perceived in Miss Gorham's eyes.

After an hour spent flirting even more outrageously than usual with Gwendolyn Campbell, he excused himself for the evening. And, once having made his excuses to the rest of the houseparty, Sir Hillary left the manor house. He had briefly considered enlisting Robbie's aid in this venture and then decided against it. Sir Hillary had no intention, if he could avoid it, of disillusioning Robert Mansfield about his childhood friend.

Hillary had his horse saddled and rode about the countryside for a bit and then, clandestinely, returned on foot to Pemmfield manor. By half past eleven Miss Gorham's lights had been extinguished, and Hillary waited, half expecting her to leave the house directly afterward. In this he was disappointed. Hillary stalked the grounds all through the long night waiting in vain for any sight of Margaret Gorham, and he was just beginning to believe that his vigil was quite useless when, just before dawn, as the light was scarcely beginning to break through the horizon, he saw Miss Gorham slip out of the house and move quickly over the south lawn.

From a discreet distance, Hillary Pendragon followed her. He was astonished, and a little shocked, that she did not behave in the least bit furtively. Miss Gorham remained, as ever, sternly erect, although she was moving with an uncommon speed. In the semi-light of dawn he followed her across the park and through to the home farm, and then he saw her disappear into the Fultons' barn. Under normal circumstances the Fultons' barn would be considered a strange place for a rendezvous, but, almost instantly, Sir Hillary's mind had pieced together yet another part of his puzzle. It was to be a very strange rendezvous. Margaret Gorham had to be the owner of the wild horse. Superficially Hillary realized that this must be the case, but he had not begun to assimilate the fact even when, a few minutes later, a lithe little figure in rough boy-type clothing emerged from the barn. Her hair was loosely tied away from her face, and she moved with an easy grace over the rough stones despite the fact that she had exchanged her sturdy walking boots for a pair of what appeared to be soft leather slippers.

In the half-light he heard the softest, gentlest of whistles, and the young stallion lifted his head, pawed the earth, and, turning, bounded for the fence and his waiting owner.

After a preliminary exchange of affection, the girl was astride, bareback, without even a halter. She must be mad, he thought. Stark raving mad. Sir Hillary seemed more than confirmed in this opinion when the horse reared its magnificent head and began to prance. Hillary, moved by a curious mixture of fear and anger, cursed silently, Damn it, bring that animal to heel! But the rider made no visible effort to bring the animal under her control—on the contrary, she seemed to enjoy his natural exuberance quite as much as he did. She simply moved with her mount and threw herself into the vitality of the animal. As they moved across the fields they seemed one creature—woman and horse—riding swiftly together into the sun.

For the next half hour Sir Hillary Pendragon watched mesmerized as Pegasus Gorham and her horse shared the morning, together in perfect freedom. Hillary had heard of riding like this before, but he had never imagined it to be so lacking in structure and in discipline. Instead of the measured precision Hillary had been taught to emulate, he saw before him a rider and a horse, one body, moving in fluid grace with no rules and no limits. And yet neither the rider nor the mount could be said to be out of control—control was in no sense relevant; instead of control there was a sort of shared communion. Hillary saw her ride under the animal's neck and off to the side, but this riding was in no way like the acrobatics one might see in an exhibit. He was witnessing an exercise in freeform exuberance. All the while he could hear,

91

drifting across the meadow, the light lilting voice of the girl singing, and then laughing, after they'd taken a fence, salaamed through the bushes, and galloped to the end of the run, where she reached out to take the imaginary trophy.

For the first time in his life, Hillary Pendragon found himself consumed with jealousy. It was not enough to witness such an event. He wished, with all his considerable will, to be a *part* of that scene, to be another wild heathen godlike creature and a partner in that ritual dance.

Then Hillary saw the girl stoop and retrieve a shapeless hat, and, stuffing her hair up into the hat, she became a boy. They jumped the fence and took off across the fields toward the east.

Half an hour later they returned, the rider dismounted, and, after another exchange of great affection, Pegasus Gorham disappeared into the barn with two pails of water which had been left waiting beside the well.

A few minutes later Miss Margaret Gorham emerged again—precise to a pin in her coarse black stuff gown and her hair pulled back tightly into a regimental bun. She moved out quickly toward Pemmfield Manor, although she did not seem to be in a great hurry. Her movements were still fluid, and she stopped from time to time to pick a flower or to admire the morning. Just out of sight of the manor house, Sir Hillary saw her stiffen her shoulders—he imagined her face hardening—and visibly bracing herself, Miss Margaret Gorham—"the General"—advanced back into the field of battle.

An hour later Sir Hillary dismounted at the stable and made his way to the breakfast room, where he joined the other members of the house party for a dilatory meal. He noticed that Robert Mansfield was examining him carefully, and once when Hillary could not quite suppress an especially aggressive yawn, he saw Robert's eyebrow quirk in a silent question.

Since the gentlemen's change in domicile, Gwendolyn had forced herself to attend breakfast with the others, but as she was still never at her best before noon, she could not be expected to allow Sir Hillary's yawn to pass without comment. "You seem a trifle weary this morning, Hillary."

"Do I?" he countered with cold civility.

Miss Campbell was momentarily nonplussed, and then she smiled innocently. "I have always been of the opinion that the English breakfast is served at a barbaric hour. I declare I do not think it is civilized to stir out of bed before eleven."

When Hillary did not respond to this sally, Lady Julia added brightly, "But surely on such a lovely spring morning you will be eager for a ride. Alicia and I have planned to take the carriage into the village, and you will join us, won't you, Gwendolyn?"

"And I shall escort the ladies," Robert offered with a flourish.

"To be sure, Mr. Mansfield," Julia trilled. "We will not want such a slow top as Sir Hillary. I believe poor Hillary is coming down with a cold, and I think he should rest in his room this morning. I shall send cook up with a posset."

"A capital suggestion, Cousin Julia. And now, if you ladies will excuse me, I shall return to my room."

He stood and bowed to the ladies, noticing that Miss Gorham, propriety itself, sat silently sipping her tea and did not even bother to disguise the contempt in her eyes.

Robert stood and followed his friend from the room. "Hillary, a moment, please. I should like to have a word with you." Once outside the room they stopped.

"Whew," the younger man said, while symbolically wiping his brow, "A bit cattish in there, was it not?"

"More than a bit. What is on your mind, Robbie my lad?"

"What's on my mind, he says. I thought that we were in this thing *together*, Hil."

"And so we are."

"Gammon. You know, Hil, I have never seen you show any signs of fatigue except when we spent the whole night on watch or on horseback. I cannot believe that a mere widow could so decimate you."

"I'm growing older, Robbie."

"Cut line, Hillary. You need not trust me, but don't take me for a fool."

"I would never take you for a fool, but there are some things that I cannot share."

"Damnation. Between you acting so *secretly* and Pegasus acting so *differently* I am coming to feel like a man who has just lost two of his last three friends in the world."

Hillary stopped and took the younger man by the shoulders. "Please bear with me, lad. I cannot speak for your Pegasus, but my disease, I hope, is passing. I have simply to work through some of this problem alone." And then when Robert did not reply, he continued, "You do see that never before when we worked together on the Continent were we *personally* involved. I am having trouble handling it."

"Yes, I can understand that. I would myself be very leery if we were working in Yorkshire amid my family."

"That is only a part of it, Robbie. I ask only that you give me time."

Robert nodded, and then, saluting smartly, he turned and went back down to the breakfast room.

"Do you ride, Miss Gorham?" Gwendolyn was asking as the ladies and the gentlemen of the houseparty were setting out for their afternoon exercise later in the day.

"Occasionally, Miss Campbell," Margaret answered as she supervised the mounting of her charges on three of the ponies so that they could, at a safe distance, and with several grooms, follow along with their seniors.

Sir Hillary was occupied in tightening the cinch of Gwendolyn's saddle, but he looked up at this answer and noticed that Miss Gorham's face was almost completely devoid of expression. Robert, on the other hand, was grinning, and even Alicia was hard put to contain a smile.

"But then you ought to follow the children and the grooms," Gwendolyn was saying.

"Oh no, Gwendolyn. Miss Gorham has other work to do at home," Julia answered.

"But that is unfair, Cousin Julia. Even a governess ought to be allowed an occasional ride, don't you think? I understand your father was a military man, Miss Gorham. I have found that military gentlemen are uncommonly fond of the hunt. Did you often ride to hounds in Yorkshire?"

"Military gentlemen on very limited incomes do not, as a rule, keep hunters, Miss Campbell, and I do not think that my father was ever truly *fond* of the sport. I have myself never been a member of a fox hunt."

Anthony Dillingham had just ridden into the courtyard. He had been invited on the afternoon expedition in order to round out their numbers. "Are you squeamish about killing the poor fox, Miss Gorham? So often women are, you know."

Margaret hesitated before answering. "No, Mr. Dillingham, I do not believe that I would be squeamish about the loss of animal life *if* it served some useful purpose."

Anthony favored them with a thin smile. "And I am quite certain, Miss Gorham, that it can make no difference to the feelings of the fox whether or not its death serves 'some useful purpose.' Death is death."

94

Miss Gorham had folded her hands and was looking directly at Mr. Dillingham. "Because the fox cannot discern the difference is no reason that I cannot."

Gwendolyn Campbell took the reins from her groom and turned her horse to face Margaret. "My dear Miss Gorham, do you not realize that you are setting yourself out against *the national sport?*"

Margaret Gorham had no wish for further unpleasantness, but she would not retreat. And so, quite without rancor, she parried, "Perhaps so, Miss Campbell, but if I am to hunt at all, I would certainly prefer to hunt alone. I find that there is something very offensive about hunting in packs."

Anthony Dillingham almost sneered. "Ah, but the pack offers protection in the hunt, Miss Gorham."

"Perhaps, Mr. Dillingham, but I do not think I need protection from a fox who is running full-bore in the opposite direction."

Hillary had tightened and tested his own cinch and had mounted his horse when he intervened, smiling at his cousin Anthony. "To tell the truth, coz, I have begun to loose my taste for our local sport. Our hunts are far too civilized. We prefer our quarry armed, do we not, Robbie my lad?"

Robert laughed lightly. "I'm afraid, Hil, that you prefer your quarry armed to the teeth and no more than three feet from your nose. If half the aristocracy of England preferred to live *that* dangerously we would all be dead."

The others laughed, and after Miss Gorham had excused herself they set out on the path toward the shore.

Sir Hillary attached himself firmly to Lady Julia, leaving Robert Mansfield to Alicia Campbell and Anthony Dillingham to Gwendolyn Campbell.

Anthony and Gwendolyn had gone on ahead and were apparently continuing their caustic conversation, and Robert and Alicia were falling well behind. Julia smiled in appreciation of this maneuver and remained silent until the other couples were so far away that private conversation was assured.

Then she looked back, smiling. "Hillary, you are so very clever. I could not have found a better husband for Alicia myself."

"I am certain the initiative was not mine, Julia. I did not know about the courtship until Robert's arrival in Devonshire. Is it *so* obvious to you?"

"But of course, you goose. It is a very properly conducted

courtship, but any ninny can see that the two of them are head over heels in love."

"Then why is it taking Gwendolyn, who is nobody's fool, so long to perceive the obvious?"

"Do you think she has not noticed? I believe that Gwendolyn is quite aware of Mr. Mansfield's affection for her sister, but Gwendolyn cannot *like* it, and therefore she ignores it. I'm very much afraid that Gwendolyn Campbell must be the center of *all* masculine attention, and then too she has always been accustomed to think of Alicia as a plain silly little girl. When one is so beautiful and when one has never become used to competition it must be very disquieting to see a younger sister so lovingly courted. Praise God that your Mr. Mansfield is merely a Yorkshire squire or we would have a Mount Vesuvius on our hands."

"And how, my wise little Julia, can you read all that into your Cousin Gwendolyn's character?"

"Hillary, for all your vast experience I do not think you have ever bothered to *understand* women. It fairly shrieks. Gwendolyn is in a very pesky humor, but of course she cannot, in public, be endlessly catty with her sister, and so she vents her spleen on a relatively helpless adversary—a woman of lower social position, who is, as Gwen sees it, a natural victim."

"Julia, do I detect a note of bitterness in your voice? It is not like you to be bitter about anyone."

"Am I bitter? Perhaps I am. I have, after all, been somewhat disillusioned—I had held out such high hopes for Gwendolyn and she has disappointed me."

Hillary, his eyes twinkling, stroked his chin in perplexity. "You no longer think I should marry Gwendolyn?"

"Cawker. As if you ever intended to.... But Margaret Gorham is my friend, and although I do not *think* Gwen's comments really touch her I do not like to have a dependent of mine treated maliciously."

They had just come to the Fulton's pasture. "Speaking of Miss Gorham, Julia—do you know she was riding early this morning?"

"But Hillary, you could not have passed the Fultons' on the way home from...oh, I see. You must have passed Miss Gorham on the road. But however did you recognize her? No one else has."

"I gather then that you are fully aware that she does ride in the mornings."

"Yes, of course, it was one of the conditions of her coming to work at Pemmfield. She keeps her own horse and has an hour or two in the morning to ride. Miss Gorham is *always* back for breakfast, you know."

"And yet you did not think to mention that arrangement to me?"

"No, I didn't, did I? I suppose it was because I knew you were bound to disapprove. And Miss Gorham is most particular about her privacy. Beyond myself and the Fultons no one knows she rides."

"Despite the fact that she leaves the home farm?"

"Indeed she does, and I glimpsed her once myself. But the villagers think she is one of our stable boys—in fact, the word is out that the strange morning rider is the Tate boy—the one they say is an idiot. Unless one knows it is Miss Gorham, she is the very last person one would expect to ride in a manner quite so abandoned. It is not at all unnatural that villagers associate the rider with a species of madness."

Robert Mansfield and Alicia Campbell had ridden up to them as they passed the pasture.

"I see our Pegasus is boarding her horse," Robbie said casually.

"You recognize the animal, Robert?"

"Certainly, Hil. I was there when she bought him from my father. Pegasus was certain that he could never be broken, and we believed her. She knows horses."

Alicia had joined the conversation. "Oh dear, I shouldn't think anyone could ride that animal unless perhaps they subdued him with a bit and a great deal of weight."

"Pegasus uses neither."

"Then she must be a magnificent horsewoman, Robert. I wish she would come riding with us some afternoon," Alicia said.

"She won't, not our Pegasus. You would never find her riding sidesaddle in a habit. Get her on a horse and neither of them can be confined. She is as free as the wind. We used to call her the heathen. Which is very strange, when you come to think of it, because in all other ways she has always been such a serious and virtuous girl."

"And how does a serious little English miss learn to ride like a confirmed heathen?" Hillary snapped.

"You've seen her, Hil?"

"Yes, early this morning. It appears that the governess takes an hour or two each day to ride about the countryside."

The two women had fallen several yards behind, and Sir Hillary was almost alone with Robert.

Robbie rode in silence for a moment before cocking an eyebrow. "I think I am very disappointed in you, Hil. If you could only have a little faith in the judgment of your friends it would save you a deal of energy. It must have been a very long cold night."

"Who taught her?"

"Silver Fox."

"Silver what?"

"Silver Fox—an aborigine my Uncle Steven brought home from America. We used to say that Silver Fox was the only man Pegasus ever considered marrying."

"An American Indian?"

"Yes, and he was a strange one. The two of them were kindred spirits, so to speak. He never talked to anyone else—and we don't know that he *talked* to Pegasus but they were always together. He taught her to ride as he did, and he taught her how to track and to hunt as well. I tell you, Hillary, our Pegasus is a good man to have about in a pinch."

"Where is this Silver Fox now?"

"Heaven knows. Pegasus was only nine at the time, but I know her mother breathed a sigh of relief when Uncle Steven decided to return to America, and of course he took Silver Fox with him. They stayed in Yorkshire less than a year, and I think *my* mother had something to do with their decision to leave."

"I suppose at nine even the redoubtable Miss Gorham could not have followed them to America."

Robert laughed. "No, Pegasus did not follow them. We discussed it one night when we had both run away from home to camp out on Tabor Hill. Pegasus said she would have gone to America if she could have been a 'brave' like Silver Fox, but she knew that within a few years they would insist on her becoming something called a 'squaw.' And squaws, it seems, do not have any fun at all. According to Pegasus, squaws do *all* the work and have to walk several steps behind the men. That did it, you know. Our Pegasus would never walk several steps behind any man."

Chapter 10

That evening Sir Hillary and Robert Mansfield met with John Paul. At Hillary's insistence, Miss Gorham was excluded from the group, an exclusion which the other two men accepted only with reluctance.

Miss Gorham could have provided a bridge between the young farmer and the gentlemen from London—without her, John Paul continued almost as reticent as ever. For much of the first hour John Paul, hat in hand, had maintained a respectful silence. Finally and with exquisite patience Sir Hillary had begun to draw him out.

"Beggin' your pardon, Sir Hillary, but there is precious little I know for certain."

"Can you not tell us what you suspect, Mr. Paul?" Hillary asked gently.

"I could if it were only myself involved, sir." The young man seemed to be concentrating on the toe of his boot.

"You are concerned for the others?"

"Yes, sir." John was looking directly at him.

"And you will need some assurances, then, that innocent folk will not be made to suffer?"

"That's it, sir. Do I have your word of honor as a gentleman that the others, the local people, will not be held accountable for what they have been forced into?"

"You have my word on it."

And still the young man hesitated as if reluctant to speak. "Well, I don't think talking will make it any worse. It's the free trade, you see. O' course, we have always dabbled in the trade in these parts—a bottle here and there, a bit of silk for the ladies—but nothing big, you understand."

"Yes, of course. And if you believe, Mr. Paul, that I would have all my farmers transported to Australia for a bottle or two of vintage brandy, you are as daft as the rest of them."

"You wouldn't then. I must be certain."

"No, of course not. I should just as soon transport the gentry folk who buy the brandy and the silks."

"Right, sir. Well, the folks here have been in the trade since the Genesis, so to speak, and no one has been much concerned about it one way or t'other. Until sometime last year when Mr. Duffy came upon the men one night during a landing, and then there was Hell to pay—beggin' your pardon, sir. Duffy, working we believe for this other gentleman, kicked up a great fuss and threatened to expose all the men to the revenuers and have them packed off to Newgate—unless, that is, the men kept mum and went to work for Duffy."

"What sort of work?"

"They were supposed to continue in the trade, only now it was to be very well organized and the hauls were going to be enormous. Our men got nary a sixpence for their labor, but Mr. Duffy and his friend kept raking in the profits. As if that weren't enough, Mr. Duffy began to claim he had made all sorts of improvements on the estate—and he no doubt charged them to the Pemmringtons—but the improvements were never actually made, and no one dared to complain."

"Why not?"

John shrugged. "Who were they to complain to? The master was dead, and they did not know a Sir Hillary Pendragon off in London."

Sir Hillary swallowed and let this pass.

"One man, Owen Pitt, raised something of a stink and tried to get to Lady Julia."

"And?"

"And one moonlit night a stranger came to his house and set it to fire. Some men saw the arsonist, but in their haste to help extinguish the flames they could not pursue the criminal. There is some slight comfort in knowing that the monster that set that fire was himself burned when he ignited the oil, but one can hardly strip every man in Devonshire to find a man with body burns."

"And the Pitts? What of them?"

"That's the worst part, Sir Hillary. Our men tried to douse the fire and save Owen and his missus, but that house was built of tinder and afore they managed to break down the locked door Owen Pitt and his wife were already dead. Most probably, by the looks of it, they were well on their way to dead when the fire was set. After that, everyone was even more leery about complaining."

"I can well imagine they were. And what of your father?"

My father was in a rage about what had happened to the Pitts. You understand that he had never been a part of the free trade himself, but he knew something of the mess the others were into, and so he and my younger brother went along on one trip to check the thing out, so to speak. My dad found that the French were involved, and no ordinary French folk at that. There was this Frenchman in charge, my brother Simon says, who was not at all the smuggling type—not a working stiff, so to speak."

"How could Simon tell?"

"This bloke smiled at everyone and yakked on about liberty, equality, and fraternity. But you could see by his hands that he had never done an honest day's work in his life. That's the sort you can never trust. He's sure to look down on working folk. No, this was some sort of French gentry—maybe even an officer."

"What did your father do?"

"M'dad started asking questions very quietly and urging the men to stand firm against Mr. Duffy. I suppose they didn't dare murder my father as they did Owen Pitt and so they set out to ruin him. First they cut off his credit and then they cut off the work at the manor. Finally, he was forced to bag a rabbit, and they had him transported. Lady Julia tried to help him, but to no avail—there is no gainsaying that Duffy had the ear of Colonel Dillingham."

"And you have no idea of the identity of Duffy's colleague, Mr. Paul?"

"I have my suspicions about the other man, but I prefer not to share them until I have some proof, sir."

"Very well, Mr. Paul." And then after a moment or two Hillary continued in a different tone of voice, "You must have made a good soldier."

"Aye, I believe I did. I was never much good with a gun, but I could think on my feet. My mother and my family need me now, and so I guess I'm glad to be back home. Anyways with this slug I have in my leg I'm no use to the army."

"You will be able to serve your king very well right here in Devonshire. Incidentally, Miss Gorham has suggested that you would make an excellent bailiff to replace the infamous Duffy, and I believe I have come to agree with her."

John Paul was kneading his cap, and when he looked up he seemed again to be the awkward young man Sir Hillary had met in the garden. "Thank you, Sir Hillary, but beggin' your pardon, I am not doing this for my king, nor yet in the hopes of being bailiff. I'm doing it to help the folks I grew up with—they are good people. And for my dad, who should not be in Australia."

"I understand, Mr. Paul—and I thank you. I did not grow up in Devonshire, but, in a very real sense, the well-being of these people is my responsibility, and I am very much afraid that Sir Scott would be rightly disappointed in my performance thus far. Well, no matter, there is no use crying over spilt milk. We will set all to rights now."

John Paul bobbed his head, made his excuses, and disappeared into the darkness, leaving Hillary and Robert alone.

"Robbie, do you think it is the free trade?" Hillary asked abstractedly.

"Aye, I do, Hil. I've noticed that the brandy at the Dillinghams was fine and very French. I do not think it could have paid duty. And there is an uncommon number of other things about these parts that are new and have come from France."

"Yes, and this among them." Sir Hillary had produced a pound note from his pocket, "I picked it up in the village, and in the light of day you will see that it is an excellent counterfeit. I cannot determine how many such bills are in circulation, but Bonaparte has made other efforts to debase our currency."

"We had better send a message through to London, Hillary."

"I have already written to his nibs and asked for Mr. Muggins. I imagine that you will not be distraught if London insists we take an extended leave in Devonshire?"

Robbie was grinning broadly. "No, Hillary, *I* shall survive quite nicely, but what of yourself?"

"And what do you mean by that, young man?"

"I should not like to see you drifting into a marriage with the fair Gwendolyn. I don't want you for a brother on those terms, you know."

"Cawker. I have been successfully avoiding marriage with the Gwendolyns of this world for better than ten years now."

"Well then, I suppose free traders and French spies are our only danger, unless of course you continue to antagonize our Pegasus and she decides to murder you."

"Robbie, my lad, do you see me quaking in my boots?"

102

"No, Hillary, but perhaps you should be." And they were both laughing as they turned back to the manor house.

A few days later, Sir Hillary came upon Miss Gorham and young Richard deep in conversation.

"Are you quite certain, Richard?" she asked.

"Quite certain, Miss Gorham. You see, I was supposed to meet him at the footbridge on the brook. He had been very upset this last day or two, and yesterday when he saw Uncle Anthony he ran like the devil was after him. I am certain he had something of particular importance to give me today, and I promised him some of the box of bonbons that Miss Campbell brought, because you must know I do not need so many bonbons. And you know how very much he loves sweets. Miss Gorham, I don't know what to do." Richard was almost in tears.

Margaret Gorham patted the child on the shoulder and reassured him, "Don't worry, Richard. I will try to find him, and in the meanwhile, you return to the footbridge. There is a good chance that Jamey was delayed."

"Do you think I should? He trusted me, and I have a horrible feeling that I have let him down."

"Go down to the footbridge. If I find no sign of Jamey I will come to you shortly." She smiled at the boy and sent him off, but when she turned in Hillary's direction her face was no longer masking her very real concern.

"Sir Hillary, I did not see you."

"What is the problem, Miss Gorham? Perhaps I can help."

"The Tate boy has disappeared. He has never behaved like a normal child, but Richard is certain Jamey has been almost preternaturally frightened these last few days. They were to meet at the brook."

"Have you asked Mrs. Tate about Jamey's whereabouts?"

"Yes, and she believes he has gone out visiting his wild things, and, pray God, she is right. In any case I do not intend to disturb her until I know more. But I confess, Sir Hillary, that I am very frightened for the boy. In an atmosphere of such tension and animosity, he is precisely the sort of victim who is most likely to become someone's scapegoat."

"Perhaps you are right to worry. Incidentally, Miss Gorham, do you intend to ride about the countryside looking for the boy?"

"I beg your pardon?"

"We have been walking in the direction of the stables."

103

"Oh yes. Jamey often hides in the loft when he is troubled. It is his place, so to speak."

"I suppose we all need some place to run to when we are troubled, don't we?"

Margaret Gorham nodded, but her attention was elsewhere. She was leading Hillary around the muddy exterior of the stables, and she appeared to be looking for some object she had lost on the ground. Moments later, Sir Hillary watched Miss Gorham climb the ladder to the loft, swish the hay about, and then lift a handful to sniff it.

Then she climbed down the ladder, brushed her hands off, and turned back to Hillary. "He has not been here today."

"How can you be certain, Miss Gorham?"

"Jamey walks barefoot, and there is no sign of new footprints around the place. And also he has about him the scent of sage. Mrs. Tate believes sage has valuable medicinal properties. There is no fresh scent in the loft. No, I am quite certain that Jamey has not been here today."

"Miss Gorham, I can well understand your concern, but perhaps it is a trifle premature. Jamey Tate is only a boy and a quite different sort of boy at that. In all likelihood he did not understand *when* he was to meet Richard this afternoon."

Margaret Gorham slowly shook her head as she absentmindedly ran her hand, in an uncharacteristically nervous gesture, along the tack supplies which hung on the side wall of the stables. "I pray that you are right, Sir Hillary, but I can feel in my bones that something is dreadfully wrong. One *can* sense such things, you know."

It was then that they heard the soft whimpering of a child and Jamey Tate, his body bloody and his clothes in tatters, came tearing into the stable and ran toward the ladder into the loft. He was followed by Anthony Dillingham, a long whip in his hand. Sir Hillary saw Anthony raise his arm to strike at the child on the ladder, and, instinctively, Hillary moved to stop his cousin.

But before he could reach Anthony, Hillary heard him howl with rage and saw him drop the weapon. Another expertly handled whip had snapped at Anthony's right arm and ripped through the exquisite coat of blue superfine. Hillary looked back to see Margaret Gorham very still, a whip in her hand and a look of grim determination in her eyes.

She was the first to speak. "I believe we have had enough violence for today, Mr. Dillingham."

104

The child had disappeared into the loft, and Anthony picked up his whip, handling it very much as if he had decided on another victim. Mr. Dillingham and Miss Gorham had locked eyes for fully a minute before Sir Hillary intervened.

"Ah, Anthony, can't have you roughing up my dependents, can I? The little brat must have done something simply awful, but he is not all there, you know. I assure you I will make good the damage."

With an effort, Anthony turned his attention to his cousin. "Hillary, keep that bastard off my land, do you understand? Keep that bedlamite away from me. If I see him again I shall kill him." Then, turning his back on Sir Hillary and Miss Gorham, Anthony Dillingham marched out of the stables.

Hillary looked back to see Margaret Gorham grimly staring at the retreating figure. When he next spoke, Sir Hillary's voice had changed—it had entirely lost that lilting charm so characteristic of him and his class. Hillary Pendragon was dead serious. "You should not have done that. My Cousin Anthony is a very dangerous man. I could have stopped him *without* unnecessarily antagonizing him."

"Perhaps you are right. I had no time to think, and I acted impulsively. I will find the Tate boy and help him. Would you follow Mr. Dillingham back to his home?"

"Why?"

"Anthony Dillingham is in a blazing rage, and when a man such as that is angry someone will be made to suffer. He can no longer whip the Tate child, and although he would like to thrash me he cannot. I am concerned for what he might do to his own children."

"Do you think he is really as bad as that?"

"Yes, I do."

"I'll go then. And Miss Gorham..." Hillary had thrown his saddle on his horse and mounted.

"Yes, Sir Hillary?"

"Take care."

Two hours later, Sir Hillary was returning from Dillingham Hall on horseback when he heard a whispered voice calling to him. Hillary reined in and looked around for a few seconds before he spotted the man standing hidden behind a clump of bushes.

"Sir Hillary, a moment, if you please." It was young John Paul. Hillary smiled. It is, he thought to himself, almost preposterous for a grown man to be showing all the customary signs of formal respect while crouching behind a rhododendron bush. Silently, Sir Hillary dismounted and led his animal to the other side of the bushes.

"I've come with a message, sir. There is to be a landing tonight. Can you and Mr. Mansfield meet me about midnight at the old fence above Johnson Inlet?"

"Certainly. Is the landing to be at Johnson Inlet?"

"No, that inlet is too public, you know. I believe they will come into a cove farther up the coast, but my informant will know for certain and meet us at the fence."

"Very well, and thank you, Mr. Paul."

Doffing his cap again, John Paul said, "You're very welcome, sir, and I will see you at midnight then."

The young man had already disappeared into the dusk, and Sir Hillary slowly made his way up to the manor house to inform Robert Mansfield of their plans for the evening.

An hour later, Hillary was still deep in thought as his valet helped him change for dinner. Despite his best efforts he had not been able to shake off the shadows of Dillingham Hall. The scene at Anthony's home had been very grim, and it had taken all of Sir Hillary's great store of determination and charm to neutralize even a fraction of Anthony's ill humor. And in the end it seemed Hillary himself had become infected with that same malignancy.

As he adjusted his neckcloth and allowed the valet to help him into his coat, Hillary tried to force himself to focus on his plans for the midnight expedition.

Mr. Muggins, with whom he'd shared his suppositions, was expected in a day or two, and with some luck they would have by then produced a juicy tidbit of information to tempt the palate of his nibs in London. But Hillary could not like the enterprise. To be a spy in France was deadly difficult and required constant vigilance if one was to escape with one's life, to say nothing of one's knowledge. Here, in his own country, the same sort of activity made Hillary feel almost unclean, as if he were occupied in the relatively harmless but totally obnoxious task of clearing out a nest of vermin— a swarm of filthy insects burrowing away in one's food supply.

Wiping these grim thoughts from his mind, Hillary pasted a smile to his face and joined Robert and the ladies for dinner.

It seemed to be a strangely subdued dinner party, perhaps because Margaret Gorham was not there.

Lady Julia explained. "Miss Gorham will be staying the evening with the Tate boy. Richard has just brought me the message. It seems Jamey Tate is in a sad condition, and Miss Gorham's calm good sense is needed."

"Cousin Julia, I think you are too permissive with your dependents. Surely it cannot be appropriate to share your children's governess with the village idiot. Can it, Hillary?"

"Do you think idiocy is contagious, my lovely Gwendolyn?" Hillary answered, smiling lazily at her.

"No, of course not, Hillary. But it is not *comme il faut*. Nor is it *comme il faut* to allow a governess, no matter how very competent, such freedom."

"But Gwendolyn," Julia was saying, "we are a family here at Pemmfield. I am very pleased that Miss Gorham has set such a fine example in her consideration for the welfare of Jamey Tate."

Robert Mansfield could not remain silent. "Miss Campbell, I was raised with Margaret Gorham, and I cannot think of another woman who could be so effective in quieting a frightened child nor of anyone less likely to abuse her freedom."

None of the women had ever seen Robert Mansfield so stern before, and Lady Julia flung herself into the breach. "To be sure, Miss Gorham is a very responsible woman, and she has done wonders with my own children, Gwendolyn. Richard has improved enormously since Miss Gorham has come to us. He has become kind and responsible, and begins to remind me now of my beloved Scott. Thomas is not nearly so irritating, and Pamela is practicing on the pianoforte every day. I never thought I should live to see the day when she displayed such discipline. It is wonderfully gratifying, I can assure you, to wake up one morning and find that one's children are pleasant people."

"Come now, Cousin Julia, surely it is preposterous to attribute this metamorphosis exclusively to the efforts of Miss Gorham?"

"But of course Margaret Gorham is responsible for the improvement."

Sir Hillary smiled across at Gwendolyn and lifted his glass in a toast. "Lovely, lovely Gwendolyn. How many women can look like a Titian Venus? And you are even more beautiful when you are angry."

Coyly, Gwendolyn Campbell returned his smile. "Hillary, I believe you are only trying to distract me."

"Never say *only*, my dear."

"Flirt!"

"Too true, but why waste precious moments in bickering when we might be discussing matters of great significance?"

"Such as?"

"Such as your eyes."

Lady Julia shook her head in mock censure. "Hillary, this is the dinner table. *My* dinner table. You must not become so *intense*. It is not, somehow, appropriate."

"Quite inappropriate. Let us retreat to the drawing room."

Once in the drawing room, Sir Hillary occupied himself, at least outwardly, in the task of smoothing Miss Gwendolyn's ruffled feathers, and Lady Julia excused herself to tend to the children. Alicia and Robert were quite pleased to be left to their own devices and soon settled into a tête-à-tête in the far corner of the room.

"Alicia, my love. I don't know what possessed me. I should not have been ripping up at your sister over Pegasus."

"I know what possessed you, Robbie. Margaret Gorham is your friend and you could not stand by and see your friend abused. I would not have you any other way. Besides, Gwendolyn did not really attend to what you were saying. She was directing her comments at Sir Hillary, you know."

"Perhaps." Robert sighed, "Do you think they will make a match of it in the end?"

"Old gloomy face. Are you afraid for your precious Hillary? Well, you needn't be."

"I should not say this, Alicia, but I don't care for your sister at all."

"Silly, neither do I, now that I come to think of it. And neither does anyone else who comes to know her—least of all Sir Hillary. He is simply, how do you gentlemen put it, *acting as a decoy* for us at the moment. He is being *extraordinarily* considerate tonight, is he not?"

Robert noticed that his beloved was examining him intently, and he found himself strongly tempted to run a finger along his collar.

"Robbie, I am not very clever, but I *feel* things, and I feel that something very deep is going on here tonight."

"Yes, you're right about that. But I can't talk about it, my love. Not yet at least. With luck it will all be over and done with before long and I'll be able to explain then."

"And meanwhile it may be dangerous?"

"Not likely to be very dangerous."

"And you and Sir Hillary are in the thick of it. I suppose you will both be running off tonight."

"Yes, but how do you know?"

"Your Sir Hillary has the look of a man who is humoring a woman while his mind is off somewhere plotting."

"Alicia, my love, you are a knowing one and my own heart's delight. Will you bear with me until this is all over?"

"Of course I will, Robbie—as if I had a choice." And then she continued almost wistfully, "But you must be in the middle of a great adventure, and it is a trifle lowering to be excluded from such fun. I hope Miss Gorham, at least, is a part of it. If anyone understands what is really happening at Pemmfield, it is Miss Gorham."

"If Hillary has his way, even Pegasus will be excluded."

Sir Hillary had taken Gwendolyn by the arm and was leading her off onto the terrace and into the gardens.

Suddenly Alicia was looking up at Robbie and attempting to smile coyly, but she looked more like a very little girl about to ask for a treat. "I think your Hillary is being very helpful, Robert. They will not know that we have gone into the garden also."

Gently he placed her hand on his arm and smiled down at her. "Alicia, my darling, if I am to have an adventure tonight I can think of nothing more appropriate than to spend the next half hour in a very dark garden telling you how very beautiful you are."

"Cawker, don't *you* start sweet-talking like your tall friend over there or I shall think *you* an unfeeling wretch."

Since Robert took this opportunity to show her precisely how very feeling he was and since he managed to convince her of his feelings in the space of a very few moments and in a language far more eloquent than mere words, Alicia was quite content to remain in the garden indefinitely.

Later she could even spare a moment's thought and a little pity for that other couple, surely no more than ten yards away, for the beautiful Gwendolyn and the handsome Sir Hillary. What did they know of happiness?

Chapter 11

Hillary and Robert silently made their way to the old fence overlooking Johnson Inlet. John Paul was already there, and, doffing his cap in the near-total darkness, he began by paying his respects.

"What is the plan, Mr. Paul?" Hillary asked, having quickly dispensed with the formalities.

"Two of us, sir, will go down and follow the path along the shoreline. We will go east about a mile."

"You mean to No Man's Cove?" Hillary asked.

"Yes, sir, although I don't rightly know if it is properly known by that name."

"You forget, Mr. Paul, that I was, as a child, a great deal in this part of Devonshire."

"To be sure, Sir Hillary. And then you will be knowing that No Man's Cove is about as secret a sort of place as can be found on the coast of England."

"It is well enough hidden to be the seat of any sort of skulduggery, to be sure."

"Yes, sir, and, as I was saying, the action will be at No Man's Cove but the leaders of the group are in the habit of meeting at the small little hut hidden a ways up the ravine that runs down to the cove proper."

"Yes, I remember the hut. We played there as children."

"Well then, it might be wise, sir, for you to be the one to make your way there on the up path—the one that runs along the ridge of the cliffs overlooking the sea. From the hut you will have an excellent view of the cove and be in a position to spy on the leaders as well. Mr. Mansfield and I will take the low path which runs along the sea to Dead Man's Cove."

"And your informant?"

"My informant is waiting at the hut, sir—on the sea side but around the corner from the footpath coming up the ravine from the cove."

"A good place. Very well, then, we will be off. And after everything has quieted down we will meet here again."

"Aye, aye, sir."

"And Robert, you will remember, and yourself as well, Mr. Paul, that tonight we are here *only* to observe. Under no circumstances are we to become involved until we know the lay of the land and have taken all the various factors into consideration. There is more here than meets the eye and far more than an isolated bit of free trading on the Devonshire coast."

"To be sure, sir—mum is the word." John Paul bobbed his head.

"Good man. I will see you both here in several hours." And after wishing both of them the best of luck, Hillary made his way along the ridge of the hills while the two younger men started down to the beach to follow the rocky coast paths to No Man's Cove.

Half an hour later, Sir Hillary was silently circling the cottage to ascertain that it was indeed deserted and to locate John Paul's informant. He had no difficulty spotting the smallish figure hidden in the bracken precisely where Mr. Paul had predicted.

Hillary barely saw a head turn in his direction, and then, very quietly, he heard the now familiar voice. "Ah, Robbie, you have finally come. Well, settle down here and make yourself comfortable—there is no action, as yet, on this front."

Silently Sir Hillary sprawled down beside the boyish figure dressed in buckskins. She continued to speak. "Do you see the schooner there in the fog just to the right of us?"

He grunted an assent, and then—quite suddenly—Sir Hillary Pendragon found himself on his back with a very deadly little knife held firmly in the vicinity of his jugular.

"Who are you?" she asked.

Hillary, moving with catlike speed, whipped her wrist so that the hold on the knife was broken and shifted to where their positions were reversed and his hands were fastened to her throat.

"My dear Miss Gorham, if you insist on becoming involved in this sort of activity, you must learn a few of the rules. First, and most important, if you are about to use your weapon, never hesitate to strike, and certainly do not hesitate in order to ask a brainless question."

111

"You would have preferred it, Sir Hillary, if I had murdered you first, before ascertaining your identity?"

"I would have preferred it if you had tried. I find nothing so annoying as relying on rank amateurs."

"You have made your point, sir, and now would you kindly release your hold on me so that we may both of us assume a more comfortable position."

Sir Hillary, who had discovered that he at least was in a vastly comfortable position, slowly removed his hands from her throat but did not shift his weight.

In her most governesslike voice she continued, very much as if they were back in the schoolroom at Pemmfield, "That, sir, is some *slight* improvement. I believe we had now better begin exchanging some information, had we not?"

"Miss Gorham—or is it Pegasus?—the proper little governess manner will not do here, you know. One cannot assume *quite* that tone of superior propriety unless one is dressed in brown bombazine—it will not work in buckskins and britches. Any more than I could lisp and smile at you charmingly while dressed as I now am. No, here you had better accept that you are not the governess. In this business, I am the superior and you are something of a subaltern. Will you take instructions or not?"

She hesitated for a moment or two. "Very well."

"Very well, what?"

"Very well, sir."

"I suppose that will have to do for now." And slowly, reluctantly, he rolled back over so that they were again side by side although they remained touching. Hillary felt Miss Gorham stiffen, and he could almost hear her gritting her teeth. Pleasant or not, their proximity was no more a neutral matter for Miss Gorham than it was for himself.

Meanwhile Margaret was experiencing a host of very strong and unaccustomed sensations, all of which she readily, but inaccurately, attributed to anger. Miss Gorham resolved not to pander to such base emotions or to this gentleman's infernal ego, but, irritated as she was, she had to *force* herself to settle down and, calmly and rationally, explain their situation.

"Jamey Tate has been haunting this cove, and he is the true source of our information. It is very difficult to make out precisely what he means, but, after about three hours of listening, so much seems clear: There will be a landing tonight and the chief men will be meeting here as they always do shortly after the cargo is offloaded. I believe that part of the cargo will be hidden in the caves, and, as is also usually the case, at least one or two men will disembark with the cargo and make their way, with full saddlebags, toward the Exeter road."

"Is that all of what Jamey knows?"

"Do you want all of it?"

"Yes. You give me the information and I will judge its value." When Margaret continued to hesitate, he growled, "I said, give me the rest of the information." Sir Hillary was speaking in a tone of voice Miss Gorham had never heard before, and it was a tone well calculated to put fear into the hearts of his bravest subordinates.

Reluctantly, Margaret braced herself and continued, "Jamey Tate believes that the big men, as he puts it, are Mr. Duffy—which we knew—and your Cousin Anthony."

"Which anyone but an imbecile would have guessed by now."

"Surely the involvement of Mr. Dillingham must affect your response to this situation, Sir Hillary."

"It is none of your damn business what my response to this situation is, Miss Gorham, and you would probably be very surprised if you knew. I will do my duty, and, in this case, my duty is clearly no respecter either of class or of blood relationship. Do I make myself clear?"

"Quite clear," she answered with just the barest hint of skepticism in her voice.

"Then the lot of you had better stop attempting to launder my information. Agreed, Miss Gorham?"

"Agreed, Sir Hillary. Hush now—there is some movement in the cove."

For the next hour the two near the hut lay silently watching thirty or so men in longboats take a cargo from the silent blackened hulk of the schooner. Two men, and then a third, moved from the ship onto one of the longboats. When they reached the shore two of these men disappeared from sight, presumably to be mounted and to set out on the Exeter road. The third man disappeared, only to reappear five minutes later on the footpath leading to the hut.

He approached the hut cautiously and peered in through the window before quietly entering through the door. Shortly thereafter, a second man, who could be clearly identified as Mr. Duffy, came trudging up the same path from the cove, called out a code word, and was answered from inside by a heavily accented voice. Mr. Duffy stepped into the hut.

Finally a third figure appeared on the ridge path. This man was heavily muffled in clothing, and he could not be identified. He approached the hut carefully, repeated the code word in a disguised voice, and was also admitted.

Margaret Gorham had begun to move. Sir Hillary watched in open admiration and with some trepidation as Miss Gorham inched away from him and moved silently around toward the upside of the hut, where she would command a view through one of the small windows. She was not walking nor yet could she be said to be crawling. Her body seemed perfectly flat, and she was, Hillary could have sworn, sliding in an unearthly silence across the open ground. At times she would stop and remain absolutely still in the way a cat will when it suddenly looks about to ascertain its direction and the attendant risks. And then she would alter her course by several degrees and work farther around the hut. When she was again partially concealed in the bracken she assumed a crouching position and seemed to race—almost silently and almost completely hidden—to her preferred vantage point. Only when she had arrived did Sir Hillary set out and cover the same territory in what he felt to be a decidedly cloddish manner. Sir Hillary had been in the business of spying for many years, but never before had he seen a human being move quite so much like a stalking animal.

He settled in close to Miss Gorham, and, as there was a single candle burning in the hut, they were able to observe the occupants as well as hear their conversation.

"*Eh bien,* messieurs, and it is still another glass-smooth landing."

"Yes." It was the voice of Mr. Duffy.

"*Certainement,* and we anticipate no problems on the next run. *N'est-ce pas?*"

"When will it be, monsieur?" Duffy asked.

"When it will be is two weeks from today. It is very important that there will be no problems on that evening, messieurs."

"You will be landing more men?" Again Duffy.

"We do not pay you to ask questions, Monsieur Duffy. We pay you to make quite certain there will be no problems."

"Mr. Duffy understands, Pierre. You and I, we will discuss this matter at the usual meeting place in Exeter next week."

The voice was still heavily muffled and could not be identified.

"Ah yes, and you are always so very careful, my dear comrade—even when you are among friends."

"But Pierre, is one ever certain one is among friends?"

"Too true, monsieur. And now I bid you *au revoir*." and with these words, Pierre casually handed a sack of coins to Mr. Duffy and left the hut, presumably to return to the beach.

The other two remained in the hut for several minutes until all motion in the cove beach had ceased and the schooner had lifted her sails and was stealing toward open water.

"It won't do, sir. You must know that," Mr. Duffy said.

"What won't do?"

"*You* must know that we cannot continue as we have been. My role in the fiddling of the estate books has been spotted, and although your ever so grand Sir Hillary has not seen fit to press charges there is no telling when he might decide to act. It is only a matter of time until our cover is blown clear off."

"And what do *you* suggest, Mr. Duffy?"

"I will need more cash. I must leave here in the next day or two. People are beginning to suspect too much. It's that bitch of a governess—that Gorham bitch. I know she is the one who put Sir Hillary on to me."

"I think you *are* becoming *excessively* agitated, my dear Duffy."

"Well and good for you. *You* have no need to be nervous. After all, I am the only man on this side of the Channel who can positively identify you."

"Is that a threat?"

"That is a request. I need money and I need to leave Pemmfield."

"Yes, you do need to leave, Mr. Duffy." And then, without any warning, there was a muffled shot and Mr. Duffy had fallen. He was writhing on the floor and moaning horribly, but he managed himself to discharge a pistol at his adversary, apparently just grazing that gentleman's neck.

With his hand to his neck, the muffled gentleman took careful aim and shot the screaming man in the abdomen and then, with no sign of haste, slowly began kicking in the head of the whimpering mass that had once been Mr. Clarence Duffy.

At the sound of the first shot, Miss Gorham had stiffened, and when Duffy fell, she found her head sheltered in Sir

115

Hillary's shoulder and her ears muffled in his protective arms. Silently, she clung to him, and while his eyes continued to be fastened on the events in the cabin, he gently comforted the woman in his arms. Within minutes it was over and the muffled figure had dragged the now still form of Mr. Duffy from the hut to the edge of the ridge overlooking the sea. And then they both disappeared from sight.

Waiting silently for several minutes, Sir Hillary continued to comfort the woman.

"They are well and truly gone now. How are you doing?"

"You must think me a child, but I could not have imagined murder—cruel and senseless murder—to have been so horrible."

"Yes—it is the ultimate horror. I would have thought you a senseless block if you had not reacted as you did."

"Does one ever grow accustomed to such things?"

"A few abnormal people eventually grow used to such things, and there are some monstrosities of nature who grow to enjoy inflicting such pain. The rest of us never grow accustomed. One grows less surprised—that is all. One learns, out of a species of necessity, to brace oneself for the worst."

"Could we have helped that poor man?"

"No, we could not have helped him even if it had been wise to do so. Mr. Duffy was shot, the first time, in the lungs. One can tell by the sound and by the blood he was aspirating. The rest was simply to satisfy the cruel nature of his murderer. Duffy would in any case have been dead in a matter of minutes."

"Oh my God, I think I am going to retch."

"Yes, go ahead. It will make you feel a little better." But instead, she began to sob into his shoulder. He let her cry herself out, and after a few minutes, showing almost superhuman restraint, Sir Hillary pulled himself away from her and dried her tears. "We had best make our way back to the fence and meet the others."

"Should we not follow the man?"

"In the dark?" he asked.

"I suppose not."

"Do you think you could? We would need dogs."

"I *could,* with some light. But let's meet Robbie first."

And together, they swiftly moved along the ridge path and came to the fence only moments after the others had arrived.

Robert Mansfield was the first to speak, and he didn't bother with the formalities. "They unloaded what looked to

116

be about twenty casks of brandy and assorted other contraband. There were about thirty local men, and all of them, every single one of them, was sulky. The entire crew of the vessel seemed to be French, and three of them were left off onshore. We quickly lost sight of the one who seemed to be the leader, but we did see the other two pack their saddlebags with small rectangular packages and them mount the waiting horses. They were riding in the direction of the Exeter road. That is about all we have to report, sir."

"Very good, Robert. We were able to observe the leader in conference with Mr. Duffy and with another Englishman— presumably the leader of this side of the Channel. The leader was heavily disguised and so we cannot be certain of his identity, but we all seem to be entertaining the same suspicions."

Robert eyed Sir Hillary for a moment and then nodded in agreement. As if for confirmation, Robert turned to Miss Gorham. "Good lord, Pegasus, you look like death warmed over."

Margaret grinned lopsidedly and almost fell into his arms, leaving Sir Hillary to explain.

"We watched Mr. Duffy's termination. It was a very bad one." Hillary tried not to speak sharply, although he found himself quite irritated to have his role as comforter usurped.

"I'm going to be all right, Robbie. And I think I can track the other man once I have some light."

"'Track'—what does that mean, Miss Gorham?" John Paul asked.

Robert answered, "Pegasus's friend Silver Fox, the American aborigine, taught her how to track—that is, follow a prey. On a clear day, our Miss Gorham is better than a herd of hounds."

"That is an exaggeration, but I have one distinct advantage over the hounds. They may have a larger nose but I have a larger brain."

Hillary said, "Mr. Paul, why don't you return to your home so as not to arouse suspicion while Miss Gorham, Mr. Mansfield, and I continue with our work here."

Thus dismissed, John Paul turned to leave, while the other three returned to the hut and talked quietly through various alternative strategies until the first light of dawn.

"Well, I believe it is just barely light enough. Shall we be on our way, gentlemen?" Margaret asked.

Hillary had stood. "How can we be of help?"

"For the most part no one helps Pegasus when she is tracking," Robert volunteered.

"What Robbie means is that the task requires *all* my concentration and until I actually ask for help I am more than likely to become confused by any interference. You need only follow me and we will see if I have retained enough of Silver Fox's wisdom to find our villain."

"Silver Fox was a very wise man, I take it, Miss Gorham?"

"You are skeptical, Sir Hillary?"

"A bit. It seems strange somehow that Miss Margaret Gorham, the intrepid defender of every single one of the ideals of civilized society, should look for wisdom in a savage."

"In truth, Sir Hillary, I have never thought of it in quite that way before. I suppose that the ideals of our civilization need not be inconsistent with the wisdom of a Silver Fox. True wisdom is not a restricted cultural phenomenon."

"I have always thought it was."

"No, I think that once we have eliminated the frenzied fanatics of this world, we would find that a truly good man or a truly wise man of one civilization would, if we could overcome our own prejudice, be seen to be good and wise anywhere."

"And your Silver Fox was both good and wise?"

"Silver Fox was wise. I am not at all certain he could provide a model for goodness." She was smiling enigmatically to herself. "In any case, his was a nonverbal wisdom, and Robbie, who knew him, never understood him. One could not expect more from you, Sir Hillary, who never had the opportunity of meeting my friend."

Hillary was about to answer when Margaret glanced out the window and said, "Good, the light is excellent now. Let us be on our way."

Sir Hillary was holding the door for Miss Gorham, and he bowed slightly as she passed through. Once on the other side of the threshold, she stood rock-still for a minute or two. Looking at her, Sir Hillary could tell that once again Margaret Gorham had become that other person.

Hillary watched as Pegasus bent to examine with almost infinite care the sides of some bushes. Pocketing a scrap of cloth, she stood and stared down toward the ridge. Her face was now totally devoid of expression, and she stood poised, her eyes almost glazed over—trancelike. Slowly, without any further discussion or even acknowledgment of their presence, Pegasus led them to the precise spot where Mr. Duffy's body must have been catapulted into the sea, and then she turned inland. She appeared to have a limitless sort of patience and would stop every few moments to examine this or that, to feel the earth, and at least once to sniff the air. Slowly they had covered almost a quarter of a mile of an irregular path coming up from the sea. Then she stopped—totally engrossed in determining in which direction her quarry had veered.

Robert had held Sir Hillary back a few yards, and now he asked in an undertone, "Hillary, do you have any idea where Pegasus is leading us?"

"I know, or rather I *think* I know, where we are going. We are circling some of my uncle's outlying land now and should be breaking through soon onto a wooded part of the estate proper."

Robert was frowning. "I see."

"Not to worry, Robert. I am not likely to make a careless mistake simply because my own family is involved."

"I don't think I am particularly worried about you, but, for the first time in my life, I find myself a little concerned for Pegasus."

"It would be exceedingly strange if you were not. Your Pegasus is damn good, but she is still an amateur."

"I suppose so, but she has always been *my leader,* you see. We were forever getting into scrapes and I never once doubted that Pegasus could pull us out. It is only a few hours ago that I ever saw that Pegasus *herself* is vulnerable. This is all so new to her. You may well smile, Hillary, but I used to think of her as a very big person—even in the physical sense. And now I see that she is really quite small and almost delicate. Still, if one must have a woman along on this sort of expedition, Pegasus is a capital fellow to have."

"She is indeed, although Miss Gorham could profit considerably from a little learning in the art of taking instructions. Incidentally, Robbie, did *you* know she was the informant?"

"Lord, no. Not until John told me after you had taken off. Had I known I would have gone along to the hut myself. I have been thinking that we will be very lucky if the two of you do not come to fisticuffs before breakfast. You are both so accustomed to undisputed leadership."

"Fortunate indeed." Hillary was recalling his encounter with Miss Gorham's dagger. "There, Robbie, she has found something now—let's get on with it."

They continued to travel in silence for a few hundred

yards, and then Miss Gorham, quite suddenly it seemed, disappeared behind a tree. She reappeared almost as suddenly—no longer the impassive animal-like savage but now a blushing English miss who was hiding her face in her hands.

With a gesture she attempted to halt the two gentlemen, but Hillary, at least, ignored her and very slowly circled the tree himself to see Miss Porter, less than half dressed, in the arms of Anthony Dillingham.

Sir Hillary was not himself a blushing English miss, and so he took a few moments to analyze the scene before turning back to his companions. Anthony and the woman were in the garden of a smallish cottage which Hillary, Anthony, and Scott had used to call the Witch's Castle. Legend had it that the cottage had been inhabited by a witch who, shortly before her own burning, had put a dreadful curse on her own home. And consequently none of the villagers approached the cottage except with great trepidation. It was precisely this aura of supernatural danger which had first attracted the young cousins to the place. And who is to say the villagers were wrong, Hillary thought grimly. Scott is dead and Anthony and I have come to this.

Hillary noted, almost in passing, that Miss Porter was to be pitied—Anthony Dillingham could no longer in any sense be said to be a gentleman.

Forcing such bleak thoughts from his mind, Hillary returned to his companions. He found Robert waiting patiently and Miss Gorham, her color somewhat subsided, resting against the tree. Taking the girl by the arm, he silently led her away until, well clear of the Witch's Castle, they were able to speak freely in quiet whispers.

"I'm afraid, Miss Gorham, you have seen rather more in the last twelve hours than you had bargained for. How are you doing?" She looked up, expecting to see sarcasm in his eyes, but saw only a gentle sort of concern.

"It was very missish of me, to be certain. I am not usually a missish sort of person."

"Believe me, no one would take you for a missish sort of person. Robert, have you ever seen her blush before?"

"Never! It must have been quite a scene, Hillary."

"It was of some interest but nothing terribly unusual. Anthony and his Miss Porter in dishabille."

"Miss Porter?"

"Yes, Robbie, the charming little blond governess who will,

120

if the need arises, ruin herself by swearing that Anthony never left her side all night long."

"In fairness to your cousin, Sir Hillary, it is not at all unlikely that I could have continued following the trail *past* that cottage. It seems very strange that a man who had committed such a brutal sort of murder should be found only an hour or two later in that sort of situation."

"Miss Gorham, you may not be missish, but you are, nevertheless, incredibly naive. I'm afraid that is precisely how a thoroughly malignant murderer might cap an evening's work."

"But sir, to go directly from murder to that!"

"Did you think that was love, Miss Gorham? I can assure you it was not. Just another sort of violence. No, I do not mean to embarrass you further, and so I will not discuss it any more, but you must not be thinking that Anthony Dillingham is now beyond suspicion." And Hillary moved the discussion onto other less sensitive subjects. "You have collected various scraps of cloth since we left the hut, Miss Gorham; would you mind meeting me later in the library and identifying the pieces and where you found them? Can you remember the information for so long?"

"Yes, I think I must...and Sir Hillary, Robert, at least, should be back at Pemmfield by now or he will be missed."

"You and I will not be missed, then?"

"I am accustomed to ride in the mornings at Fulton's farm, and we are nearly there now. I shall ride again this morning."

"Is that wise, Miss Gorham? You must be exhausted."

"Perhaps it is not wise, but it is nevertheless essential. And you, Sir Hillary?"

"I have spent other nights out, and my absence will not occasion a great deal of comment. I will not be expected back until later this morning, and so I shall find someplace to rest and wander back in time for a lazy luncheon. I will meet you in the library directly after lunch."

And so, while Robert returned clandestinely to the manor house, Pegasus Gorham spent an hour astride the horse in Fulton's pasture, and Sir Hillary, himself hidden from sight, sat silently observing her.

Only after she had changed back into the uniform of a governess did he find himself a secluded spot and settle back for a few hours of needed rest.

121

Chapter 12

Two nights later, three men were gathered in a private parlor in one of the city of Exeter's less distinguished inns. Although all three seemed to fit into their disreputable environment, one man was particularly noticeable for his apparent lack of distinction. Mr. Obediah Muggins was a seedy-looking little man on the far side of forty with the manner and the appearance of a pitifully down-and-out petty criminal—the sort of man who seemed cursed with ill luck, had drifted in and out of Newgate several times, and was now waiting patiently for an inevitable death to put a period to his calamities. Appearances not withstanding, Obediah Muggins was, in actuality, one of the chief liaison men for the head of British intelligence—a fearful individual whom Obediah invariably referred to as his nibs.

Mr. Muggins's two companions could never have claimed his almost absolute lack of noteworthiness. The two husky, garishly dressed ruffians seated at the table were too large to achieve total anonymity. Fortunately, however, whatever else they might appear to be, neither the disguised Sir Hillary nor the almost overly disguised Mr. Mansfield would ever be taken for a gentleman.

Sir Hillary had taken charge of the meeting. Technically he was not and had never been a subordinate of his nibs. Sir Hillary worked occasionally for his nibs and, more often, for Wellington, but in neither case had he ever accepted a rank which would render either of these gentlemen his superior. Sir Hillary had managed a thriving career in the military while successfully avoiding most forms of army discipline.

"Is the innkeeper in your confidence, Obediah?"

"Nay. The innkeeper is a shady sort of cove."

"And what then is the official explanation of this meeting?"

"I let it slip, so to speak, that ye gentlemen were me fences for some very prime goods I'd acquired in a sommat less than honorable fashion."

Robert was grinning. "Obediah, you will have us all established in Newgate yet."

Mr. Muggins sniffed his disdain. "Nasty mind you have there, young man. I'm more likely to see you launched tonight on a new and highly profitable occupation." Obediah lifted his glass to toast Mr. Mansfield's new career opportunity.

The three of them had settled in over a bottle of very inferior gin—half of which Sir Hillary planned to dispose of in the nearest gutter. The other half of the bottle was being consumed single-handedly by Mr. Muggins. It was a well-established fact that Obediah Muggins could drink anything. *He* had not been born a gentleman, nor had he ever aspired to such rank. Mr. Muggins liked to describe himself as a Wapping-born bastard thrust into the world without a shirt or a crust of bread and nursed throughout his infancy on blue ruin. The description, although poetic, was reasonably accurate. Obediah Muggins could and would drink anything, and alcohol seemed to have no apparent effect on his mental abilities.

Having put young Mansfield in his place, Mr. Muggins turned back to Sir Hillary and addressed that gentleman with a respect which could not be due to social standing. "Well now, guv'nor, you wrote his nibs that you knew these blokes to be hand in glove with them frogs. Have you learned ought else?"

"During the last landing three Frenchman were left on-shore, and at least two of them seem to be responsible for the counterfeit currency being circulated in Devonshire. They do have some other agents in the area, and so it is not unreasonable to assume that some sort of sabotage operations are under way. We know there will be an important landing next week."

"And what are your plans, guv'nor?"

"I will need you and a half-dozen well-trained men. We will intercept all the French and hope to trap their English contact with a minimum of noise and bother. I think it can be done—ideally, with no loss of life. Those captured will, I am certain, provide us with a great deal of valuable information. Incidentally, I have also guaranteed, as I have explained to his nibs, that none of the local farmers who have been forced into this will be made to suffer."

"His nibs don't like it much, but he'll go along on that. I

agree wi' you. Don't see any cause at all for cluttering up our fine Newgate with a pack of illiterate plow pushers. Tell me, were all of them sods forced to it wi'out making a single complaint?" Mr. Muggins asked while casually blowing a cloud at the ceiling and one hand still slowly nursing his glass.

Sir Hillary smiled grimly. "There were some objections from my people—and as a result there are now two dead, a man and his wife burned to death. And one very good man transported."

"If one man be lagged, then the beak must be in on it."

"The beak, my Uncle Dillingham, is a conscientious magistrate but he has been misled by his son."

"Are we speaking of the fashionable fribble, guv'nor?"

"No, not Claude. You know, Obediah, I am still, after all these years, amazed by the quality of your research."

"Then it is t'other one. The aspirin Corinthian. That one always was an ugly customer—a loose screw."

"Precisely."

"Do you have proof, sir?"

"Not yet, Mr. Muggins—not proof positive. But I witnessed the murder of Mr. Duffy, and these pieces of cloth belonged to the murderer. I believe they can be identified as Anthony's if he has not already destroyed the garments."

"Here, let me see 'em. A moment while I top this glim so's I can look better." He trimmed the candle and produced a magnifying glass from his pocket.

"It's little enough to pin a toppin' offense on, guv'nor. But you say in a couple of weeks there is to be another landing from across the ditch?"

"A big landing."

"Will half a dozen men be enough, then?"

"They should be, since we are all agreed that the locals will be allowed to escape. Besides, half a dozen men are all we can safely move, without notice, into the area."

"That's the thing for sure. We don't want the thing getting buzzed about—it might queer the nab. Can't let the frogs twig to our being on to them."

"Precisely, and that is one of the reasons that I specifically requested that *you* be sent. I want my Cousin Anthony followed. He will be meeting his comrade Pierre here in Exeter in a few days. It will be impossible to set you up at Dillingham Hall, but there are places from which Anthony's departure for Exeter can be monitored. Are you up to it, Mr. Muggins?"

"'Course I am. I'm up to anything you like, guv'nor." And, for punctuation, Mr. Muggins toasted Sir Hillary with another gulp of gut-destroying daffy.

The next half hour was spent in discussing the broad outlines of Sir Hillary's plan for the night of the landing, and then the two gentlemen took their leave of Obediah Muggins and left the inn.

Later, on the road back to Pemmfield, Sir Hillary noticed that his young companion was in something of a brown study.

"What's ailing you, lad? Out with it."

"I don't suppose its serious, Hillary."

"Have you spotted a fly in the ointment, Robbie?"

"No, it has nothing to do with the plan, Hillary. It is just that I have been thinking we should have brought Pegasus with us tonight."

"Miss Gorham to meet Obediah Muggins? You must have taken leave of your senses," Sir Hillary snapped.

"I don't think so, Hillary. Look at it reasonably."

"I am looking at it reasonably. One look at your Pegasus and Obediah would have packed her off to his nibs. And his nibs would have sent her off across the Channel on the next tide. His nibs would never release his hold on a woman of Miss Gorham's abilities."

"But don't you see, Hillary? That is precisely why I think Pegasus should have come tonight."

"Do you want to see her placed in such danger? She would be courting death."

"No, I don't want to see her working with his nibs, but don't you see, Pegasus herself would want it. I think we may be very unfair to her in not allowing her to have a chance at the kind of life she wants."

"Rubbish. I have no intention of giving her an opportunity to throw her young life away."

"It would be better than spending the rest of her life as a governess."

"Surely, Robert, there are other alternatives."

Mr. Mansfield shook his head sadly. "Are there, Hillary?"

For the next two weeks Sir Hillary was determined to maintain the facade of normalcy at Pemmfield. Alicia, and even young Richard, may have begun to suspect that something was very wrong, but the other members of the Pemmrington and Dillingham households seemed almost totally ignorant of any undercurrents of a serious nature. And

Hillary was determined they should remain ignorant for as long as possible. Toward this end, he attempted to foster precisely those social contacts between the two families as would exist were the situation entirely normal. It would not be difficult to have the families meet on a regular basis and exchange dinner invitations, but even his Aunt Augusta would need to be supplied with a plausible reason for Hillary's extended stay in Devonshire. Gwendolyn Campbell was to be that reason.

Sir Hillary let it appear that the only cause of his dallying in Devonshire was the pursuit of the fair Gwendolyn. It tickled Hillary's lively sense of the ridiculous that while it was necessary for Alicia and Robert to act as if they were *not* madly in love it was equally necessary for Gwendolyn and himself to act as if they were fast approaching that state. Gwendolyn, unwitting, played her part in the comedy with great skill, for although it would be inaccurate to describe her emotions as deep, she was nevertheless quite determined to cap her brilliant career as a debutante with the capture of Hillary Pendragon. Sir Hillary played his part with his customary savoir faire, which concealed, in this case, even more than his customary degree of boredom.

Hillary Pendragon was bored with Gwendolyn. In fact, *young* ladies had always bored Sir Hillary. He had lived to see hundreds of blushing schoolgirls grow up to be faithless wives, and he did not take their proclamations of innocence seriously. Of course, he never crossed the invisible line in all his flirtations with young ladies, least of all with Gwendolyn. Sir Hillary was no fool, and he knew that one step too far and he might find himself wedded for life to some rapacious debutante. It was all very well to satisfy the mamas by flirting with the young ladies, but Madelaine Quincey and her colleagues had satisfied all his creature needs while not in any way entangling him in a lasting commitment.

Now Sir Hillary was finding himself equally bored at the thought of courting either his debutante or his full-blown widow. Madelaine Quincey could, of course, be avoided, but it was still necessary that appearances at Pemmfield be maintained, and so Sir Hillary Pendragon was condemned to spend much of his time smiling down into the beautiful eyes of the exquisite Miss Gwendolyn Campbell.

Hillary's performance was excellent, but not everyone at Pemmfield was fooled. One morning Hillary was alone in the small parlor with Lady Julia. They had been discussing a host of trivial sorts of things for the better part of an hour when Julia set aside her needlework and regarded him with a woebegone look—a look which would have suited the six-year-old Pamela.

Julia sighed audibly. "Poor Hillary!"

"I beg your pardon?"

"No, don't fly up into the boughs, Hillary. I have come to know you quite well over the years, and I know when you are endeavoring to suffer nobly. Much as I would like to evict Gwendolyn and spare you your heroic labors, it cannot be done."

"Labors?"

"And do not try to convince me that you are momentarily about to become enamored of my Cousin Gwendolyn. Don't cut a wheedle for *my* edification....I could evict her, but it would not be fair to Alicia and to your friend Robert."

"Not fair at all. And I will manage, Julia." Hillary was smiling now, and he reached over to pat her hand reassuringly.

"To be sure you will manage, Hillary....By the by, I cannot imagine why we were all so certain that Alicia was the slow, rather plain sister. It is strange how one's perceptions of people change over the years. Now I can see that Alicia is not at all slow—she is only a bit silly, as I am myself. How are you intending to bring my Uncle Campbell around, Hillary?"

"Now that you mention it, Julia, you might be of some assistance—if you would."

"Well, I have been waiting forever for *someone* to ask. I think I shall begin by writing to my uncle, and I shall need to have all the details about your friend Robert. It will be a very casual silly sort of letter—somewhat empty-headed—and my poor Uncle Bruce will not be able to make out whether Mr. Mansfield is about to marry Alicia, Gwendolyn, or even myself. But the letter will certainly set him thinking, and he is bound to make inquiries. In the end, he will be delighted to accept Robert Mansfield for Alicia. After all, Gwendolyn has been out these last three years and she has not settled on a husband—it must have been frightfully expensive for poor Uncle Bruce."

"Julia, I had never noticed what a devious little mind you have. I shall leave the planning of the entire campaign in your hands."

"That might be for the best, Hillary. Because when you

and Gwendolyn return to London, still both fancy-free, you will not be in particularly good odor in the Campbell home."

"Too true."

"Yes, and while we are at it, Hillary, I would like you to notice that I have *not* asked you about anything else. I have *not* inquired about Mr. Duffy's disappearance or your late-night excursions with Mr. Mansfield, which, incidentally, have nothing to do with Madelaine Quincey, whom I happened to meet just the other day in the village, and who made it very clear that she had not seen you in weeks and weeks and that she had expected better of you."

"Thank you, Julia, for *not* asking. But please believe that if I felt you should know I would tell you."

"How pleasant it is to have a strong man to lean on, and yet I can imagine that such solicitude would drive a more determined woman than myself to distraction. Can you imagine what our Aunt Augusta would say if you told her, 'If I felt you should know, I would tell you'? Miss Gorham, for another example, would skewer you alive for just such a comment."

"It is truly not a matter for you to worry your pretty little head about, Julia."

"Now don't go ripping up at me, Hillary. I am not a child, and if I cannot know what is going on in my own home I suppose I will survive. I am pleased that at least Miss Gorham is in your confidence despite the fact that she is a woman."

"Rather say I am in her confidence, and she is not, in some relevant sense, a woman."

"Then you, dear Hillary, are in some relevant sense *quite* blind. Funny, somehow I have always taken you for a knowing one."

"Darling Julia, I am decimated by your loss of faith."

"Oh, I understand *some* things well enough, Hillary Pendragon.... Ah, here is Gwendolyn, and we were just discussing our planned expeditions with the Dillinghams to the Swansdown Abbey ruins. Hillary thought we might manage the excursion this Thursday. Do we have other plans for that day, Gwendolyn?"

"No, Thursday should do very well."

"Good, and I hope this fine weather holds. I have promised the children they might come as well, and it would be a pity for them if it rained."

Gwendolyn did not seem entirely pleased with the prospect of sharing her outing with the children, but she was willing to accept the inevitable gracefully. "How will the children travel? Surely they cannot ride so far."

"I think my boys could make it to the abbey. They have become quite confident in their riding. But as we have invited the Dillingham children as well, Richard decided that he ought to travel in the carriage with them. Richard seems to have grown quite close to his cousins this last month or two."

Gwendolyn had seated herself beside Hillary. "Julia, are you saying that all five of them will go in a single carriage? There will be havoc."

Lady Julia laughed in a delightful trill. "I don't *think* so, Gwendolyn. Miss Gorham will be riding with them, and I am convinced that she could manage half the house of Barth while traveling through the jungle on the back of an elephant."

And so, two days later, early Thursday morning, several sets of riders set out from Pemmfield with two carriages. One carriage contained Miss Gorham and all five children, and the other carriage contained Lady Augusta and her son Claude. Augusta had insisted that her Claude was far too delicate to ride such a great distance and, in her concern for his health, she would keep him company in the Dillingham carriage.

Sir Hillary was mounted and was riding beside Gwendolyn Campbell, Robert had found his place beside Alicia, and the colonel was escorting Lady Julia. Anthony Dillingham had fallen behind and seemed, in a way totally out of character, to have taken an interest in the occupants of the nursery carriage.

The party arrived at the Swansdown Abbey ruins and spent a delightful hour exploring the picturesque structure before settling down for a pleasant luncheon on the grass.

After lunch, Claude assumed responsibility for the children and took them off to skip stones on the pond.

"I think we really ought to let Miss Gorham rest, hadn't we," he had said. "Truth to tell, I have worn my most ghastly-colored coat particularly in anticipation of a romp in the woods. If I am very fortunate, I will have ruined it completely before the afternoon is out."

Margaret watched as her charges ran off after the graceful little elflike man in periwinkle blue. And then, allowing herself to relax, she sat up against one of the ancient battlements and settled back to view the tableau before her.

Having long lived the life of the uninvolved observer at

129

such gatherings, Margaret did not expect to be disturbed, and least of all did she expect to have her observations interrupted by Anthony Dillingham, and so she was somewhat taken aback when Mr. Dillingham seated himself beside her. Instinctively, Miss Gorham pulled herself bolt upright.

Anthony inclined his head in greeting. "Do not disturb yourself on my account, Miss Gorham. You have earned your rest."

She studied him for a few moments, not knowing how to reply to an Anthony Dillingham bent on civility.

He continued to speak. "My apologies. We should have brought Miss Porter to help you with the children. But Miss Porter's health is not what it should be. I'm afraid we have been a little disappointed in her work thus far. My children, I think, need a less delicate governess."

Margaret knew she must respond. "On the contrary, Luke and Sarah seem to be very easy children to manage. I expect Miss Porter is simply suffering from a bout with the influenza that has infected the village. It is, I am told, accompanied by the most dreadful headaches."

"You think it the influenza then, Miss Gorham?"

"Most probably, Mr. Dillingham, and if that is indeed the case it is just as well that the children are not with Miss Porter. I have heard that the disease is dreadfully contagious."

"Then by all means we will keep dear Miss Porter away from the children. Sarah and Luke are such strange nervous little fellows and really quite sickly. Their mother was a sickly woman, you know."

"The death of a mother is of course a great loss to small children, and one would expect that Sarah and Luke would be a little more timid than most other children their age, but I do not think of them as weak youngsters. On the contrary, their suffering seems to have given them inner resources and a strength of character rare in ones so young. I admire your children, Mr. Dillingham, and I know the Pemmringtons have been looking forward to this outing with their cousins."

"Perhaps, Miss Gorham, you will come to Dillingham Hall and replace Miss Porter. My children seem to blossom in your company, while Miss Porter does not get on with Sarah and Luke at all."

"Nonsense, I am sure you exaggerate, Mr. Dillingham. Look how well Sarah and Luke play with your brother, Claude."

"Claude *is* very good with them. Strange, is it not?"

"I do not think it is strange at all. Claude is a gentle man with exactly the sort of vivid imagination to appeal to children. He is also very fond of them, and the children can sense such things."

Anthony flicked a speck of dust from his sleeve and guided the conversation into safer waters.

"And a lovely day for skipping stones, is it not, Miss Gorham?"

"True, Mr. Dillingham, we are fortunate that it did not rain."

"Perhaps, but I for one believe that the atmosphere of the ruins are wonderfully improved in the rain. I'm certain that the hundreds of clerical spirits that infest such places would prefer to see us shivering, wet, and properly repentant."

"What a strange notion, Mr. Dillingham. I am not so severe in my notions, and, for myself, I find the act of repentance even more genuine when performed in the warm sunlight. It is far too easy to repent in the rain."

"But surely, Miss Gorham, *you* do not approve of such bucolic idleness?"

"And why should I not, Mr. Dillingham?"

Robert Mansfield and Hillary Pendragon had wandered over to join the two by the wall.

Robert spoke casually. "Strange that you should ask, Mr. Dillingham. I for one have discovered that such harmless idle sorts of pleasure are not as sweet, for me, as they once were. It seems wrong somehow that I should be so fancy-free, even for a single afternoon, when so many other people in the world are suffering. Of course, after one has lived with the war nothing ever again seems entirely free or innocent. Don't you agree, Hillary?"

"No, I don't agree, Robert. I do know how you must feel, but it is precisely because of the war that I believe we ought to enjoy our little harmless pleasures when we can. I certainly have no intention of allowing some French martinet to destroy my life. The war is not everywhere, and in Devonshire one is allowed to enjoy oneself. Do you agree, Anthony?"

"Having never been off to war, I cannot know whether I agree or not. But it seems to me, Hillary, that you are endorsing a policy of 'live, drink, and be merry, for tomorrow we die.' Miss Gorham, do you think *that* a noble sentiment?"

"In general, I think it is not an ignoble sentiment provided one does not interpret it as an endorsement of excess. I believe
131

one ought to live one's life, day to day, in the fullest way possible."

"And what, Miss Gorham," Anthony asked, "is your idea of enjoyment?"

The other members of the party had gathered in closer, and Lady Augusta took this opportunity to express her views. Her voice fell ponderous and heavy on the conversation. "You must know, Anthony, that Miss Gorham, and I, find our greatest enjoyment in fulfilling our responsibilities and in our charitable works."

There was a moment of silence, and then Anthony turned back to the governess. "Do you really, Miss Gorham? Does it not, at times, grow tedious, all this charity? And surely it must become somewhat less than pleasant to spend all one's time ministering to the needs of other people's children. I cannot think good works are at all what my Cousin Hillary means when he speaks of harmless pleasures."

Gwendolyn could not keep silent. "But of course *you* do not appreciate Miss Gorham's sterling qualities, Mr. Dillingham. Miss Gorham seems to thrive on self-sacrifice and is even wonderfully concerned for the children of the lower classes—paupers and idiots. Just the other night she spent hours ministering to the idiot Tate boy."

There were another few moments of silence. "Did you indeed, Miss Gorham? How very noble of you. I have myself found the boy to be a mischief maker and a malingerer, but, I confess, I can barely tolerate dealing with the *canaille* myself. I believe it is better to lead these people than to minister to their every whim. They would be happier for it, and the nation would be stronger. And that, after all, is precisely what our nation lacks—leadership."

"Do you think so, Cousin Anthony?" Hillary asked quietly.

"Of course I do. Instead of leaders we have a pack of old fat lecherous dukes together with their brother, an old fat lecherous prince. We have ourselves a parliament, to be sure, but that is nothing more than a disorganized litter of bickering soi-disant gentry."

Anthony's mother could not allow this to pass. "My dear son, you know *I* cannot approve of the excesses of our regent, and I have always taught my children to follow a righteous and abstemious course. But one should nevertheless not describe one's government in such terms. Even if it is the *truth*, it is *not gentlemanly* conduct to speak in such a way."

"It is gentlemanly, my dear mama, to suffer stupidity and incompetence in silence?"

Margaret Gorham had shifted and was addressing Anthony Dillingham directly. "I myself think leadership is a vastly overrated quality. I would rather see a nation of responsible citizens than a nation of well-led sheep. Surely it is better to live in a land of free individuals with an absolute minimum of what you choose to call leadership than to live in a land of slaves, be they ever so devoted and content with their lot."

"And are you *so* free, Miss Gorham? I would not have thought it. It appears to me that you lead a very restricted, drab sort of existence. Your sentiments, however, are noble—if misguided—and I'm certain that in the extremely unlikely event of your ever being ushered into the presence of the crown your virtue will be properly applauded."

Robert started in to defend his friend, but she silenced him with a nod and then with an almost tranquil smile Miss Margaret Gorham addressed Mr. Anthony Dillingham.

"Your sarcasm is quite wasted on me, Mr. Dillingham. As a mere governess, I do not expect ever to be ushered into the presence of the crown, but I do, most assuredly, expect that someday I shall be ushered into the presence of the Lord. And I for one shall continue to live my life in the anticipation of that day."

Chapter 13

Sir Hillary met with Mr. Obediah Muggins several times during the course of the next few days, and he met with that gentleman again after Mr. Muggins had returned from Exeter in Anthony Dillingham's wake.

"O' course, guv'nor, I couldn't hear all that was being said and all; but the innkeeper, being a friend of mine, so to speak—whose friendship was wonderfully improved by a fiver—allowed me to listen from a particularly choice spot."

"And what additional information do we have, Mr. Muggins?"

"They will land at least ten men. Two of them will proceed with the counterfeit currency to Exeter, but the other eight are concerned with some other grand bit o' espionage. The leader, an Henri chappie, has been entrusted with delivering some very precious papers. Incidentally, your Anthony seems to be completely in that Pierre's confidence, but, in my opinion, Pierre don't know more than a bit hisself of what is going on."

"Do you think Anthony was ever aware he was being followed?"

"I don't think either of them was fly to me, if that's what you mean, guv'nor. But I'll tell you this. That Anthony Dillingham is a surpassin' nervous man with a foul personality. Not the sort to make hisself welcome with any decent folk. I don't suppose that even without his frogs, that one is destined to die in bed."

"Yes, Obediah, I am beginning to suspect as much. In any case, my Cousin Anthony bears watching."

"Aye, that he does. But he's not like to do anything afore the next landing. And by then, God willin', he'll not be in a position to do anything more."

"Let's hope so.... You are going to report back to his nibs now and collect our half-dozen men?"

"So I had planned, if you have no need of me here, guv'nor."

"I think we will manage without you for now. But before you leave I should like to clarify a bit more of our plan, and I would also like to convey to his nibs my suspicions about the other espionage efforts in the area."

"Very good, guv'nor."

Much later, as Hillary was preparing to leave, he hesitated at the door and, as if in an afterthought, he said. "Incidentally, Mr. Muggins, there will be a woman with us that night."

"A woman! What sort of a woman?"

"A governess."

"Damn it all, you cannot be wanting to take a blimey governess on a mission?"

"No, Mr. Muggins, I most certainly do not *want* to take a governess on a mission, but we do not have an effective choice in the matter. The governess in question is the source of much of our information and has been in the habit of attending these gatherings uninvited. I cannot like it myself, but, with-

134

out our cooperation, her presence is almost certainly assured."

"Then why do you mention the matter?"

Hillary remained silent for a moment or two, and when he did begin to speak his voice was almost totally devoid of expression. Obediah Muggins had been privileged to see that look in the guv'nor's eyes before—this particular Hillary Pendragon was an exceedingly dangerous man to cross. Hillary spoke quietly. "The governess, despite her appearance, is damn good, and I wish to be certain that under no circumstance will his nibs make any attempt whatsoever to recruit her."

Mr. Muggins did not hesitate. "Understood, Sir Hillary, and you have my word."

"Thank you, Mr. Muggins." And Sir Hillary quickly took his leave of that gentleman and set out for Pemmfield.

"Come along, Luke, you can make it."

"I don't think so—it is still such a long way, Sarah."

"No, it is only a little bit farther."

"You go ahead without me, Sarah, I can't see anything."

"Yes, there is still blood in your eyes, but I don't think it is *from* your eyes. Hold tight to me and I will lead you ...Shush!" And then a whisper: "I hear someone."

"Sarah, Luke, is that you? Can I be of help?" It was a clear cool familiar voice.

"Oh, thank goodness it's you, Miss Gorham," Sarah answered.

The two children came out into the clearing, and even in the dark Margaret could see that they were each of them a wreck. Sarah's left arm hung loosely and awkwardly from her thin shoulders, and Luke's face was covered with contusions.

"Oh my God!" was all even the very cool Miss Gorham could manage. And then the children rushed into speech.

Sarah began, "We have come for a visit, you see," and then after a moment's hesitation she added, "We had a mishap."

"And we don't want to go home right away," Luke interjected while he was trying to rub his eyes clear.

"Please God, Miss Gorham, may Luke and I stay at Pemmfield?"

Margaret had just gathered the two small figures to her when they heard the sound of still another intruder.

"Hush now, my loves. Someone else is coming. I think you
135

had better go toward the house—cook will let you in the kitchen door. I'll catch up. Hustle now, my darlings."

The two children disappeared instantly into the darkness only moments before their father appeared in the glade.

"Ah, fancy meeting the redoubtable Miss Gorham at this time of night. Have you been here long?"

She was smoothing her skirts when she answered, "About half an hour, Mr. Dillingham. Why do you ask?"

"Has anyone, in that time, passed through this way?"

"Five minutes ago I heard some prowling noises toward the south—in the vicinity of the home-farm fields. I don't think it was anyone—more likely to have been some sort of small animal."

The clearing had been freshly tilled, and so, even in the moonlight, it was obvious that either Miss Gorham had been very agitated or other people had been through that way recently. Margaret hoped that Anthony would not notice.

Slowly, he bent to pick up a handful of soil, and casually he sifted his hand through it. "Strangely moist soil, is it not?"

Margaret could almost see the blood sticking to his long fingers. "It has been freshly tilled, Mr. Dillingham."

"And I will ask you just once more, Miss Gorham, did anyone come through this way?"

"I have answered you as best I could, sir."

"Tell me, Miss Gorham, are you in the habit of wandering alone in the gardens after dark? Or, perhaps, you did not intend to remain alone.... Well, answer me."

"I shall not dignify that question with an answer, Mr. Dillingham."

Slowly sifting another handful of soil, he continued, "Such a touching sight—virtue in arms. The ramrod-straight little governess. Tell me, my ever so respectable Miss Gorham, are you real or do you have a filthy stinking peasant lover waiting in the shrubs?"

Without a moment's hesitation, Margaret turned in the direction of the house.

"Don't you dare to turn your back on me, Miss Gorham."

She stopped but did not turn to face him. "Mr. Dillingham, if you cannot address me with even the pretense of gentility, I see no reason to remain here and have my ears abused."

Suddenly she felt herself caught, wrenched around, and literally struck in the face by a balled fist. Momentarily, Margaret felt herself grow faint, and she fell back against a

136

tree. Then she had pulled herself away from the support and was standing very straight.

Anthony was livid. "I shall not warn you again. Don't act superior with me, woman. I detest starched-up, smug females."

She had folded her hands before her but remained thoroughly alert. "Mr. Dillingham, you are a very *sick* man."

He seemed about to lunge again, only now Pegasus was prepared to defend herself. Then they both heard a disturbance in the bushes somewhere off in the direction of the house. It seemed to be only the sound of a rabbit or a rock falling, but it was enough to set Mr. Dillingham on his guard, and, with a sneer, he turned in the direction of his own house, saying, before he left, "I have all the time in the world to settle our differences, Miss Gorham. Don't push me."

Margaret remained immobile until Anthony was not only out of sight but also out of hearing. Then, slowly, she turned and started for the manor house.

"Psst, Miss Gorham, we are still here."

"Sarah, is that you? Haven't you gone?"

"No, we thought it better to stay close. We threw those rocks and made the noise a while back," Luke said.

"Then you heard the conversation?"

"Indeed we did, Miss Gorham," Sarah said. "And you were so very brave. You're a *trump*. You're a regular out-and-outer. Isn't she, Luke?"

"She's a Corinthian too," Luke added in awe.

"Yes, well, I have never been called an out-and-outer or a Corinthian before, but Mr. Mansfield always used to call me 'the Trump.' Come, children, if I bend a little, Luke can ride me pig-a-back and Sarah can hold onto my hand."

An hour later, Margaret, Julia, and nurse were tending the wounded children. Lady Julia had sent for the doctor to set Sarah's dislocated arm and stitch up young Luke's face, but he had not as yet arrived. Fortunately Robert had taken both the Campbell sisters into the village to visit the rector and they were not scheduled to return for an hour or two.

Sir Hillary had just returned from his meeting with Mr. Muggins when young Richard fetched him to the sickroom.

Hillary knocked quietly and came into the room. He glanced at Sarah and Luke. "Young Richard has chased after me. He said there was trouble and I was needed. Good Lord, what has happened here?"

Lady Julia and nurse silently excused themselves, leaving

Miss Gorham, who could not, in any case, leave since her hand was still clutched, almost convulsively, in Sarah's good one.

"Uncle Hillary, you see, we were running away from home and we took a terrific fall—didn't we, Luke?"

"Yes, that is just what happened, Sarah."

"And Uncle Hillary, can we stay at Pemmfield? Can we please stay here?" The tears coursed silently down Sarah's cheeks.

Hillary Pendragon tilted one little battered face and then the other up into the candlelight. "Yes, you may stay, but first you must answer one question with perfect honesty."

"Cross our heart and hope to die," Sarah said.

"Is your father responsible for your condition?"

There was a long still silence, and then Luke spoke. "No, it wasn't our father."

"It was not Anthony Dillingham?" Hillary persisted.

"If we tell you who it *really* was, will *you* promise to keep the secret?" Sarah asked.

"We cannot swear, but we will promise to do our best, won't we, Miss Gorham?"

Margaret nodded her agreement.

Sarah sighed and began, "It has taken a very long time, but we know the truth now. We found this book among his things, and the book explains everything."

"What book?" Hillary asked in great seriousness.

Luke's voice was hushed. "The Book of Monsters."

"And how did the book help you to find the truth?" Margaret asked quietly.

"Now we know *how* they did it," Luke announced as if this statement clarified the matter.

"Our father was a very good man." Sarah had again taken the lead. "We saw a painting. He was beautiful and gentle and good—it was all right there in the painting. And our mother, she was gentle and beautiful and good as well. We remember our mother a little, but I don't believe we remember our *real* father at all. You see, when we were very tiny, our *real* father must have died or disappeared, and Grandmama was very desolate so she went to the graveyard and put together a thing that looked for all the world like our real father, and then, in the dungeon hidden in the east wing, she put electricity into the thing. We found the platform. Do you know what electricity is, Uncle Hillary?"

"I think so, Sarah."

138

"Well, it's this magical sort of thing like lightning—it can make things alive you see."

Luke continued, "And the monster came to life—well, sort of life. And, to begin with, it must have been beautiful, almost as beautiful as our real father, but underneath it was *really* a monster, and soon it began to sicken and decay. Ordinarily, you wouldn't notice it, since the monster mostly acted like a real human being, and only sometimes it would break loose and do horrible things. We think the monster killed our mother."

"And we have proof it's a monster, Uncle Hillary," Sarah said.

"Proof?"

"Yes. You know, the monster in the book began to rot and its skin began to get all pocky and horrible. We surprised it once in the dressing room and its whole belly is covered with rot." She shivered. "It was ghastly awful....And you know, its teeth that were once so white in the painting are going black, and its hair is coming away from its head, and then finally, just the other day, a seam was exposed."

"A seam?" Hillary asked.

"Yes, where its neck has been attached to its body. We saw the welt of the seam just under its collar yesterday," Luke explained.

"Don't you see what Luke and I have been trying to tell you? The thing the world knows as Anthony Dillingham is *not* our real father, he is Grandmama's monster. Our real father, wherever he may be, is a good and beautiful and gentle man."

Hillary and Margaret were silent—dumbfounded. And, before they could frame any sort of a reply, there was a lyrical voice speaking from the doorway.

"You know, I think you are quite right, my gems. Queer that I never thought of it myself." Claude Dillingham came into the room. Slowly he examined his niece and nephew. "You see, I knew your father—your *real* father—very well. He was a rather good sort of chap, and then suddenly he up and clean disappeared. Went on a trip to London and he didn't come back. I can tell you that both your mother and your grandmother were quite frantic with worry. And then, a few weeks later, someone showed up who looked so much like Anthony Dillingham that we all assumed he *was* Anthony Dillingham. I should have known better, but I'm afraid I am

139

not very bright. Of course, I would never have been bright enough to find the proof."

"You do believe us then, Uncle Claude?"

"Completely. And another thing, your mother knew the truth as well. When she was dying she called me to her and begged me, on my solemn word of honor as a gentleman, to protect you children from 'that monster'—those were her very words, 'that monster.' She knew it was a monster, but you see, *I* didn't understand what she meant exactly, and I didn't know where to look for proof, either. But now, thanks to you two, we all have proof positive that the thing is truly a monster and not a father at all. All we have to do now is sit tight and this monster is bound to disappear and decay just like the monster in the book."

"And we don't have to go home just yet, Uncle Claude?"

"No, Sarah. I will explain it all to your grandfather—he is very much wiser than he looks, you know. You will not have to go home as long as the monster is still there. I promised your mother and I swear to you on the word of a gentleman, on my sacred honor"—he smiled broadly—"I swear on my new silk lavender waistcoat, on all my waistcoats, that you will never be in the power of that unnatural thing again."

"Thank you, Uncle Claude." Sarah sighed and relaxed back into her pillows.

Luke took hold of Claude's hand. "Uncle Claude is a trump too. Miss Gorham is a trump—she stood by us. She is very brave. Miss Gorham protected us from the thing and it struck her hard and she didn't even flinch—not for a moment. She looked it straight in the eye and told it it was sick."

"Miss Gorham thought it was human, you see. Monsters are not sick, properly speaking. They decompose," Sarah explained.

Sir Hillary had lifted a candle from the bedstand and was slowly examining Miss Gorham's bruised face. He took his own hankerchief and, with infinite gentleness, wiped the blood from her lip and ran his finger along the hollow of her cheek.

"Well," he said. "I expect the monster will descend on Pemmfield any moment now. I will go down and turn him away from our door."

"Sir Hillary, should we, Claude and I, come with you?" Margaret asked.

"No, no, Miss Gorham, you will both be needed right here when the doctor arrives. Besides, we must not let on that

Claude knows the truth, because he will have to continue to live in the monster's house....By the by, Miss Gorham, I think you can be classified as wounded in battle, and, at least temporarily, you ought to leave the field."

"Not to worry, Miss Gorham," Luke assured her. "Uncle Hillary is the strongest, bravest soldier in the British army. He is Wellington's right hand, and it stands to reason that Wellington's right hand can floor anyone—even Grandmama's monster."

Hillary smiled at the boy, "Just so. And having traveled to all sorts of strange and exotic places, like Bavaria, I have come in contact with a wide variety of monsters, and I have yet to meet one I could not handle. Still, forewarned is forearmed. I will be back soon, my little ones." And he kissed them both and left.

Hillary returned to the room an hour or so later to find the doctor slowly completing his work. Luke had already been stitched up and the doctor, with nurse's help, was winding linen about the brace which supported Sarah's arm. Dr. Hugh Belding was a jolly sort of man who had tended all the children of the neighborhood for over thirty years. He was exchanging pleasantries with nurse and the children when he lifted his head and asked Hillary, in an excessively casual manner, whether he might have a word or two with him after a bit.

"Of course, Dr. Belding. And will you join me for a well-earned glass of cordial in the library?"

"A man after my own heart, Sir Hillary. I shall be down shortly."

"Meanwhile, doctor, do you think you might spare me Mr. Claude Dillingham and Miss Gorham?"

"Of course. The worst is over now and the children have been very very brave. I am certain they can manage without their supporters for the balance of the night."

Nurse had turned to see the little figure creeping through the doorway after Sir Hillary, "Dick Pemmrington, and what are you doing in this room now? You ought to be in your own bed this minute."

"Miss Gorham, nurse, may I *please* stay? I've been awake all this time and all I saw was Luke and Sarah come in looking awful."

"I think, nurse, that just this once we might make an exception for the sake of Master Luke and Miss Sarah. I remember once when I hurt myself as a youngster that the

141

presence of Robert Mansfield, my very best friend, was all that sustained me."

"Yes, Luke and I would so like it if Richard could stay by us."

Nurse humphed. "Very well then. If you all agree to sleep now and not to chatter the whole night through, I will set up a cot for Master Dick. Now be good children and listen sharp to Dr. Belding."

As nurse was clearly in control of the situation, Claude, Margaret, and Hillary were able to slip, almost unnoticed, from the room. Hillary led them into the library and offered each of them a sherry before he began.

"Robert Mansfield and the Campbell sisters have returned, and the sisters, at least, have been packed off to bed none the wiser."

"And Anthony Dillingham?" Margaret asked, setting aside her sherry untouched.

"Anthony has been and gone. I was as civil as possible, but I did explain, without equivocation, that the children must stay here at least temporarily. Anthony may fight it, however, and I think it best if Claude could return home now and explain the situation to his father."

"Do you think it safe for him, Sir Hillary?"

"Thank you, Miss Gorham, I do appreciate your concern, but it will never be any safer for me, and I'm likely to lose what little courage I have if I put it off any longer. Besides, I have become *too* wrinkled, positively shabby. I would be mortified if Lady Pemmrington or the Campbell sisters were to see me in my present state."

Margaret took his hand and smiled. "Good luck to you, Claude, and thank you."

With a great show of affection, Claude bowed low over the hand that held his and kissed it. "It is rather we who must thank you, Miss Gorham. I bid you adieu."

"Au revoir, my friend," Miss Gorham whispered as Claude minced off down the hallway.

Miss Gorham watched him take his hat and cane from Thackery before she turned back into the library and addressed the other occupant of that room. "Sir Hillary..."

"Do you think you might ever be able to manage 'Hillary' without benefit of the honorific?"

"Sir Hillary, *that* would be a mistake."

"A mistake? Surely you exaggerate. I do not hang on ceremony, you know. Men have shared the greatest of dangers with me without ever knowing that my name is prefixed with a 'Sir.'"

Miss Gorham, determined to maintain her hold on some sort of reality, looked skeptical. "Perhaps *you* do not care for such conventions, but I do—most governesses do, as a matter of fact. I pay you respect of title, and I expect, in return, some respect for Miss Margaret Gorham, governess. Without my profession, and the formal recognition of its dignity, I am nothing but a shabby-genteel spinster named Maggie or Peg."

"Never Maggie." He smiled. "Robert calls you Pegasus."

Without a hint of humor she replied, "Pegasus was a myth. She disappeared some years ago on a trip to London."

"Strange, I could have sworn I saw her just the other night slipping along the side of a white-faced cliff."

"Like Luke's monster, she reappears from time to time."

"I begin to think it is the other Miss Gorham who is the artifact and the monster."

"Rubbish—don't *you* be childish." And then determined, at all cost, to change the direction of the conversation, she continued, "I have been thinking about the rotting flesh and the neck 'seam.' Do you think they can be entirely coincidental?"

"No, I don't. You are really very clever to have picked it up."

"Thank you, Sir Hillary. I am customarily held to be clever enough," she replied quite stiffly.

"No, really! Now, don't fly up into the boughs! I did manage a look at his neck when he found it expeditious to loosen his collar a bit. I believe it is a relatively new wound and could well be a flesh wound from a small-caliber pistol."

"And the puckered flesh of the belly may well be a burn."

"Quite likely. I have made inquiries, and, as near as anyone could tell from a distance, the arsonist had burned, or at least was clutching, his midriff."

She shuddered. "It is all so horrible....Should we have allowed Claude into our confidence on these matters?"

"Claude has known for some time that something is amiss, at least with his brother's finances. He has been dropping me hints since I arrived in Devonshire. Claude Dillingham understands a great deal more than we have given him credit for. I wonder how I have so underestimated him all these years."

Margaret nodded. "Claude is terribly affected, to be sure, but affectation seems a modest price to pay for sanity in that

143

family. He is not only intelligent, he is a caring, compassionate human being."

"Just so, Miss Gorham, but how you managed that speech without ever once departing from the perfect rigidity of your profession, I cannot fathom."

"I suppose you think me ridiculous?" she countered.

"A little, yes." And he broke into a grin.

Margaret was now desperate to maintain some sort of control over the situation. "I think, Sir Hillary, that the events of this evening are too grim to occasion laughter."

"To be sure, Madame Governess, but it is precisely at such times when one must needs learn to laugh. I have seen men waiting for an almost certain death, convulsed with laughter. Yes, and I have even been one of those men."

She shook her head. "And yet man is held to be the rational animal."

"But Miss Gorham, your philosophers have it all wrong. I am convinced that there are other rational animals in the universe, but man is the only animal capable of laughter— he is the only one of God's creatures blessed with a sense of his own ridiculousness...And believe me, Miss Gorham, we are both of us ridiculous. In fact, at this precise moment, you and I, my dear Miss Gorham, are two of the most ridiculous people on the face of this planet."

Fortunately for Margaret, the doctor had come to the door and she was able to excuse herself and escape to her room, leaving Sir Hillary to explain the situation with the Dillingham children to the older man.

Chapter 14

The night of the anticipated landing they gathered together at the old fence just after dark. It was a small group—Robert Mansfield, John Paul, Hillary Pendragon, Mr. Muggins and a half-dozen of his men, and toward the rear of the troup in a sturdy brown walking dress stood the redoubtable Miss Margaret Gorham.

Looking every inch a blimey governess, Obediah Muggins thought to himself, and certainly not the sort at all to interest his nibs or Sir Hillary, either professionally or otherwise.

Hillary had divided the group into three units. John Paul and Robert Mansfield would again be waiting at the actual landing site or in the caves. It would be their task to alert the locals. John had already notified two or three of the most trusted Pemmfield men that there would be trouble and that, at a prearranged signal, the whole group would be quietly and quickly dispersed. Once Robert Mansfield had been assured that the local people were safely out of the way, he would make his way to the second group—Mr. Muggins and his six men. Sir Hillary had instructed this group to remain concealed at a crossroad just the other side of Pemmfield proper.

That particular crossroad had, since time immemorial, been a favored haunt of highwaymen, both because it offered concealment and the opportunity of surprise and because it was necessary for all travelers in and out of the area to pass by that place. Tonight the highwaymen would be king's men, but the principles of the ambush would be the same. Mr. Muggins would set his trap and hope to catch his quarry alive. Violence would not be in the best interests of anyone and was, Sir Hillary insisted, to be avoided if at all possible. If somehow the French had been alerted of the danger there would be a bloody confrontation, but failing that, Mr. Muggins was instructed to take most of them alive or to follow them until they could be run to earth.

Meanwhile, Sir Hillary would station himself near the abandoned hut, where, according to Mr. Muggins's information, the Frenchmen were to collect their horses before traveling across the Dillingham estate to intercept the Exeter road. In the unlikely event that the French had a change in plans, Sir Hillary would know of it and would be in ideal position to notify Muggins in time to make pursuit feasible. And, as an added advantage, Sir Hillary would have the opportunity to overhear the French in their last unguarded conversations.

Margaret Gorham was to go with Sir Hillary. For their own reasons, neither Sir Hillary nor Mr. Muggins wished to see her involved in the crossfire of an ambush, and her presence in the cove with Robert Mansfield and John Paul would have exposed her to almost certain recognition by the locals.

Sir Hillary, having thus explained his plans in detail,

dismissed them all. Each was to make his own way to his post some time short of midnight. Even Mr. Muggins's men would be traveling in pairs so as to avoid comment should they be seen.

Sir Hillary himself did not intend to return to the manor house that evening. He had again used the implied excuse of Madelaine Quincey; his departure, earlier that evening, had been quite public and his return before the next morning was not anticipated. Robert and Pegasus were not near so fortunate in their choice of alternative excuses, and so, with some foresight, Sir Hillary had sought Lady Julia's aid.

Hillary had quietly informed his hostess that there was to be a critical maneuver that evening and that the greatest caution must be used in disguising their plans. It would, he suggested, be very convenient if neither of the Campbell sisters was at Pemmfield that evening.

Lady Julia had agreed readily and had arranged, almost on the spur of the moment, to ride out early in the afternoon with both Alicia and Gwendolyn. They were to take the afternoon to visit, together with Lady Augusta, one of that lady's friends in the village. Augusta's friend was a women of unimpeachable lineage, fairly respectable income, and two rather plain daughters on the shelf. No sooner were they through the door than the Campbell sisters realized it was to be an exclusively feminine and stultifyingly proper gathering where the younger women, Julia included, were expected to maintain a strategic silence while Lady Augusta and her friend vouchsafed to instruct them in the ways of the world.

Alicia managed quite well with the two plain daughters, but Gwendolyn was bored to tears and could see that even Julia was looking decidedly peevish. It came as no surprise, therefore, to Gwendolyn at least, that Lady Julia, in the midst of the most inconsequential drivel, should take the opportunity to faint dead away. It did come as a surprise to Miss Campbell when her cousin did not revive immediately. Lady Augusta insisted on having one of the servants fetch Dr. Belding, and, on his arrival, the doctor examined Lady Julia privately for a few minutes and came out of the room to announce that she was not in a fit state to travel. Thus rather than providing a speedy escape, Julia's collapse had ensured that the ladies from Pemmfield would spend at least another twenty-four hours in that dreadfully stodgy company. Gwendolyn was not even spared Lady Augusta, as that

146

lady graciously volunteered to stay and nurse her deplorably sickly connection. The balance of the evening was spent over an unpalatable dinner served up with an almost equally unpalatable lecture on the excellent health of the blood members of the house of Barth and the rather indifferent health of those people the Pendragons had chosen to marry.

Lady Julia's opportune illness allowed Pegasus and Robert a fair amount of freedom, although it was still necessary to proceed with a certain amount of stealth so as not to unduly advertise their actions to the servants.

Robert left Pegasus at the fence where they were to meet Sir Hillary, and while the younger man made his way down to the caves, Sir Hillary and Pegasus started out for the hut. Swiftly they moved along the ridge with the lush plateau to one side of them and the stark fall to the sea to the other. When they came to the ravine in which the hut was located they slowed their pace in order to ascertain that it was still unoccupied. Hillary had decided to skirt past the hut itself and take up their position farther down the ravine. From there they would command an excellent view of Dead Man's Cove and would be in a position to observe every movement of the French.

It was only when they were settled in to wait that either of them broke the silence, and then it was only to begin a trivial sort of whispered conversation in an effort to dispel the growing tension—tension which could only in part be attributed to the anticipated landing.

"Miss Gorham, I did not inquire, but I assume you speak French?"

"Yes, I do."

"A competent schoolgirl French?"

"At the Wolverhamptons the eldest daughter had married into a family of émigrés. I do not know precisely what the social position of that family was in France, but their use of their native language was highly idiomatic. During my eight months as governess to the Wolverhamptons my command of the language was considerably expanded beyond what would ordinarily be considered schoolgirl French."

"How well you phrase it. I am acquainted with that brood, and it is comforting to know, Miss Gorham, that you are quite capable of expressing yourself in French with all the color and panache of a stevedore from Marseilles."

"I believe, Sir Hillary, that both my French and my English are adequate to any occasion."

"That, Miss Gorham, sounds remarkably like a challenge, but I shall let it pass. Still, somehow I cannot imagine you speaking with anything less than perfect propriety. You may look and act the part of a stableboy or an American heathen, but you have only to open your mouth to be revealed as a superlatively proper English governess."

"Thank you, Sir Hillary."

"I'm not certain I meant it as a compliment."

Instead of responding to this sally, Pegasus drew his attention to the beach. "Look down into the cove—they have begun to move."

The black hulk of the schooner had moved in quite close to shore, and men were disembarking. There was a flash of a lantern from the ship and an answering flash from the hut, indicating that Anthony had arrived with the horses.

The offloading of the men and goods was again accomplished with an almost military precision. The Devonshire men, as they had done in the past, almost immediately disappeared with their goods into the caves. The Frenchman had started up the hill and were about halfway to the hut—and fifteen feet from the hidden observers—when they halted.

Pierre had stopped to look back, and then, waving the rest of the party onward, he remained in conversation with another Frenchman.

"Ah, Pierre. I see you are concerned. *Pourquoi?*"

"I do not know, Henri. But I feel in my bones that it does not go as it should. The peasants are almost too silent. They have disappeared almost too quickly. Perhaps I am suffering a crisis of nerves because Mr. Duffy was not at the cove to welcome us. But of course I had expected that.

"Monsieur Duffy?"

"The bailiff who managed the activities of the peasants. Mr. Dillingham found it necessary to eliminate the man because, or so we are told, Monsieur Duffy grows puffed up with greed."

"And you, Pierre, think there is more to the matter than greed."

"I think so, yes. Our Mr. Dillingham has a great deal of sang froid, but I believe there may have been some other more pressing reason for disposing of his assistant. Our activities may have begun to draw attention."

"Perhaps, Pierre. . . . And do you have some suggestions?"

"Henri, you are in command of this mission, and it is only

148

with the greatest of reluctance that I express my concern at all. In your place, however, I would give serious thought to sequestering the pouch before we advance to the hut; we may be marching into a trap."

"*Mais oui*, Pierre. Please have the men wait up ahead. I have the pouch here and I will find someplace in the rocks where it can be safely hidden."

Pierre continued up the hill to where the main party of Frenchmen were standing, and they all began to walk very slowly toward the hut. Once they were out of sight, Henri walked to the edge of the ravine path and over onto the steep cliffs. He looked about him for a moment or two and then, lifting a small boulder, prepared to hide his precious pouch. Unfortunately, he had been walking in the direction of the hidden observers, and it was at this instant that he glimpsed Sir Hillary.

"*Alors*, Pierre!" Henri managed to shriek a moment before Sir Hillary had rendered him unconscious.

A bright oilskin packet had fallen from the Frenchman's hands and was tumbling down the cliff toward the water with Pegasus Gorham behind it. She just managed to retrieve the packet before it reached the last precipice, and she raised it high to show Sir Hillary. But he had not been following her.

Then, from a distance, she heard his voice: "Run, Pegasus, run!"

Pegasus looked up to see Hillary Pendragon expertly holding off half a dozen Frenchmen who had returned at the sound of their commander's call.

Her first instinct was to return to help him, and so she stood for a moment in indecision until he shouted, "Run damn you, run. I'll follow."

Still clutching the pouch but with great reluctance, Pegasus turned and ran amid the rocks parallel to the ridge. Somehow, Sir Hillary managed to avoid his attackers—or what was left of them. He leaped onto the rocky cliffside and quickly made his way toward the place where Pegasus had last been seen.

"After them!" Pierre was shouting. "They have the pouch."

Sir Hillary had spotted her in the moonlight, but instead of continuing to work his way toward her he moved along a parallel path several yards up the cliffside. The French had begun to fire.

But Henri's men were no fools. They realized they could see only one of the culprits, and they knew that man did not

149

have the pouch. The Frenchmen also knew that the two of them would probably come up off the cliffs and onto the ridge. And so the French reasoned, not inaccurately, that their best chance of retrieving the papers would be for them to mount and fan out along the ridge and wait to pursue their quarry, who would, almost certainly, be on foot.

Hillary was aware that the shooting had ceased, and he signaled for Pegasus to join him.

"You still have it?" he asked.

"Yes."

"They will have gone for their horses and will be waiting for us to appear up on the flat land. I suggest you remain with the packet down below and I will decoy them."

"We can both remain here on the cliffs."

"Not if we wish to get word to Muggins. We know the packet is worth a great deal to them, but it is not enough. I want the men as well, and I want the English traitor."

"I won't stay here alone."

"Yes you will."

"Sir Hillary, you can hardly force me, and I don't think you are being reasonable. They already know that you do not have the packet or they would not have abandoned their trap shoot. They will not waste more than a man or two following you, and therefore neither I nor the packet will be safe."

"And your suggestion?"

"We might hide the thing, but I am inclined to go it together. All three of us—you, me, and the packet."

They had been moving steadily upward during this conversation and now were within a few yards of the level.

"Very well, Miss Gorham. I know a fairly sequestered place up ahead where we might break through onto the upland with a minimum of notice."

"How many of them are there?" She swallowed.

"I believe that I have dispatched two or three of them, but there will still be at least six or seven men pursuing us on horseback."

"And the Englishman will be among them."

"Undoubtedly, and we must remember that my Cousin Anthony knows the terrain far better than we do. But be brave, child. We are not his accustomed sort of easy prey. This particular fox hunt will not be played by Anthony's rules."

"Don't worry. I don't think I will fall to bits on you."

"Good girl. Quiet now. Here is the place. We will find

ourselves in a very thickly wooded grove, and I will take the lead until we are on open ground."

Silently they came over the top of the cliffside and moved swiftly through the woods. Always they listened for the sounds of their pursuers, but for at least a quarter of an hour the woods were silent around them. Both Hillary and Pegasus knew their luck would not last. Anthony, at least, knew the lay of the land, and he would know where to look for them. They ran on and were almost a third of the way to the ambush site when they first heard the horses.

Silently, the two of them continued to run ahead, making some efforts to conceal their path. It was only when the first shots were fired and they knew they had been sighted that they began to dart in and out of the brush in an attempt to shake off their pursuers. At moments they almost seemed to have succeeded, and then they would hear the guns again coming closer. Sir Hillary had motioned Pegasus to take the lead, and twice he threw himself over her when the firing increased, but each time they were able to escape again into a wooded area. Finally, within sight of the Pemmfield home farm, Pegasus began to feel that there was hope. The French could follow, because with the moon clear and with the ground soft two pedestrians would be easy to track. But if the two of them could elude the pursuers for a few more precious minutes, they would have reached safety.

Pegasus noticed that the firing had stopped—in fact, the silence was almost too complete—and she turned back sharply. Sir Hillary had fallen to the ground fifteen feet back. Pegasus was by him in a moment.

"Are you wounded?"

"Yes. In the thigh. I've lost too much blood. I can't continue."

"Oh, my God."

He was very weak, and she had to lean close to hear him. "Pegasus, my best chance, and yours as well, is for you to leave me here and take the pouch—continue on your own— you can make it. Leave me the pistol and get some help. I shall wait right here for your return. Now run along, my love."

She looked down at him for a moment. "Yes. Wait here. I will come back." And, stooping quickly, she smoothed back his hair and kissed him on the brow.

It occurred to him only moments afterward that she had taken the pistol. He saw her darting off into the darkness, and he lay back and waited. The French, he knew, would arrive in minutes, and they would not hesitate to kill him once they had assured themselves that he did not have the packet. It was not a pleasant thought. Hillary had been near death many times, and he thought it almost comically ironic that now, when death seemed certain, he should so very much want to live.

Hillary's senses were beginning to grow dim when he thought he heard a soft whistle and then, a little later, the sound of an owl. The owl! It was always Robert's signal. No one else could reproduce it. But there seemed suddenly to be two such owls, because there was an answering call from up the road. And then a double call returned by a double call. And then the sound of a horse. A single horse and a single rider broke through just beyond the tiny clearing where Sir Hillary was hidden.

"Goddam," he muttered to himself. It was Pegasus.

She took a few precious minutes to roughen the paths around his hiding place so that it would no longer be possible for anyone to follow the tracks made by a pair of boots and a pair of moccasins. And then she waited.

The first of the French were in sight, and they saw her. Indeed, they could not have missed her. Her coat had been opened to reveal a white linen shirt—it sparkled in the moonlight—and around her waist, firmly tied, was the unmistakable oilskin pouch. She had made of herself, and her horse, the perfect target.

And still, for what seemed to Hillary like hours, she did not move. Only when all the French were in sight did she turn herself in the direction of the Exeter road and call out in a low-pitched scream, "Hey, wait. They're here. Wait for me." And she began to ride.

To the French it must have appeared that she was attempting to elude them as she darted in and out of the bushes, but Hillary knew otherwise. On that animal she could have escaped her pursuers in moments. They shot at her several times, and she returned the fire once, and then she just rode, with the oilskin pouch flying out at her side. It was, even in the moonlight, an incredibly beautiful picture, the figure of a woman and a horse moving with an almost supernatural wild grace. The French, to whom it was all totally unexpected and very new, were mesmerized.

Sir Hillary saw only one man halt and then yank at his

mount until the beast was turned back in the direction of the Dillingham estate. The others followed Pegasus blindly.

Hillary Pendragon lost consciousness just as he heard the clear sound of the owl repeated in the distance.

Later he was dimly aware that he was being gently lifted, and he knew when his brow was kissed and when his leg was being bandaged by very tender gentle hands.

He heard the sound of Dr. Belding's gruff voice, and then, briefly, he saw the fleeting image of Obediah Muggins and Robert Mansfield. It would have been minutes—it could have been days. But always he knew that she was there. Her presence—the love in her touch—seemed to surround him. With an almost infantlike trust Hillary Pendragon allowed himself to fall back into a healing sleep.

Chapter 15

She watched him sleep. There had been a moment of blinding relief when she had returned with Robbie to find him alive although unconscious, and then there had been the long wait until Dr. Belding passed judgment. Hillary Pendragon had lost a great deal of blood, but the wound was superficial and there was every reason to suppose that, with responsible care, he would live. Lady Julia and the Campbell sisters had returned the next morning, but it was assumed that Miss Gorham would continue as nurse, and so she did.

Margaret Gorham would, under any circumstances, have made a more than competent nurse, and she performed her duties well—almost automatically. At first she was still awash in relief—relief from the terrible blinding fear which seemed to accompany the thought of living in any world without Sir Hillary Pendragon. But Margaret was not a stupid woman, and the flood of relief could no longer protect her from the recognition of the emotions underlying that fear. At twenty-four Margaret Gorham realized that she had, for the first time in her life, fallen in love. It was a shattering revelation.

She had, in those twenty-four years, never had such an assault on her psyche. She had come to this experience totally unprepared. Nothing had ever touched her in this way. She had had friends—good friends—but their existence had never threatened her independence of spirit. She had had a species of hero worship for Silver Fox, but she would have never dreamed of loving him in this way. Margaret had thrived and prospered because she had been strong. People had always depended on her and looked to her for leadership and guidance. It had been a splendid aloneness and a safe one.

As the hours passed, Margaret began to beat herself into submission. The figure in the bed, she reminded herself again and again, was Hillary Pendragon—the nonesuch. The man who juggled half a dozen feminine hearts at one time, and she, Margaret Gorham, had become one of those hapless hearts—just one other victim of his vacuous charm. Worse, because Margaret Mellicent Gorham had nothing to offer him—not youth or beauty or wealth—she could expect nothing in return.

Margaret had changed back into her brown bombazine before the doctor had arrived, and with the change of clothes she had assumed she could return into the person of the governess. With the same ruthlessness with which she suppressed the weakness and lack of discipline in her charges she set out to suppress those within herself. She would not—could not—allow herself to become a victim to what must be nothing more than an infatuation. A stupid senseless ignominious attachment to a puffed-up, hypocritical London dandy.

A woman of lesser will might have allowed herself the indulgence of a dream or two and perhaps the great luxury of tears, but Margaret Gorham had always been a woman of iron will, and with that iron will she was determined to stamp out any spark of a love she could not control.

When Hillary regained conciousness, she was standing over the basin preparing some medication. She turned slowly and saw that his eyes were open.

"You're awake."

"Yes."

"Good. I'll find Lady Julia."

And she turned and left the room. He settled back to wait for her, and when Julia returned alone he suspected that Miss Gorham might be avoiding him. After he had waited for

154

several hours, he knew instinctively that she would not be back.

If Margaret had had no experience with love, Sir Hillary had had no experience with rejection. That she had in some sense rejected him was very clear, and the knowledge began to fester and infect his system far more effectively than did the wound in his thigh.

Robert Mansfield came later in the evening when Lady Julia judged that Sir Hillary was well enough for conversation.

"Hil, except for your wound, it went off wonderfully."

"The documents! She had the documents with her?" Sir Hillary found himself almost too tired to speak and certainly too tired to engage in repartee.

"Not our Pegasus. She hid the documents near the Fultons' well and carried the empty oilskin pouch. She led them straight to us, you know. But for a while it looked like they might escape. Our men were as certainly bewitched as the French. I had, of course, alerted Muggins, but I think he expected to see a matronly figure in brown bombazine. Hillary, I tell you it was one of the high points of my life to see Mr. Muggins thoroughly nonplussed. 'Be damned,' he yelled, 'it's the blimey governess.' The poor man has been in something of a daze ever since."

"Is he still here?"

"No, he left with the prisoners and the packet before Lady Julia and the Campbells had returned. We got back to you as soon as we could—Pegasus and I. But of course you had lost a great deal of blood. I don't suppose you were even aware of us."

Hillary let this pass. "And Anthony?"

"Anthony Dillingham has disappeared. We captured the others alive except for two you dispatched near the hut. There were two more wounded in the hut, for which you were also responsible. Hil, you look exhausted. I'll give you the rest of the information tomorrow when you are up to it."

Hillary settled back into the bed. "Robbie, she saved my life. I want to thank her."

Robert was looking aside, busy with adjusting the pillows.

"Yes, I know, Hillary, but she was never any good at taking thanks or praise of any sort."

And while Hillary suspected that this was the truth, he knew it to be only a part of the truth. He waited for Robert to continue.

155

"Hillary, I don't know how to explain this, but all this has been a great shock to Pegasus's system, so to speak."

"Rubbish."

"I think she may be afraid of you."

"Robbie, you take unfortunate advantage of me. I am too weak to laugh. Go away. I want to sleep now."

Gwendolyn called on him the next morning, and he remained closeted with her for the better part of an hour, long enough to mend, in part, the inroads on his ego made by Miss Gorham's continued absence. Hillary had never in his life had to concern himself with *attracting* a female. His concern had always been in avoiding entanglements, and now when he lay helpless and waiting passively for Miss Gorham he began to look for and quickly found some method for bringing her to heel—or so he thought. Hillary began to flirt ever more outrageously with Gwendolyn Campbell and to encourage her to repeat her visits ad nauseam. It did not occur to him that he was very unfairly using Gwendolyn as a means for making some other woman jealous. Had it occurred to him, he would have shrugged it off. Gwendolyn's heart, he knew, was not in danger, and she had herself proved quite ruthless in crushing the hopes and hearts of others. And so he continued to pay an obvious and heavy-handed court to Gwendolyn Campbell, and if that courtship was a hollow mockery they both of them refrained from publicizing the fact.

In the meanwhile, news of Sir Hillary's illness had been spread about the countryside. The lower classes were perfectly aware that Hillary had been wounded during that glorious night when the French had been apprehended and the yoke of terror had been lifted from the community. The gentry, on the other hand, had to be supplied with an excuse. It was Hillary himself who suggested that he had been shot at by a gamekeeper who took him to be a poacher. He had been shot, he said, as he was stealing across the fields on his return from an evening assignation.

As an explanation it was not without fault, and it was modified, by his friend Robert, so that Hillary himself took a shot at the mythical poacher, who shot back at him. "You see, Hil," Robert had said, "you have been defending Sir Scott's ancestral domains."

To Hillary it seemed six of one and half a dozen of another—just so that there was manufactured some excuse for his being bedridden with a hole in his thigh.

On the third day all the children had come at once to visit

him and to indulge in idle speculation about the *real* cause of his wound. Between Richard, Sarah, and Luke they had invented so many preposterous adventures that Hillary himself was convulsed in laughter. Then he noticed a shadow in the hallway.

"Do come in, Miss Gorham. Your charges are vastly entertaining to a sick man on the verge of collapse. I shall insist that you do not drag them away so soon."

She stood in the doorway. "I am certain we can, in this instance, delay the geography lesson for another quarter of an hour. I will return then." And she turned.

He said to her back, "Thank you, Miss Gorham. Thank you for everything."

"Think nothing of it, Sir Hillary. We are honored to be of assistance."

In her haste to leave, Margaret Gorham almost collided with another woman. The visitor was tawny-haired, lush, and dressed in an azure silk walking dress which revealed virtually almost every square inch of her very considerable charms. Margaret was familiar enough with the gentry of the neighborhood to realize that here, in the flesh, was Madelaine Quincey.

Mrs. Quincey looked clear through the governess and seemed to ignore the children as she swept through the room to collapse in Sir Hillary's arms. "Oh, my poor dear Hillary. What have they done to you?"

"Madelaine, my sweet, you should not have come."

Richard, taking the initiative, helped Miss Gorham herd the younger children from the sickroom, although Pamela seemed absolutely enthralled by the tableau before them. "Dick," she whispered once in the hall, "was that Mrs. Quincey?"

"Yes, you gudgeon—who do you think it was, the Archbishop of Canterbury or the queen mother?"

"No indeed. Even the queen mother could never have arrived in so *ravishing* a dress. She is splendid."

"Come, children—the geography lesson," Margaret said as she hurried them along.

But Pamela, who had always been relatively resentful of Miss Gorham's authority and immune to her methods, continued, "Why ever did Uncle Hillary not introduce us, Miss Gorham?"

"Your uncle, Miss Pemmrington, clearly had other more weighty things on his mind."

Pamela giggled, and Richard pinched her. Lord, he thought to himself. Uncle Hillary could hardly have introduced his mistress to his wards. It would not be the thing. It was shabby of the woman to appear at all—quite shabby. He looked up to see, by the rigid look in her eyes, that Miss Gorham agreed with him, but her obvious disapproval of the scene in the sickroom did not sit well with Richard. He so wanted Miss Gorham to think well of his uncle—he wanted Miss Gorham to think well of all his friends.

Margaret Gorham had engraved that picture of Madelaine Quincey and Sir Hillary on her mind. She dredged up that picture and others like it as a sort of penance any time a softer thought about Hillary Pendragon struggled to break through her own defenses. For another woman, jealousy might have worked toward making her declare and appreciate her own feelings, but Miss Gorham was not just any woman, and in her case jealousy served simply to reconfirm her conviction that Sir Hillary was not for her. She used that jealousy as a weapon to drive every thought of him from her mind. Sir Hillary could have any woman. She had heard him say as much himself. She imagined him with Gwendolyn and with Madelaine Quincey, and with a daily regimen of such thoughts she managed to convert her very real love of the man into something very like hatred.

Hillary Pendragon was allowed out of the sickroom within a week, and although he could not manage to move about without a cane he spent his days quite profitably visiting with the ladies in the library and working several hours a day with his new bailiff. Margaret Gorham continued to avoid him. She could not have avoided dinner in his company, but he noticed, as did everyone with the exception of Gwendolyn, that she had retreated even more completely into the role of governess and seldom spoke or even looked up from her plate during those dinners.

Except for meals, she had hoped to avoid him for the rest of his visit, but events moved against her.

The day before Sir Hillary and the Campbell sisters were scheduled to leave Pemmfield, Margaret Gorham received an unexpected letter in the post.

My dear sister Margaret,

I am writing to inform you that all is well here at Ashby and with our beloved mother at home.

I continue fortunate in being able to discharge with more than average competence my duties as a curate, and, of course, I am greatly blessed in having the affection and respect of my dearest Lucy to sustain me in all my endeavors, as well as the encouragement of her beloved father—the vicar. Both Lucy and I continue to pray that God in his infinite charity will see fit to bless our efforts with those meager earthly rewards which will enable us to end our long betrothal in marital bliss.

It is with respect to this matter that I most particularly wished to consult you. It has come to our attention through an old friend of Lucy's father's that a living has become vacant in a place called Mormount in Lancashire. It is not a large living, but it will more than suffice us, since, with God's aid, our needs will prove to be very modest. Providence has meant that very living for me, my dearest Margaret. You will see that this is so when you read that the patron of Mormount is that very same Sir Hillary Pendragon who is the guardian of the sweet children entrusted to your care.

I am fully cognizant of the fact that as a *mere* governess you cannot hope to impose your views on such a profound and elegant gentleman as Sir Hillary is known to be, but, as a sister, you will naturally be most anxious to do all in your power to advance my career.

You will of course wish to speak to Sir Hillary of this matter. Assure him that I am a worthy and a God-fearing man with a great devotion both to the Church of England and to the God who bestows great fortune upon that Church. Do not, I pray you, neglect to mention that at Oxford I was accounted a brilliant scholar and that I have just completed a book of most edifying sermons— a copy of which I should be delighted to send to Sir Hillary.

Dearest Margaret, my Lucy and I have great faith in you. It has occurred to us that perhaps Sir Hillary is already somewhat in your debt because of the services you have rendered with respect to his sweet wards, who are, most probably, dreadfully difficult children. In any case, we feel certain he will at the least be willing to give you an audience, as Hillary Pendragon is known to be a very condescending gentleman—a truly liberal and enlightened aristocrat. Such men do, occasionally, speak to governesses.

We pray that you approach him for us and that you do so with all the humility due to the considerable differences in your stations. Do not, we beg you, destroy this our greatest hope by one of your ill-advised displays of immodest pride.

Your devoted and loving brother,

Phillip H. Gorham

Pegasus read this letter through twice and then, in a gesture of suppressed violence, she folded it over several times and crammed it into the pocket of her starched gown. Fortunately, it was the hour to begin classes, and she could therefore defer for a while the consideration of the contents of the letter and her own response to her brother's request.

During the short morning recess, Robert Mansfield found Miss Gorham pacing the hallway by the schoolroom.

"Good Lord, Pegasus, you look *grim* this morning."

"Do I, Robbie? I suppose I am. Nothing serious, you understand, but nevertheless annoying."

"If there is a problem, perhaps old Squire Mansfield's first-born might be able to help you fend off the dragon."

"The dragon is Phillip." She smiled up at Robbie. "I received a letter from him this morning. You know he is betrothed to Lucy Crawford, and he has been a curate this last year to her father, the vicar at Ashby."

"I had heard as much."

"They have been holding off the banns until Phillip obtains a living. Mr. Crawford is quite hale and hearty—not likely to vacate in the foreseeable future."

"How unfortunate."

"Just so."

"And Phillip, as always, looks to you to conjure up a solution to his problems. They all look to you, Pegasus."

"Yes, and you will be saying that I fostered their dependence, but I do not think I could have done otherwise.... In any case, Phillip has discovered that a living has just become vacant on one of Sir Hillary's smaller estates, and he has asked me to put a word or two in with Sir Hillary himself."

"And will you ask Hillary?"

"I don't know, Robert. I expect I must, but it is a very difficult thing for me to do. If only Phillip could have found a living in some other way."

Robert Mansfield stood silent for a few moments. "If you ask him, he will come through—you know that. Still, Hillary is a good sort, and it is a pity to wish Phillip on him."

"Robert!"

"Phillip may be your brother, Pegasus, but he is nevertheless a very tedious young man. He was always nine years old and going on eighty. Does he still act as if the weight of the world were on his poor spavined shoulders when all the while you have been cheerfully taking upon yourself all the family responsibilities?"

"Phillip is not a *bad* sort. And you know, it is those prematurely old fellows that most people prefer in their clergy."

"No, I don't suppose he is a *bad* sort. Is it useless for me to point out that he can manage on his own—that you cannot go on forever solving all of your family's problems?"

Deep in thought, she seemed to have scarcely heard him. Margaret was twisting her hands together, and, very uncharacteristically, she took a turn or two about the room before speaking. And then with a frown of concentration and a great deal of humility she began. "Robbie, I cannot explain to you how very difficult this is for me. It does not seem to make any sense at all, and you will think me very silly, but I can't do it. I simply cannot bring myself to it. Can you... would you help me in this?"

"Are you asking me to approach Sir Hillary for Phillip?"

"No, Robbie, I am not asking, I am begging."

Robert hesitated a moment longer. "It's against my better judgment, Pegasus, but I will do it. Nor do I think that my speaking to him will suffice, but I will give it a try."

"Thank you, Robbie—you're a brick."

"True. Just call me Robert Mansfield, Old Brick. I think, though, Pegasus, that you may have deteriorated into something of a fool. A proud fool but all the more a fool."

After luncheon during the mathematics lesson, the butler came to the schoolroom.

"Sir Hillary has requested that, at your convenience, Miss Gorham, you come to the library."

"Thank you, Thackery. I will come immediately." And the children were dismissed for an unscheduled recess.

She came into the library and saw him standing at the window leaning heavily on his cane. The cane, she thought, did not seem like an impediment and did nothing to adversely effect the lounging grace so characteristic of the man.

Neither of them spoke for several moments—it was the first time they had been alone together since Sir Hillary had recovered consciousness the week before.

Margaret broke the silence. "You should not be standing, Sir Hillary. May I find you a chair?"

"Miss Gorham, you are a governess, not a nurse. And I prefer not to be seated, thank you." There followed another awkward silence, and again she forced herself to speak. "You wished to see me, Sir Hillary?"

"Yes, yes, I did, Miss Gorham. Robert spoke to me this morning about a brother of yours. Incidentally, how many brothers do you have?"

It seemed an irrelevant question, but she answered him. "I have two brothers, Michael and Phillip. Michael is in the navy."

"And two sisters as well?"

"Yes. One is married and the other betrothed."

"I see. So that with this living in Mormount you feel the last of your siblings will be settled for life."

"I hope so, sir."

"It occurs to me that there is something of an inequity here."

"An inequity?"

"Does it not seem something less than perfect justice to have all of them settled but yourself?"

"I have my work, sir."

"To be sure you have your work. But on your own testimony, Miss Gorham, you do not remain in one place for upward of six or eight months—half-year incarcerations, first in this household and then another, cannot precisely be described as settlement for life, can they?"

"No, sir."

He waited for her to continue and to argue the point. She remained silent. Hillary toyed with his cane for a moment before proceeding. "As it happens, Miss Gorham, I owe you my life, and so I think I will grant your brother the living at Mormount. But I shall require more information, and, in particular, I must know what sort of man your brother is. Robert was surprisingly reticent on that point."

It was Margaret's turn to hesitate a moment. She had anticipated the question and knew her answer, but it was difficult to gather herself together and begin. "My brother Phillip is studious and serious. Perhaps he is too serious for such a young man. But he has always been determined on the Church, you know, which is strange in a military family such as our own. Phillip's very considerable strengths, I believe, lie in his great stability of character and in his quite remarkable faith in the Church of England."

"He has, of course, done splendidly at Oxford."

"So I have been led to believe."

"And his betrothed—Lucy Crawford—is a pattern card of all the feminine virtues?"

"I have met Miss Crawford only two or three times, and each time she has impressed me by the modesty and propriety of her manner and the seriousness of her conversation."

"In short, a perfect mate for your brother?"

"They are certainly well matched, Sir Hillary."

Hillary Pendragon silently thanked the Lord that Mormount was one of his minor estates so that he would not be exposed at length to this clerical pompous ass. He reminded himself as well that the people at Mormount were very conservative in their thinking and had always preferred dry vicars. Still he persisted, "The Mormount living is not precisely munificent. Can your brother manage on two hundred and fifty a year?"

"I rather think such a sum would represent luxury for Phillip. Both he and Lucy have been accustomed to live very modestly, and he is not, I believe, an *ambitious* man."

"Not an ambitious man? I understand your brother has written you and virtually demanded that you plead his cause with me. Since he cannot know of the great debt I owe you"— he watched her flinch—"your brother's request strikes me as the action of a very ambitious and somewhat unreasonable personality. Governesses as a rule do not make such requests of their employers."

"Phillip has always turned to me for guidance and support. I think he believes that, whether or not there is a chance of success, I *ought* to extend myself in such a matter. He made no demands, he merely requested that I at least *ask* you to consider him."

Hillary hesitated for a moment, deep in thought.

"And will you ask?"

"I beg your pardon?"

"Come now, you are being uncharacteristically obtuse. It is really quite simple. All you need say is, 'Sir Hillary, would you please consider my brother Phillip for the vacancy at Mormount.' You hesitate, Miss Gorham. I'm certain you might manage those few words—is *asking* so very difficult for you?"

Again she was strongly tempted to look away from him, but she did not. "Yes, for some reason it has always been difficult. Between friends such formality should not be necessary."

"Very true. But we are not friends, are we, Miss Gorham? You have made that abundantly clear, have you not? Were we friends you would be calling me Hillary. Were we friends you would not have asked Robert, who was obviously most reluctant, to intervene on your behalf. Miss Gorham, you have in fact consistently spurned my friendship."

Margaret almost instinctively had turned toward the door. "Miss Gorham, you are not excused. Just this once in your life you will have to remain and listen to a little unpleasantness. Your precious brother will have his living, but I shall exact as payment the next half hour of your time—is that clear? Now please be seated."

"I prefer to stand, sir."

He did not raise his voice. "I said, sit."

She sat.

"And don't look so damned pious. I do not intend to be duped again. Whatever illusions you may harbor, please to remember that you are not *my* governess."

"I never supposed I was."

"The deuce you didn't. You, Miss Gorham, continue in spite of everything to rule everyone with a sort of uniform intimidation. The intimidation exercised by a governess on a pack of imbecile seven-year-olds."

"Sir Hillary, much as I hold my brother's interests dear, I cannot and I will not remain here to be abused. Good day."

She made to rise and found herself effectively countered by an expertly wielded cane. "I said I am leaving, sir."

"And I said you are not. Sit."

She sat and glared up at him.

"Wonderful, Miss Gorham. I suspect you are now genuinely angry. You have even abandoned your stern schoolmistress pose and you are looking almost human."

"We each of us make our way through this world as best we can, Sir Hillary. As a governess I may seem stern, but I, at least, have never stooped to manipulating my fellow humans by means of a false charm and a mindless grin."

"Smile, not grin. And it was never mindless—a trifle empty at times, but never mindless."

"At the moment, sir, you do not precisely radiate charm."

"I, at least, am not a hypocrite, Miss Gorham." Hillary smiled.

"Nor am I, sir."

"Of course you are. You strut about the place hidden behind your starched blacks and browns. You are a fraud."

"Rubbish. Like you I simply exploit an actual facet of my personality."

"A facet of which I have become thoroughly sick."

"Bravo. Fortunately I do not seek to be guided by your opinion in such matters. I was thoroughly sick of your idiot grin and vapid attempts at charm within five minutes of making your acquaintance, Sir Hillary. Now may I be excused?"

"No, you will not be excused. You will be an excessively sweet little woman and listen politely to everything I have to say. And I in turn will award your pompous little ass of a brother the living in Mormount. It is a more than fair exchange, and despite all your noble sentiments to the contrary you will bear with me quietly. You will listen because if you do not your sweet little Phillip's chances of acquiring my plump little living are not worth a tinker's damn."

Her eyes were blazing, but she made no attempt to stand. "I am listening."

"Good. I wish you to leave Pemmfield at once."

"Is my employment being terminated?"

"No, it is not. The situation here has, at least temporarily, become too dangerous for you. Do you understand?"

"I understand that you are overwrought. I have work still to do at Pemmfield. The children will need me until they can be settled in the school. And John Paul will not be able to manage these first months without my help."

"Miss Gorham, you try the patience of a saint. Will you attend to me, or must I cane you? That sort of cruelty is said to run in families, you know."

"You are referring, I suppose, to Anthony."

"How wonderfully clever of you to deduce so much, Miss Gorham. Anthony is dangerous—very dangerous. Have you in the past few months grasped even that much?"

"We all know that he is dangerous, but on the other hand he does not appear to be in Devonshire at the moment."

"No, my information is that he is in France. We cannot, however, know when he will return, and I will not have you here when he does return."

"You believe I cannot manage Anthony."

"You have managed him very poorly heretofore."

"I have done what has to be done," she retorted.

"And you have been damn clumsy about it."

"We do not all have your remarkable charm. My methods are more direct and less adorned, but they will suffice."

"Fool! Your methods have set a determined murderer against you."

"And what of the rest of you? Your cousin is guilty of grievous crimes. You know it, Sir Hillary, I know it, a slew of people know it, and yet Anthony Dillingham goes free."

"He goes free not, as you seem to imply, because he is my cousin or because he is a gentleman of standing in this community. Because he is a gentleman we needed proof positive, and once we had it we needed Anthony to bait the trap for the others. He evaded that trap. Should he return to England he will be apprehended, and you must trust me in this."

"I seem to have little choice."

"None at all. Meanwhile you must realize you have unnecessarily taunted him time and again. He is no fool, and he will discover, if he has not done so already, who the rider of the wild horse is. He will undoubtedly seek revenge, and his notions of revenge have never been pretty. I am asking you to leave this place and avoid Anthony until he is apprehended."

"Not unless you terminate my employment. In which case, of course, I shall leave. I shall go to America and be free of the whole lot of you. I am heartily sick of the house of Barth. But I will not run home to Yorkshire simply because I am afraid of what Anthony Dillingham might or might not do if and when he returns to Pemmfield. I am no coward, sir. And, at the risk of seeming ungracious, I will remind you that I have been managing very difficult people quite successfully for as long as I can remember. I am not afraid of your cousin or of any other man."

"You damn well should be. Do you expect to stare him down or to appeal to his nonexistent tender mercy? You will succeed in neither."

"Again, Sir Hillary, I pray you not to concern yourself in these matters. I am held to be a very competent person."

"Oh, to be sure, Miss Gorham, I concede that you are wonderfully competent as a boy in britches, but as a woman in skirts you are a total failure."

She could not recall ever having experienced so wild, so volcanic, an anger. She was on her feet and half inclined to physically attack him with his own cane. With a stern effort she regained some sort of minimal control over herself and turned toward the door. He had thrown the cane aside and came to stand not a foot from her.

She stood rigid and straight and waited for him to stand aside. He did not stand aside. She looked up to see his eyes narrowed and a certain grimness about his mouth. And then he reached out with pantherlike swiftness and pulled her toward him.

In her youth she had been kissed once or twice, and, except for a slight queasiness, it had not affected her. She was totally unprepared for this kiss. Every instinct in her body cried out to plummet him, and then quite suddenly and equally violently she wished to return the ardor of his embrace. To have done so would have been to concede defeat, and Margaret Gorham would not be defeated. Summoning every atom of will, she forced herself to remain perfectly rigid in his arms and to endure the embrace in silence. He moved away—mockery, bitterness, and some understanding in his eyes.

The mockery and bitterness she could have tolerated, but the understanding was unbearable. She clenched her hands together and forced herself to look up at him. "I should like to murder you."

"But you won't, Miss Gorham. You have done remarkably well thus far, but if you reach out and touch me now—even slap me—you will be lost."

Then he smiled down at her. The wicked charming devastating smile of Hillary Pendragon. "Come, Pegasus. I offer you a wager. Strike me if you can."

She turned and ran from the room, slamming the door on the sound of his laughter.

Dear Woody,

I hate Sir Hillary Pendragon. I have never detested any man near so much—the ingrate—the imbecile. He shall not be my hero nor my villain nor even the dense sort of disbelieving respectable fellow. No, I shall make him appear to be a normal charming fellow but in reality he will be a blith-

167

ering charming idiot—a bedlamite protected from ruin by his mother, Lady A. He shall in his idiocy be a smiling charmer convinced he can seduce any woman, and he will suffer countless humiliating rejections. Finally after Lady A is destroyed in the cataclysmic fire of the grand finale, we shall have Sir H locked up in a home for the hopelessly mad.

He will leave tomorrow, and I pray I will never see him again. Tonight I shall set to work revising my manuscript, *The Witch of Firth Island,* and it will be in the hands of the publisher within the week.

Pegasus

And then she penned still another letter.

Dear Phillip,

I have discussed your desire for the living in Mormount with Sir Hillary. I do not believe the discussions went well, however, and, in your place, I would not anticipate anything good coming of it.

Your sister,

Margaret

Chapter 16

The next morning the houseparty was disbanded. Robert'
Mansfield left to return to his home in Yorkshire, and Sir
Hillary left for his estates in Somerset. Gwendolyn and Alicia
stayed on for a day or two until their father came into Devonshire to escort them to London.

Anthony Dillingham had not returned, and, within a fort-
night, it was being rumored about the countryside that he
had gone to London, to Paris, or even to America. In any
case, no one, save his mother, seemed greatly interested in
his whereabouts, and, after the initial spate of speculation,
no one even bothered to discuss him.

For Margaret Gorham the balance of the summer and the
early fall seemed relatively uneventful. The two Dillingham
children were allowed to remain at Pemmfield, ostensibly so
that Margaret could remedy the deficiencies in their education. Miss Porter had disappeared, and now no one, least
of all Lady Augusta, argued that she had ever been even a
competent instructor of the young. On her own initiative,
Margaret set out to convince Lady Augusta that the children
would be best off in a school atmosphere. Indeed, there were
schools in Bath, Margaret claimed, that were of such intel-
lectual superiority that they rendered education in the home,
indeed education anywhere but in Bath, dismally inadequate. Actually Miss Woodruff had suggested the two schools
in question because they were modest sorts of places run by
friends of her youth. The pair, a man and wife, had earned
a reputation not only for their academic superiority but also
for the gentle humanity which leavened their treatment of
the young. And so, for the balance of the summer, Miss Gorham found herself devoting hours of her time each week to
the tiresome task of discussing with Lady Augusta strengths
and weaknesses of various educational theories until that
lady came to suggest, entirely on her own initiative, the very
two schools that the rest of the family was quite set on send-

ing the children to. In fact, it was understood that Richard would accompany the Dillingham children and within a year or so the younger Pemmfield children would also be sent to Bath.

During this time, Claude Dillingham was in almost constant attendance at Pemmfield, and a bond, gratifying to everyone, was fast developing between him and his brother's children. Where they had lost such a father and gained such an uncle, the children could not long remain unhappy, and in the atmosphere of general good health and vitality at Pemmfield, Sarah and Luke had soon recovered the natural buoyancy and clear good spirits of normal children.

Madame de la Coeur's novel was completed within days of Sir Hillary's departure and was published before the end of the summer. Still, in Devonshire, there was no great stir made by the publication of *The Witch of Firth Island,* yet another novel by the infamous Fleur de la Coeur. For over three years Margaret's novels had been the talk of London, at least in part because they seemed so accurately to reflect the characters of the leading lights of the ton. But the author of these same novels, buried in the guise of a governess in first this rural community and then the other, saw only the royalties and unwittingly avoided all the attendant publicity. In fact, Margaret Gorham did not seem to require the admiration and acclaim that has always sustained the typical vain scribbler.

She had received her copy of the finished work and had, as a matter of habit, read it through for errors and omissions. There were none. At least none which could be attributed to the publisher. The errors and omissions were all in the drawing of Sir Randolph, the hapless individual on whom she had vented all her wrath. Her portrait of Sir Randolph had been devastating and, as she now realized, grossly unfair to Sir Hillary. In the cool light of late summer she understood why she had drawn Sir Hillary as she had, but to understand why is not to excuse. She had behaved the part of a mean-spirited, bitter, jealous woman, and she was now deeply ashamed of herself—although she did not believe for a moment that anyone else reading the novel could even associate Sir Randolph with Sir Hillary Pendragon.

The other characters had been softened, since Margaret invariably found that she could not *dislike* her own creations, but in Sir Randolph she had created a biting satire worthy of a Swift or a Fielding, and in so doing she knew she had done a grave injustice to a gentleman and a friend. And so Miss Gorham was filled with a sort of remorse which was quite independent of any fear of reprisal. And still she knew that somewhere and somehow there would be a reprisal. Margaret Gorham had always believed in the efficacy of divine justice, and she believed that even if no one ever knew, except of course Rachel Woodruff, there would still be a price to pay for such a dishonorable act and that she, Margaret Gorham, would be called upon to pay that price.

Fortunately she was not a woman to be completely cast down even by such feelings of remorse, particularly since the book had already been commended to posterity, so to speak, and there was no way now to influence the resulting course of events. In fact, because the book had been completed, Margaret knew that she should be moving on. But curiously, despite the dangers of remaining in Devonshire, she seemed reluctant to leave Pemmfield. For the first time since she had become a governess, Margaret Gorham found herself almost a member of the family.

It was therefore with a heavy heart that she approached Lady Julia one day early in September and announced her plans to leave that lady's employ soon after the family was removed to London. "To be certain, Lady Julia, I shall stay until you have found a suitable replacement."

Lady Julia shook her head. "But my dear Miss Gorham, after you there can be no suitable replacement."

"Thank you, Lady Julia." Margaret smiled ruefully. "But I have always had a sort of wanderlust, you see, and I cannot remain in any one place long."

"Promise me you will reconsider the matter, my dear. We are, to be sure, very dependent on you, but we are, as well, terribly fond of you. It seems so dreary and unnecessary for you to leave what has become to you a home only so that you can think of running off to some other obnoxious family as their governess."

"Quite honestly, Lady Julia, I have thought of abandoning the profession entirely. I have saved some money, and I think I will set up house with my own governess and a few horses. We have purchased a cottage in Yorkshire, you see.... And, if that does not work out, I have seriously considered emigrating to America. It has always been a dream of mine to see America."

"Oh, my dear Miss Gorham. You have such strange and

such heroic notions, to be sure. Only don't, I pray you, move too quickly. You are young and you have time."

For the moment, Margaret did not pursue the matter. Lady Julia was agitated. In fact, Margaret found her concern quite touching. People in general had never worried about Miss Gorham—she had worried about them.

Margaret would have been astounded to find that Lady Julia was not merely concerned, she was genuinely distraught—so distraught that she immediately sent off a missive to Sir Hillary informing him of Miss Gorham's plans and aspirations.

Hillary Pendragon received her letter when he was already in a foul humor. He had just survived a harrowing interview with Mr. Phillip Gorham, and he felt he deserved better from Phillip's sister. Hillary read the letter in grim silence and then, ripping it to shreds, he threw it into the fire and barked for his valet. His ill humor had come to be expected by members of the household staff. Sir Hillary, who had always been an exemplary employer, had deteriorated, since his return from the country, into a very erratic and often foul-tempered gentleman. His valet was convinced that the disease would pass, but in the meanwhile these sudden turns of the master had the effect of putting the household into a frenzy. The night he received Julia's letter was the worst. Sir Hillary was in a towering rage, and it took the valet over an hour to dress him, after which time, without so much as a thank you, Sir Hillary stalked from the house and spent an evening indulging, or attempting to indulge, in every one of his various libertine propensities—simultaneously. He woke the next morning with a splitting headache and in an even fouler humor, having accomplished only the one goal of becoming completely intoxicated. And, after divesting himself of the greater part of the last night's dinner, Sir Hillary Pendragon swore a horrible vengeance on the person of Miss Margaret Gorham.

Miss Gorham, for her part, could not think of Sir Hillary without experiencing a great deal of pain, much of which she attributed to remorse. But Sir Randolph could not account for *all* that pain, and Miss Gorham did not have much trouble in diagnosing the bulk of her complaint as an advanced stage of lovesickness. She was still in love, and she knew the proper treatment for that disease was to exercise the very thought of Sir Hillary from her mind. Miss Gorham continued to spend a great deal of her time in the determined pursuit of *not* thinking of Hillary Pendragon. This was made even more difficult, not only because Lady Julia, Claude, and the children seemed forever to be discussing Sir Hillary, but also because Margaret herself could not clear from either her mind or her heart the memory of his every gesture, his walk, his smile, his touch.

Eventually, Margaret had almost entirely obliterated the image of Sir Hillary from her waking moments only to find that she was unable to keep him from invading her dreams.

The situation was further exasperated when, days after her interview with Lady Julia, she received still another letter from her brother Phillip.

My dear sister Margaret,

How happy I am, how truly blessed, to be in a position to inform you that you were quite wrong in your reading of Sir Hillary's mind on the subject of yours truly.

That noble sir vouchsafed me an interview today, and I can now say I am quite disappointed in you, my dear sister, I cannot think that you did very much to plead my cause with the noble Pendragon, since he repeatedly assured me that he had not been led to expect a great deal from our interview. How you must have misrepresented my abilities I cannot comprehend. Fortunately, with God's aid, I was able to impress upon that great nobleman the profoundity of my intellect, the Pindaric heights of my sermons, and my absolute devotion to God and His Church, etc.

Sir Hillary is a man of great discernment and perfect powers of observation as well as of an Adonislike countenance, which latter I am certain is responsible for his otherwise completely unmerited reputation as a libertine. Such manly beauty and grace cannot fail to melt the hearts of countless women, and we cannot hold him responsible for the devastation wrought by this beauty which God has granted him.

Sir Hillary for his part was most impressed with my credentials and with my person, saying often that such wisdom in one so young was almost beyond belief.

Straightaway he offered me the living in Mormount, and I humbly accepted his offer. I ask you, dear sister—could anything be better?

Afterward we exchanged pleasantries about the Mansfields and about yourself. I feel my patron was most graciously condescending in his evident concern for your well-being, and I can only agree with his wisdom in censoring the often inappropriate prideful and headstrong nature of your character.

Sincerely,

Your brother Phillip

This letter, far from reestablishing Sir Hillary in Miss Gorham's regard, simply led her to put in motion her previously tentative plans to liberate herself from the whole house of Barth and its descendants both collateral and otherwise. The cottage in which Miss Woodruff was living was finally purchased outright, and one of the servant girls, recommended by Lady Mansfield, was engaged to attend to the cooking and cleaning. Now Pegasus spent much of her time working out her plans for the renovation of the existing barn and the fencing of a small pasture. In fact, Miss Gorham spent an inordinate amount of time on these plans, so she found herself to be fully occupied with her responsibilities to five children, to Lady Julia, and to the day-to-day running of the estate with Mr. John Paul. It had always been an object with Miss Gorham never to *waste* time. Consequently, although she could not bring herself to begin a new novel, she found ways of absorbing her otherwise considerable energies. With every waking moment occupied she would not and did not think of Hillary Pendragon.

But the world did not stand still for Margaret Gorham. She must of necessity meet Sir Hillary at least once more. Late in October the Pemmrington family would travel en masse to London to attend the marriage of Robert Mansfield and Alicia Campbell. Despite his flirtation with Miss Gwendolyn Campbell—or perhaps because of it—Sir Hillary had maintained a great deal of influence with that family, and with Lady Julia's assistance he had been as easily able to settle Robert Mansfield for life as he had been able to settle Phillip Gorham.

The wedding was to be a relatively modest affair, but it would provide for Margaret an opportunity to see many of her Yorkshire friends, and in the hustle and bustle of the major social event she did not feel that the newfound and still precarious control of her feelings for Hillary Pendragon would be seriously threatened.

Everyone except perhaps Gwendolyn Campbell was delighted with the match, particularly since it was so clearly a love match between two people who were almost universally liked. The wedding promised to be a happy occasion, after which the Pemmringtons would return to Devonshire and the bride and bridegroom would leave for a three-month honeymoon in Ireland.

Lady Julia could not wholly approve of at least this aspect of the plans. "Ireland, you understand, is no place for a wedding trip. It is so unfortunate that the cursed Boney has been interfering so much all over Europe and there is no place else to go. There is no romance in Ireland, Miss Gorham. Only fog and potatoes."

Miss Gorham set down her tea and answered, "I expect, though, that Robbie and Alicia will find Ireland a very romantic country."

"I expect"—Lady Julia was laughing and blushing simultaneously—"that they will not give it a thought one way or the other. Marriage is a wonderful institution if it can only be combined with love."

As Lady Julia seemed suddenly lost in memories, Miss Gorham did not comment. But with some determination Julia shook herself free and seemed to attack another subject. "By the by, Miss Gorham, you are not going to wear one of those horrid brown things to the wedding, are you? After all, at this wedding you will be a most honored guest—a lifelong and dear friend of Robert's! To appear in the garb of a governess would be entirely inappropriate, don't you think?"

"Perhaps you are right, Lady Julia."

"Of course I am right. I understand about these things. Shall we go into Exeter next week and purchase you something more fitting to the occasion?"

"That won't be necessary, Lady Julia. My brother Michael has sent me a length of blue silk from the Orient. I am beginning to think a brother in the navy is worth ten in the clergy."

"But, of course," Julia trilled, "why would anyone wish to have her soul saved if she might only go to the devil in blue silk? Besides, Miss Gorham, I rather suspect you are quite capable of saving your own soul without the aid of a clerical brother, no matter what the degree of his virtue."

The two ladies looked up and smiled as Claude Dillingham was announced, and after giving him his tea they discussed their plans for the wedding with him. He threw himself into the enterprise with enthusiasm, insisting that he see the length of silk on the spot so that he might plan his own wardrobe and the wardrobes of all the children so that they would harmonize.

"For I am determined," he said with a flourish and a bow, "that we shall all attend ensemble."

The trip to London was begun in the best of good spirits. Too many good spirits, as it turned out. Miss Gorham was kept so occupied she could not spare a thought for the coming festivities. Both Claude and Margaret spent the whole of their journey dampening the soaring spirits of the exuberant children, monitoring the intake of bonbons, and providing Pamela with gentle loving care when she became horribly motion-sick. But at last they all arrived and the children were handed into the care of one of the nurses in Julia's sister's home.

The next day the wedding itself went very smoothly. It almost seemed, Margaret thought, as if no one had ever been the least bit opposed to the match and Robbie and Alicia's months of meeting in relative secrecy had somehow been completely unnecessary. The whole Mansfield clan had descended on London, and Margaret herself was greeted by them as one of the family. In truth, she scarcely looked the governess. The silk of her gown was a thing of splendor, and if she had had it cut on lines far more severe than either Julia or Claude would have preferred it was nevertheless quite flattering to a ramrod-straight neat little spinster lady.

Hillary Pendragon was the groom's man, and Margaret could not help but notice that most of the female eyes in the room seemed pinned to him. Margaret Gorham had forgotten the strength of the magnetism that seemed to radiate from him, and the force of it shook her resolve. Somehow she had succeeded in muting and softening his image, at least during her waking hours, so that it no longer seemed to pull at her with a primeval power. Margaret was in the same room with Sir Hillary for less than ten minutes before she realized that she was nowhere near cured of her disease; try as she might she was almost intoxicated by his mere presence.

After the ceremony, Hillary and Margaret had welcomed each other almost gingerly, and then he had been rushed off with the rest of the wedding party. The wedding party itself did not seem to be in uniformly high spirits. Margaret could almost feel the chill wind that blew between Hillary Pendragon and Gwendolyn Campbell. In fact, Gwendolyn Campbell seemed to be the only person in the room determined to ignore Sir Hillary. Instead, she seemed totally intent on nabbing herself a fat little middle-aged earl who was reputed to be distressingly plump in the purse—as plump in the purse as he was in the person.

As the reception continued, the wedding party was disbanded and the social fabric of the group seemed to have stretched itself thinner until there seemed to be about twenty smallish clumps of people circled about the room. Many of the men seemed slightly on the go, and some were behaving almost foolishly. Out of habit, Margaret Gorham, the novelist, was observing them very carefully when she looked around to find herself suddenly face to face with Sir Hillary Pendragon.

For a moment Margaret was nonplussed, and it was Sir Hillary who spoke first. "Good afternoon, Miss Gorham."

"Good afternoon, Sir Hillary." She stared at the glass of champagne in her hand before continuing. "I had meant to thank you for granting my brother Phillip the living in Mormount. He has written to me and has explained all you have done for him."

"I did nothing for him. I did it for you." As she uncharacteristically refused to lift her eyes from the glass in her hands, he turned the conversation. "Have things settled back down in Devonshire?"

"Yes. We are managing quite well, and the estate may even show a very small profit for the year."

"I was not intending to lose any sleep over the matter one way or another, Miss Gorham."

"True. But if one is to do anything, it is, I think, more rewarding to do it well." She hesitated. "I do not mean to presume, but..."

"Yes, Miss Gorham?"

"Do you happen to know anything of Anthony Dillingham? We do not speak of him, but he hangs like a shadow about Pemmfield."

"I do not *know,* but I suspect he is in France. In any case the powers that be have decided that, should he return to England, he will be watched rather than apprehended immediately. Mr. Muggins and his superiors are of the opinion that if we allow our Anthony a little more line we will pull in a whole basket full of frogs."

"Yes. I suppose you might. Sir Hillary, I have come to agree with you on the matter of Mr. Anthony. I would just as soon be out of Devonshire when he returns. I have completed my work there—we are hoping that the children will all be able to attend school in Bath after Christmas. I think it best that I give my notice to Lady Julia, and, of course, to you as well."

"Have you found another situation?" There was a barely discernible tightening of his jaws, and the smile had left his eyes. Miss Gorham, who had not lifted her own eyes from her glass, did not notice.

"No, Sir Hillary, nor will I seek one immediately. I am largely undecided about my future. I shall return, at least for a time, into Yorkshire and live with Miss Woodruff, my old governess. We have purchased a cottage, and I hope, on a modest scale, to raise horses."

"Somehow it seems a trifle unchallenging for someone of your disposition, Miss Gorham. You seem to ask very little of life."

"True, but then I am not like to be disappointed, am I? If it grows too dull I have also thought of emigrating to America."

"I see—you will sail to America and join the other heathens?" he asked.

She looked away from her glass and out across the room. "Or, more likely, I will become what they call a schoolmarm and roam about the frontier bringing the ideals of Christian civilization to the wilds of the Western Hemisphere."

Just then Gwendolyn and her portly new swain walked past them. Gwendolyn barely nodded in only the slightest acknowledgment of Sir Hillary's existence, and there was no acknowledgment of Miss Gorham at all.

Hillary was smiling. "I am very much afraid I deserved that frigid stare. I used Gwendolyn poorly, and you know. Fortunately Lord Hamwich is reputed to have almost twice my income. They will make an admirable couple, don't you think, Miss Gorham?"

"They seem to enjoy each other's company."

Her companion was chuckling. "Rubbish. And you are still a lovely little hypocrite. You know, in the beginning I entertained a fantasy that you were not a governess at all but some sort of an exotic spy for Napoleon. You would sit at the dinner table observing us all so carefully, and I would imagine you running up to your room and committing all your mental notes to paper, then mailing the information off to France. But, of course, that was before I came to know that although you may be a trifle hypocritical in maintaining the guise of innocent little governess, you are nevertheless scrupulously honorable."

He saw the glass tumble from her hand, and she instinctively stooped down to retrieve the pieces. Hillary motioned to a servant to clear the floor while he slowly raised Margaret by the elbow and moved her away.

"For a fellow of such remarkable address, I think I have botched it, Miss Gorham."

"I *am* a hypocrite, you know. And in some ways I am not an honorable person."

"Is this the invincible Pegasus? Brave and true? You know, you have not looked me in the eye since I greeted you."

"Sir Hillary"—she was making a valiant effort to look at him—"I am not very brave at the moment. Moreover, I have a vicious temper, and Phillip is always saying that my temper or my pride will be the end of me. I think for once he may have the right of it." And then she pulled herself together and, straightening, looked at him very seriously. "Sir Hillary, I have something I must tell you."

She seemed so upset that his only instinct was to reach out and soothe her. Instead he chuckled and said, "Next you will be confessing that you really have been a spy for Napoleon and that you have sold us all for a handful of golden guineas."

This was so near the truth that Margaret was, for once, speechless, and before she could reply he had continued.

"Next month Julia will be having a ball at Pemmfield as a sort of grand send-off for her return to London society. All of Devonshire will be there, and I shall come as well. We will be able to settle things then. You do need time, Miss Gorham, don't you?"

He spoke, she thought, with all the assurance of a man who was the catch of the town and knew himself to be irresistible. It was her slight irritation at his obvious self-as-

surance which stiffened Pegasus sufficiently so that she did
not then and there collapse into tears and confess all.

Instead she smiled up at him a trifle awkwardly and hur-
riedly excused herself while Lady Mansfield came to introduce Sir Hillary to one of the octogenarian Mansfield uncles.

Chapter 17

Once returned to Devonshire, Miss Gorham found herself
looking forward to the ball with something less than uniform
enthusiasm. On the one hand she was eager, despite her own
better judgment, to explore the growing friendship between
herself and Sir Hillary. But just when she began to allow
herself to dwell on such pleasant thoughts she would be assaulted by a sharp pang of remorse when she remembered
that deep within the pages of *The Witch of Firth Island* was
an erstwhile portrait of Sir Hillary which might, in itself,
preclude any possibility of ever establishing a closer, more
amicable bond with that gentleman. She must, Margaret
knew, confess what she had done, and then she must be willing to leave Pemmfield free of any emotional entanglements.
The world, of course, would never have perceived that Miss
Gorham was in a state of great psychic agitation, because
she managed to continue, at least outwardly, calm as always.
But inwardly she was finding it more and more difficult to
control her violent vibrations from elation to misery. There
was so much which would keep a Sir Hillary and a mere
governess apart; the existence of the novel seemed nothing
more than a *coup de grace*. Still, the thought of a single
unblemished evening in the company of Sir Hillary was ex-
hilarating. To live a dream for a single moment was infinitely
better than not to dream at all.

For his part, Sir Hillary was looking forward to the same
evening with an undiluted eagerness. It had dawned on him
in the weeks since he had left Devonshire that his attraction
to Miss Gorham was wonderfully different from his attraction
to countless other ladies over the years. For no other woman

had he ever experienced such feelings of friendship and respect, and never before had he so wanted a woman that the prospect of a lifetime without her seemed unbearably bleak. Hillary Pendragon knew that, for the first time in his life, he was very much in love. Once having realized the state of his own emotion he naturally assumed he would marry Margaret Gorham. It did not occur to him that she might refuse him, even if she were properly approached, although he recognized that his attempts to arouse her jealousy in Devonshire had been heavy-handed and ill-advised. He would, he swore, do better now. He would maintain control over the situation and over himself. And so having resolved on his course of action, Sir Hillary settled back into an unblemished contemplation of the future.

A week before he was scheduled to go into Devonshire, Hillary was met outside his club by Obediah Muggins. Sir Hillary, Mr. Muggins explained, had been summoned into the presence of His Nibs.

For once, the summons to adventure was not an entirely pleasant experience for Sir Hillary. He discovered when he met with his nibs that he was scheduled to return to the Continent shortly after Julia's ball, and *his* services would be required because it was an extremely delicate and dangerous mission. His nibs, who refused categorically to use married men, had made no effort to disturb Robert in Ireland. Sir Hillary would manage this mission alone, and it was this very aloneness which seemed to chill Hillary Pendragon's soul. It was not that he wished to avoid hair's-breadth escapes and courageous rides across the French countryside, it was simply that he could no longer imagine such adventures without simultaneously imagining a lithe boyish figure riding beside him and laughing into the wind. Sir Hillary shook himself loose from such thoughts and began to discuss the details of his assignment with his nibs.

An hour later, as he was preparing to leave, Hillary remembered to ask Muggins whether Anthony Dillingham had finally been located.

"Aye, he has been that, guv'nor. The rotter is in France selling out his country and his king."

"I should have thought you would have prevented that, Muggins."

"Pshaw. The man has nothing to sell. His nibs is in favor of keeping the gentleman alive and well for a bit. He may still lead us to a few more frogs or at least scallawags before

181

he himself departs this world. That is what his nibs is thinking, and p'raps he has the right of it."

"He may be right."

"To be sure, guv'nor. But I for one shall rest easier when our bird is safely in hand and the matter is finished."

"And so will I, Mr. Muggins. Much easier."

Sir Hillary took his cane and was shrugged into his coat. He pinned the perennial smile to his face and left the elegant home of Lord ——— by the front door. Hillary had the look of a man who had just come from a pleasant exchange of crim cons managed over a very superior brandy.

His mind, as he strolled down the street, was not on crim cons nor on brandy. He was not even concerned with the details of his new assignment. Instead, Sir Hillary was thinking that he would have only a single evening and perhaps a morning with Margaret Gorham, and he was not at all certain this would be enough time. Somewhere in the back of his mind he began to fret. He was disturbed not only by the necessity of this unplanned excursion to the Continent, but also by his nibs' decision concerning Anthony Dillingham.

Hillary was certain it would have been far better for Sir Anthony to have disappeared quietly and finally, instead of which Anthony would remain alive and well at considerable risk to his family and to Margaret Gorham.

Ordinarily, Hillary would have actively questioned his nibs on the matter, but this was not an ordinary set of circumstances, and Hillary was the first to realize that where his own cousin and his own loved ones were involved he could not be objective. His nibs, he knew, was not concerned with the well-being or the embarrassment of a single family or with any handful of mere mortals. His nibs was concerned with the well-being and safety of Britannia herself. For his part, Hillary had found such devotion to an abstract entity slightly offensive, even idolatous. Hillary Pendragon had always felt awkward about such grand displays of allegiance; instead he had been in the habit of ensuring the safety of a handful of people at a time. For him there had never been a Britannia—he fought for Englishmen, and when he thought about it he fought not for Englishmen in general but for the many individual Englishmen, of every description, whom he knew and who knew him. Hillary Pendragon's humanity and sense of duty extended only to people and not to abstract entities like the state.

Beyond fretting, however, he would not challenge his nibs

in matters concerning his own family. Nevertheless, instinctively Hillary agreed with Mr. Muggins in this instance. A bird in hand was worth several on the wing, and a world in which a period had been put to Anthony's existence would be a safer world for everyone.

Hillary had a week in which to have his affairs in order, and he spent that week in discharging various business matters and bringing his papers current. That is, he spent the week precisely as the weeks before each assignment had been spent. And although the accomplishment of these rather mundane tasks had never been precisely exciting, the tediousness on the other occasions had been more than balanced by thoughts about the coming adventure. Hillary's new ambivalence made such considerations appear a trifle empty. What seemed of overriding importance was not the coming weeks in France but the single evening in Devonshire, and much of Hillary's energies were concentrated on his hopes and plans for that evening.

Hillary set out for Devonshire the day before the ball. He had some business to attend to in Chippenham and planned to spend the night in that town. Accordingly, after having completed his business, he found himself, quite early, alone and unoccupied in the private parlor of the White Hart Inn. He should, he knew, take the opportunity to have a long and restful night of sleep unencumbered by any of his always pressing social engagements, but a man in love is very often a victim of insomnia. And at eleven o'clock Hillary returned to the parlor in search of some sort of distraction. In one corner of the room he found two or three books which had been obligingly left behind by some other patron. He returned to his room with a bottle of excellent wine, a brace of candles, and the books, which had, he decided, been the property of a person of rather indifferent taste. One of these books seemed precisely the sort of catchy, empty frivolity guaranteed to induce sleep in any mind of a better than average intellect. And so with a yawn and a glass of wine at his side he opened the book to the first pages of *The Witch of Firth Island*.

Sir Hillary was not a devotee of either romantic or of gothic novels. Had he been the least bit familiar with either genre, he would have instantly recognized the superior virtues of a Fleur de la Coeur novel. Actually, it came as something of a surprise when he found himself hugely enjoying the book. The plot moved along predictably but with a certain dash of imagination, and the characters, on the whole, seemed to be remarkably true to form. In fact, the characters were, he felt from the very beginning, people he could come to know—in fact people he had come to know already. Here was an author of mysterious and outrageous tales who peopled her novels with quite ordinary types of men and women. It took Hillary to the tenth page to accurately identify the hero, the villain, and the heroine. Having done so much, he could safely concentrate his energies on the minor characters. These he found vastly amusing. In particular, he enjoyed the arch-villainess, who appeared in the guise of a pompous, vastly autocratic aunt, and the empty-headed, vain Sir Randolph, who had been cursed in having her for a mother. Hillary would have read through the book from cover to cover and set it aside without a second thought had he not, almost immediately, discovered in the autocratic aunt an almost uncanny resemblance to his own Aunt Augusta. And then, almost in spite of himself, the other characters began to come into focus, and they all of them seemed to be distressingly similar to his companions in Devonshire. Quite suddenly, Sir Hillary Pendragon experienced a revelation. With an expression here and there and with the repeated assertion that "he could have any woman in the world," Sir Randolph, mad, benighted, and pathetic, was revealed as the author's opinion of Sir Hillary Pendragon. It was six in the morning, and Sir Hillary found himself in a towering, staggering, unquenchable rage. Only one person could have written that book. And that person was the pious scheming spying little governess to whom he had blindly entrusted his heart. Only now he remembered the saga of Mrs. Treakle and the letters to the *Yorkshire Times*. Only now he understood the source of her newly acquired funds. In an instant, the love in Sir Hillary's heart had been converted into a blinding, unreasoned, and unquestioned hatred. Within an hour he had taken to the road armed with a kind of intent determination to be avenged on Miss Gorham—totally and completely.

He rode steadily toward Pemmfield and stopped only once at an apothecary in Exeter to acquire a flask of an exotic but particularly effective drug.

Between Chippenham and Pemmfield he noticed nothing, his mind being totally engrossed in his plans of vengeance. He could have passed half a dozen burning buildings or as many ravishingly beautiful ladies without once pausing to observe the scene. It was only at the gates of Pemmfield that Hillary Pendragon wiped the grimness from his countenance and replaced it with that charming smile the world had come to expect. It was thus, apparently without any evil intentions, that he arrived at Pemmfield Manor.

In the confusion and bustle of last-minute preparations, his arrival was not noticed and he had just enough time to dress for the ball and lead Julia out for the first dance.

In honor of the occasion, Margaret Gorham had again dressed in her blue silk gown. It had been primarily her responsibility to arrange the logistics of the evening, but all the while she worked she waited and watched for Sir Hillary. Her heart missed a beat when she saw him come into the room, and she had the very fleeting impression that he was angry, and attempting to conceal that anger. But then his impersonation of the charming gallant gentleman seemed so to dominate his presence that Miss Gorham became convinced that her first impressions must have been erroneous.

Margaret would have liked to seek him out, but instead she remained standing in the background, conversing quietly with several of the neighborhood matrons and dancing occasionally with one of the local gentlemen. She smiled a little whenever her eyes met Sir Hillary's, and he smiled back at her, ushering into that smile many years of skill at devastating the hearts of femalekind. Slowly, as the evening progressed, he worked his way gradually into a position where he could talk to Miss Gorham.

And then, just as he was coming to speak to her, he saw her stiffen and frown. Simultaneously it seemed that almost half the assembled guests had suddenly fallen silent. Turning toward the door, Hillary saw the reason for their change in mood as well as Margaret's. Anthony Dillingham had returned from his travels and was calmly surveying the room. Just as clearly, he was not being wonderfully welcomed by his assembled neighbors. Few of the local gentry knew precisely what sort of activities Anthony had been involved in, but there was not a shadow of a doubt in their minds that life in the vicinity of Pemmfield had become a great deal more pleasant since Anthony's departure.

The awkward silence continued until Mr. Dillingham made his bow to his hostess, then the conversations and dancing resumed—almost as before.

Margaret Gorham was determined to avoid Anthony. She knew she could not dissemble her own contempt and hostility should he approach her, and it seemed quite pointless to leave

185

Devonshire under a cloud of evil spirits. In a few days, she would be gone and Anthony Dillingham would be only a part of her past—dead and buried.

Hillary saw Margaret turn toward the nearest door opening into the gardens and silently retreat from the room. Just as silently, almost unobtrusively, he followed her into the gardens. Her back was to him when he whispered hello.

Candlelight sifted through the windows, and when she whirled about he saw a tremulous welcome on her lips.

"Shall we remain out here in the moonlight and leave my Cousin Anthony the ballroom?"

"If you wish, Sir Hillary. I would like to avoid him as much as possible."

"Just so. And so would I. Come sit beside me and join me in a glass of champagne. I have escaped with the better part of a bottle and two glasses."

She sensed that there was something strained in his voice, and she hesitated.

"Come, a glass to the future. I shall be leaving for France within a week, and I should very much like us to part friends."

She seated herself beside him and took the glass. Not being a connoisseur, Margaret did not notice the off taste, nor is it likely she would have noticed it in any case. Not only was the drug a very subtle one, but Miss Gorham was so wholly intent upon confessing her transgression to the man beside her that nothing short of a blazing fire would have made her aware that all was not as it should be.

"Sir Hillary, I think there are some things which you ought to know."

"Still *Sir* Hillary? I give you fair warning I do not want to discuss *serious* things tonight. I am a man about to face danger and possibly death. Let us be friends tonight, Margaret, and give over discussing anything which might be construed as unpleasant."

The prospect of Sir Hillary single-handedly confronting all of Napoleon's armies was suddenly very real to Miss Gorham. She felt herself almost against her will sinking into a kind of maudlin fear for his safety and an almost equally maudlin wish to assure him that she was indeed his friend.

"You will be careful, won't you? I am quite afraid for you. You know I am not usually so chicken-hearted. I expect it is the champagne."

"Then another glass will clear your head."

After another glass and a half hour of very intense conversation, Margaret Gorham's head was far from clear. She found that she could not think at all—only feel—and that her feelings for the man beside her were very sweet and very powerful. She offered no objection when he, still smiling down into her eyes, asked her to waltz. The strains of the music were coming from the ballroom, and she found herself in his arms waltzing around the rose garden. There in the moonlight the harmony of their motion seemed perfect, and in that moment Margaret knew that she was living her dream. She was almost divinely happy.

They had stopped dancing. He began very slowly, to kiss her, and she did not object. It was all so exceedingly pleasant—so right. Within moments she found herself first melting into his arms and then beginning to return his kisses with an ardor she had never known was possible. Dimly Margaret knew that her heart and her mind were completely out of her own control and that she had entrusted all of herself to the man who was embracing her. But if she had lost her insular self-control she seemed to have gained so much more. And there was no resistance in her—only a swell of blinding passion and total surrender.

Very suddenly, he pulled away from her. His hands were still on her shoulders, but she felt herself resting against one of the trees. Margaret looked up, expecting to see his easy understanding smile. Instead she was confronted with a grim mask of hatred and anger. Slowly she tried to shake her mind clear as she looked up at him. There was tenderness, love, adoration in her eyes—and a certain curiosity.

And then she heard him speak. His words came with slow merciless brutality. "You see, my dear Madame de la Coeur, I really *can* have any woman in the world."

And then he turned his back on her and moved, without another word, to the ballroom.

Behind him Sir Hillary left a figure in blue silk slowly sinking into the ground.

She was aware only of a blinding pain and humiliation.

Margaret did not know how long she remained there. Slowly, she pulled herself to her feet and made her way to the back of the house.

An hour later a small figure in boy's clothing left the manor house through the kitchens. Only one person noticed

Pegasus moving out across the south lawn. Anthony Dillingham had been standing alone on the terrace blowing a cloud and thinking his own dark thoughts. He saw her as she slipped across the moonlit garden, and quickly he extinguished his cigar, made his way to the stables, and set out to follow.

Chapter 18

Sir Hillary forced himself to return to the ball—to smile and to chat with the matrons and the old gentlemen and to dance with the local belles. Once or twice, in the course of the evening, he surprised a look of curiosity—even concern—in Julia's eyes, and then he would quickly look aside.

Well before the midnight collation, his revenge, which should have been sweet, had turned to wormwood, and during the early hours of the morning, when the rest of the household slept, Hillary could not rid himself of the memory of Margaret's eyes in the moment before he had turned his back on her. He felt as if he had just murdered his best friend or even the very best part of himself.

He remembered then that she had tried to confess on at least two occasions and that he had not allowed her. Not even last night, when he knew what she was trying to say. No, he had preferred to have his little revenge go off perfectly—and, of course, it had.

At the earliest possible respectable hour Sir Hillary went in search of Miss Gorham with some vague intention of totally abasing himself and pleading for her forgiveness. It had not occurred to him that in one moment of unguarded rage he could have lost her forever.

In passing through the house he noticed a stir around Julia's apartments, and then the lady herself in the hall, coming toward him a note in her hand.

"She has gone, Hillary."

Silently he took the scrap of a note and read it:

My dear Lady Julia,

I have been called away on the gravest of emergencies.

I would have liked to inform you personally, but there was no time.

I cannot express my gratitude to you for allowing me to become a part of your family. I shall always remember you as a friend, but the time has come when I must move on.

I will write again when I am settled.

Margaret Gorham

As if in a distance, Hillary heard the women around him speaking, and while he knew he ought to listen to what was being said, his mind was strangely unresponsive—opaque.

In a daze he heard Julia say, "She has left almost all of her things."

Then they were in Miss Gorham's sparse room. He saw the several brown-and-black gowns hanging stiffly in the little closet. The writing materials. The handful of personal artifacts that even a governess needs to establish a temporary home. He saw too in the grate the ashes of the papers that had been torched and the remainder of at least one partially burned book. Almost unconsciously, he stirred the coals and watched the spine of the book consumed in flame. It was little enough, but he would protect her at least in this.

The cook was speaking. "I saw Miss Gorham before she left. Looked terrible, she did. Certain I am she received word of the death of a dear one, but she shouldn't have gone off in the night like that. Miss Gorham was not fit to travel, My Lady—not fit at all. I had no notion at all she was bent on leaving or I'm sure I would have stopped her. In such a dreadful state she was."

Hillary had turned away from them and started down the hall to his own room. He knew he had to think, but his mind was still so incredibly sluggish—he felt as if he himself had been drugged. But there had to be *something* he could do.

He knew she would have left with the horse, and so he walked down to the Fultons. Yes, the horse was gone, but the Fultons had been out the evening before and had not seen Miss Gorham.

Hillary knew that if she had started back for Yorkshire he could no longer easily follow her. No one would have noticed a young boy riding through the fields in the dead of night. And she could have as easily gone in some other direction. The first necessity, Hillary kept reminding himself, was to think calmly and rationally, and yet it was precisely this sort of thinking which now seemed impossible for him.

He remembered seeing Anthony at the ball and then not seeing Anthony again, and so he thought he ought to check at Dillingham Hall. Half an hour later he found himself face to face with his Aunt Augusta—possibly the last person on earth he wished to talk to.

"I can tell *you*, Hillary. *You* will understand that I was never so shocked in my life. My son—Anthony—is finally returned to his home, and at his *own cousin's* house he is virtually shunned by the neighborhood. I cannot think what could have caused it. Anthony is so sensitive to such things, and he was crestfallen, of course. He would not stay where he was not welcome."

"Left the ball early, did he?" Hillary asked.

"Yes he did. He went riding over the countryside. Poor boy."

"Poor boy?"

"Why, yes. Didn't I tell you? He was in a dreadful accident. He fell from his horse and only just made it back to the hall. We have called the doctor, and Anthony will be bedridden for several days. He cannot have visitors, although if I must say so myself he is taking it all very bravely and is in the best of spirits."

Hillary had heard enough to know that he would not see Anthony, and, excusing himself to his aunt, he made his way back to Pemmfield Manor to plan his next move.

He was not really surprised to be intercepted on the way by Obediah Muggins.

"Morning, guv'nor. You seem a bit under the weather."

"Do I, Mr. Muggins?" Hillary managed in a creditable imitation of a drawl. Mr. Muggins was warned not to make any further inquiries. "I expect you have been here, Mr. Muggins, supervising the activities of my Cousin Anthony. As you undoubtedly know, Anthony met with an accident last night and has been laid low. I am only surprised that one of his enemies did not dispatch him outright. As it is, he will be bedridden for the better part of a week."

"Is he back then? The little rotter slipped right in past our guard. Well, I shall pin two or three good men to him. We will have the drop on him now."

"You did not know Anthony had returned?" This in icy civility.

"No. Fact is, I came to find you, guv'nor. There has been a change in plans. You must leave immediately from the coast here."

Hillary found himself fighting for a delay, but when the matter had been fully explained to him he knew he must go. Scores of lives depended on his being in France that night and on his making a particular rendezvous. He had no real choice but to go.

They were almost back to Pemmfield Manor. "Very well, Muggins, I will be with you in half an hour."

"Half an hour?" Mr. Muggins knew it would take only half that time to pack whatever essentials a man in Sir Hillary's line traveled with.

"I will be back in half an hour," and Hillary was off.

He found a quill and some ink in the library, and he sat down to write a quick note to Miss Margaret Gorham, enclosed in an envelope addressed to Rachel Woodruff care of the Manfields in Yorkshire. Before he left he would find some way of posting the letter.

My dearest Miss Gorham,

I beg you to accept my apologies for my despicable conduct of last night. There is and can be no excuse for what I did.

Believe only that I love you. Had I loved you less, your portrait of Sir R would not have so angered me. Had I loved you less I should not have been lost to all reason and to all feelings of humanity. I see now that Sir R was merely a clever little parody and a well-deserved one at that. My conduct in Devonshire did not, at times, merit any better.

I must now leave for France. It is the gravest of emergencies and I have been allowed no choice. I should far prefer to follow you and to throw myself at your feet.

Please believe that I love you, and in the name

191

of that love I ask you, despite last night, to accept me as your husband.

God bless you.

Love,

Hillary

Three weeks later, when Hillary had broken through the lines and joined Wellington on the Peninsula, there was an answer, forwarded by his secretary, waiting for him. He had left the other officers and sequestered himself in one of the staff tents alone in the near-dark with a single sputtering candle. When he opened the letter his hands were shaking.

Dear Sir Hillary,

I cannot accept your very generous offer. You owe me nothing for your conduct of that night. I received no more than was due me.

I had humiliated you grievously and now you have humiliated me as well.

Let us be quits.

Sincerely,

Margaret Gorham

He sat there alone, casting a shadow against the canvas wall of the tent. His back was to the entrance and no one would see his tears.

"Bad news in the mail, Hillary?"

He wiped his eyes and turned quickly. "Arthur, I did not hear you enter."

"No, you were preoccupied. How bad is it? Anyone dead or dying?"

"No—not that bad," and he forced himself into a half-smile.

"If I did not know better I would say that the woman you love has just run off with another man. But of course you have never loved a woman, and if you did she would not be choosing any other man."

"No."

"Well then, lad, there is no one dead and no one irretrieveably lost—it cannot be *that* bad. Everything else can

192

be remedied, you know. Come join me in a toast to your future."

"Of course, Arthur. Always supposing I have one."

"Smile, Hillary—we are getting old, and soon, if we live that long, we will both of us be retired to the War Office. Let us make the most of life while we still may."

And the two friends spent the rest of the evening sharing a bottle of excellent French brandy and discussing trivialities.

Two weeks later Hillary found a pencil in his supplies and sat down to answer Miss Gorham's letter.

December 25th

10:00 P.M.

My dearest Pegasus,

I am sitting at a campfire in the vicinity of Calais. It is a cold night and I am having a lonely Christmas with only thoughts of you to keep me company.

We have just outrun a pack of French and smuggled several gallant people out of Napoleon's reach. They will even now be safely out to sea while I prepare to return to Wellington in the Peninsula.

You would not recognize me now, my love. I am dressed like a gypsy. My hair is blackened, together with a handful of my teeth, and there is so much dirt in my fingernails and in my ears that any day now I expect to begin to sprout.

I have everything on my back that I shall need to survive, except of course that I do not have you with me. We should make a splendid pair of gypsies, don't you think?

2:00 A.M.

They forwarded your last letter to me and I received it two weeks ago.

How could you write such a letter? You gave me nothing to hope for and nothing to live for. You must know how very much I love you. I did not offer for you out of any sense of honor. I want you to be my wife, and I have wanted only that for months. I came into Devonshire only to ask

193

you, and I would have done so within minutes of seeing you had I not come across that wretched novel in the inn in Chippenham. I curse the evil genius who left that book for me to find.

Had I not loved you so much I would not have been so hurt, and had you not loved me—as I know you must—you would not have created Sir Randolph and you would not have melted in my arms.

Please believe that I love you more than life itself. I see your face in the flames of my campfire and in my dreams each night. I ride across the countryside with you beside me always—and no matter what, you shall always be beside me.

On this earth I can imagine no greater happiness than to have you for my wife.

Please wait for me and God bless you.

                    With all my love,

                    Your Hillary

Chapter 19

Sir Hillary had intended, upon his return to England, to go directly into Yorkshire. He was deflected from his course, however, when he found a letter from Colonel Dillingham waiting for him in London.

My Dear Hillary,

I need to speak with you. I beg you to come into Devonshire or I shall come myself to you in London. The matter is most urgent.

                    Sincerely,

                    Reginald Dillingham

Without bothering to unpack, Sir Hillary ordered his groom to follow with some changes of clothing while he himself left on horseback to travel back to Devonshire. Early in the evening of the next day, he arrived at Dillingham Hall and formally requested an audience with his uncle by marriage.

In the space of a few months Reginald Dillingham seemed to have aged twenty years. He was now gray and stooped and seemed literally to have shrunk into the frame of a relatively small and very old man. The uncle whom Hillary had always remembered as bluff, hale, and bosky was no longer any of these. Colonel Dillingham seemed like a man being slowly consumed by a cancer—a man patiently waiting for death. Perhaps most incredible of all, for the first time in Hillary's recollection, Reginald Dillingham was stone sober.

The butler was excused and the two men were left to themselves.

"Sit down, Hillary, please sit down. I shan't take much of your time but it is proving difficult, very difficult, to say what I have to say. I believe you must know why I have asked to speak to you."

"No, I don't know, Uncle Dillingham."

Colonel Dillingham shrugged his shoulders and began.

"You never called me uncle even when you were a very little boy, and here you are expecting me to be avuncular when *you* seem to be dead set on protecting *me*. Why did you not tell me earlier? Surely I had a right to know about my own son."

Hillary fingered the stem of his glass and noted in passing that his uncle had refused the sherry. It was with a great reluctance that Hillary began to speak. "It didn't seem appropriate to voice what were little more than suspicions." And then at the look of mockery on his uncle's face, "Very well, I knew about Anthony, but I saw no reason to cause you unnecessary pain. I felt that it could have been handled without being generally known."

"Not *generally* known, of course. There was no need, in the beginning, to disgrace the family. But *I* am his father. *I* should have known. It is my right and my responsibility. I have discovered from strangers that my firstborn son is a villain, a monster, and a traitor to everything you and I have fought for. All of these many years I have been allowing him to become what he is. I had lost myself in drink and I shirked

195

my responsibilities as a father, as a soldier, as head of this family, and even, in the end, as a magistrate. By the by, I have had William Paul brought back from Australia. I did so, originally, at your request, but of course since I have come by at least a part of the truth Mr. Paul's record has been cleared. He has been completely exonerated and he has been indemnified for all of his losses. That much I could do to begin with, and such things are quite simple. The rest of the things I must do will not be so simple."

"Uncle Dillingham, *you* do not have to do more. There are others who will do what has to be done."

"Yes, there are always others, are there not?.... But first, Hillary, I must know the whole of it. I have convinced young John Paul, on his word of honor, to tell me what little he knows, although he was most reluctant to do so. He is a good man and a good son of a good father. But of course you must know that."

"Yes, I know it."

Colonel Dillingham seemed lost in thought for a few moments before he began to speak again. "I have heard of places in the East where a father would suicide himself in such instances to atone for the guilt of a son. I haven't long to live, anyway, and, the gesture would be futile. Nor do I suppose my death would prevent my precious Anthony from assuming the power he has so long coveted, or prevent him from continuing in his vile ways. In fact, my death would only facilitate matters for him. If he were a gentleman and a soldier I would lock him in a room with myself and two primed pistols, but of course he is neither a gentleman nor a soldier."

"Reginald, *we* will catch him and he will be dispatched with little or no fanfare. But do you truly wish it to happen?"

"Wish it? My God, no. I wish him to be a saint, a slayer of French dragons, anything but what he is. I am telling you that if he returns he will not live here again. And I am asking, no, I am begging, you to tell me the whole. It is difficult enough to tell his mother what she will need to know. *I must know it all.*"

Gently, slowly, and with absolutely no embellishment, Hillary repeated all he knew to Anthony Dillingham's father. In pity he watched the man before him shrink still farther into himself. There was a change, however, after Hillary had completed his recital of the facts. The colonel straightened himself to his full height and began to look as he must have twenty years before in the army. Within moments Reginald Dillingham was glaring at Hillary precisely as he must have glared at all his subordinates when, in the course of a particularly bloody campaign, the full extent of the losses were being reported.

Hillary waited for his uncle to speak. "To be sure, Hillary, it is far worse than I had thought. Have you reported all of this in writing to the government?"

"The people who need to know do know."

"You irregulars are all alike. Never anything out in the open if you can avoid it."

"Just so. We irregulars are a sorry lot."

"But *I* was always a regular army man. Military tradition and training is not something one can outgrow. I have always reported everything promptly and accurately—and in writing—to my superiors. I shall, of course, continue to do so. A full report of this matter will be in the post tomorrow."

"And what of the family?"

"The family is no better than the honor of its members. We must each of us act with honesty and integrity even if we receive the odium of our fellows for doing so. There is little enough honor in admitting that you have been a fool and a delinquent father and that your son is a murderer and a traitor. No, Hillary, don't try to stop me. Leave an old man whatever claims to honor he still has. We have been very fortunate here in England, and we, the whole of the family, have been blessed by birth with affluence and with status. For these we owe a great debt, and I have tried to discharge that debt with a career in the military. But now I have found that in the most horrible way my own son has been false to everything good and decent. He has been vicious, dissolute, traitorous. I must report him, and should he return to Dillingham Hall, God forgive me, he will die by my hand."

There were several minutes of silence. There seemed very little to say.

"If I believed I would survive the journey—if I were a few years younger—I would go up to Yorkshire to find him."

"Did you say Yorkshire? Is Anthony in Yorkshire?"

"Yes, he went up about two weeks ago. I believe he wishes to marry that young woman, Margaret Gorham. Of course, she is far too good for him and knows him for what he is, but he cannot know of her part in his exposure. In any case, he

197

has assured his mother that he is going to Yorkshire and will be returning with a wife."

Unconsciously Sir Hillary had arisen, and had the old man been looking he would have seen Sir Hillary Pendragon monstrously transformed. Within a moment, however, Hillary had made his decisions and his features had returned to their normal pleasant pattern. There remained, of course, much to be explained, but Hillary knew he would do what must be done.

"It is late, Reginald, and I must sleep. I will be leaving for Yorkshire in the morning."

"Yes, yes, of course. Oh, and my wife has asked that you join us for a late supper. You cannot have eaten today. She and Claude are awaiting us in the dining saloon. You will be kind to her. She need not know yet."

"Of course not."

Fifteen minutes later Lady Augusta was holding forth at the table in her usual manner, totally unperturbed by the unnatural silence and somber expressions of her three companions. "You will never guess, Hillary, how busy we have been here since we saw you last. Julia has gone off to London and now I am the only lady in the vicinity—not that I am lonely, you understand. Julia was always too silly to bear a sensible woman company. No, but I declare I cannot rest from dusk to dawn. All the responsibilities of the parish fall to me, and we are always having to visit the poor and entertain the vicar or the doctor or some such person. I do not cringe at accepting the responsibilities of my station, of course, but I cannot help thinking that Julia has sadly spoiled these people. They have come to expect too much of us."

"I'm certain, Aunt Augusta, that they all appreciate your efforts," Hillary said automatically.

"Well, I am not near so certain of that. They all seem to be forever bemoaning Julia's absence, although she was *never* more than a very silly woman. But never you mind, I anticipate that soon I shall have a staunch supporter and another lady's aid. Did Dillingham tell you that my Anthony is to be married?"

"Married, Mama? I'm afraid that is news even to me."

"Of course it is news to you, Claude. If you had not, against my better judgment, been running off with my grandchildren you would have been informed. And then of course you found it necessary to remain in Bath for weeks on end when you should have been more concerned with what was toward with your own brother. Do not think that I haven't noticed how disagreeably you have been behaving toward Anthony. And *why* did you stay so long in Bath?"

"I have explained it to you, Mama. At least three times. The people who administer the schools specifically asked me to remain in Bath. The children needed me, you see. And I was delighted that I could spend some time with them and bring them both together. Although why children of that age should be segregated by sex I do not know."

"There is a great deal *you* do not know about children of that age or of any other age, Claude. *I do* know, and you would do well to be guided by my judgment."

"Yes, of course, Mama, but what or who in blazes is my brother planning to marry?"

"Anthony has gone into Yorkshire."

"Yorkshire be damned. He told me he was for London."

"Do not interrupt me, Claude, and never use such language in my presence. I don't know what has come over you lately—you were always such a sweet harmless sort of boy. Your brother, Claude, has gone into Yorkshire and he will marry Miss Margaret Gorham."

"Preposterous, Mama! Has he asked her?"

"Of course he has not asked her—why should he go into Yorkshire otherwise? But she is not likely to refuse such an offer, and I consider myself most enlightened and liberal to be willing to welcome her into our family. I trust you will behave yourself properly when she arrives here as your brother's wife."

"And I, Mama, hope to God that never happens."

"Claude! I am shocked."

"Mother, may I be excused?"

"No, of course not. Finish your meal."

"Leave the boy be, Augusta. Claude, you are excused," the colonel barked.

Claude left the table and in passing placed a hand on Sir Hillary's shoulder. "Hillary, I must speak with you before you leave."

"In my room in fifteen minutes."

"Agreed." Claude turned his back on his mother and left the saloon.

Sir Hillary entered his room a scant quarter of an hour later to find his Cousin Claude already there. The younger man was glaring out the window, his arms braced on the frame, and he turned as he heard the door close quietly behind Hillary. Almost unconsciously Hillary noted that he had never before seen Claude in such a thoroughly masculine posture.

In fact, Claude was looking at him with a directness and an intensity that seemed quite at odds with his normal personality. Slowly the younger Dillingham began to speak.

"You are going into Yorkshire tomorrow?"

"Yes."

"I am going as well."

"If you are asking me, Claude, I can tell you it will not be necessary."

"No, I am not asking you, nor do I intend to burden you with my presence. You will travel much faster alone, but I too will set out in the morning."

"I see. Claude, how much do you know?"

"How much do I know? I know, of course, that Anthony is a thief and is cruelly depraved. I've known that much for years. I know now that he has been terrorizing this community and that he is very likely both a traitor and a murderer."

"He is both."

"Thank you at least for being honest. Few people think it necessary to inform Claude Dillingham of anything."

"But Claude, surely you realize that Margaret Gorham knows these things as well. Even if he has gone into Yorkshire to propose marriage, I cannot think her in any danger of accepting. Indeed, I do not believe her to be in any considerable danger at all, surrounded as she is by family and friends."

Claude did not answer. Instead he turned to pace the room. He hesitated, looked up at the ceiling for guidance, and then began to speak. "I'm afraid, Hillary, I am not so sanguine on any of those points. There is a great danger, think, but I hope to God that I am wrong."

"Why don't you tell me what you know, or suspect, Claude, and let me be the judge of it?"

"Hillary...Hillary, do you love her?"

Hillary knew it was his turn to hesitate and to stare at the ceiling, but he simply locked eyes with his cousin for a second before answering very slowly, "Yes, I love her."

"Have you asked her to marry you?"

"Twice, by letter, and she has refused."

Claude sighed. "You know, Hillary, I owe that woman a

very great deal. I believe I owe her the lives and the health of Sarah and Luke, and those children are more dear to me than anyone else in the world is or is likely to be. I shan't have children of my own, and Sarah and Luke will be my patrimony. I owe Margaret Gorham the world."

"I know. So do I."

"Did she refuse you before or after Julia's ball?"

For the first time Hillary stiffened, and his face was a mask when he answered. "After. Dammit, Claude, out with it."

"The night of the ball Anthony was in an accident."

"Yes. I came by here the next day and he was too ill to be seen."

"It was the same night that Miss Gorham disappeared. I think the two may be connected."

"Connected?"

"I looked in on Anthony that day. You know, I believe I understand him. He told Mother it had been a riding accident, but his clothes were covered with straw and his face was marked with scratches and bruises that I do not believe could have been administered by a horse."

"I suspected that he had come across one of the multitude of his enemies and had been beaten."

"That, of course, is a possibility. But he had been scratched at, you see, and he was nevertheless in the very best of humor. I asked him what had happened and he repeated the business of a riding accident. Then he said, 'Claude, it was worth it— it was the best damned ride I have ever had in my life.' That's all, nothing much really, but I remember thinking that if Anthony was so very bruised his victim must have been near death." And then after another glance at Hillary, "You know, Hillary, it is all inference on my part—there may be nothing to it."

"And I rode into France without trying to find her or to ascertain her safety."

"You could not have known, and you had no choice."

"And now I have *her* confounded sense of honor to contend with."

Claude shrugged. "I have never understood such things. Will it make a difference to you?"

"Don't you be an ass. No difference at all."

"No difference at all?"

"Only that instead of killing Anthony out of some sort of necessity I shall kill him with pleasure."

201

"I suppose someone must kill him, if only to spare my father the necessity of doing so. I shall go into Yorkshire and help to pick up the pieces, if there are any."

"And I shall appreciate your support."

Rachel Woodruff was sitting by her window when she saw the tall gentleman open the gate and make his way up the walk toward her cottage. For a moment she appeared flustered, but the moment passed and then she began to smile. Miss Woodruff remained seated until she heard the firm knock on her door. Rising slowly, she went to greet her visitor.

"Rachel Woodruff?"

"Yes, I am Rachel Woodruff. And you?"

"I am Sir Hillary Pendragon." And when she nodded he added, "You do not seem surprised, Miss Woodruff."

She greeted him warmly. "I was surprised—at least a little surprised a few moments ago when I saw you at the gate. I knew, of course, who you must be, and I am delighted you have come. Come and sit down. I see that you are confused, but we will have a friendly chat over some tea."

Sir Hillary allowed himself to be seated, and, armed with his tea, he began to speak. "I have come into Yorkshire to find Margaret Gorham—this is her home, is it not?"

"It is her home, but she is not here at the moment."

"I would very much like to see her if it would be possible."

"Why?"

Hillary had not expected such a direct question, and he hesitated for a few moments while looking intently into Miss Woodruff's eyes. Apparently he was satisfied with what he found there. "I have come because I love her and I wish to marry her."

"A good answer. Have you told her?"

He stared down at the teacup. "I'm afraid I did not handle it as I should have. I wrote her and she refused me. I was unreasonably and stupidly angry about that ridiculous book, and I may have done irreparable damage."

"I do not entirely blame you. Pegasus was bound to run into someone eventually who could identify her as the author of those novels. It was always a calculated risk. It was only unfortunate that you were the first to see the truth. She did not mean her portrait of Sir Randolph, you know. She knows now that she wrote what she did because she was very jeal-

202

ous—you *were* behaving shabbily. Sir Randolph was simply a way of defending herself."

"From me?"

"From you, from herself, from the world. Have you noticed, Sir Hillary, that for all her strength of character, my Pegasus is a remarkably defenseless person?—She has always lived too hard."

"Just so. And she is so good that there will always be those who will try to drag her down. But what is to be done now? What can *I* do?"

"Yes, that is a problem. You know she has not been well since she left Devonshire?"

He nodded, and a look of understanding passed between them as he said, "I suspected as much."

"She arrived here in the worst of health. She had somehow managed to ride into Oxfordshire, where the Twinings live. The Twinings use a Dr. Thorne—a man whom she had befriended. Pegasus found him, and although she was near to death he managed to patch her up a bit."

Again Hillary nodded. He could not trust himself to speak.

"She was not fit to ride, and Dr. Thorne brought her to me in a wagon. He would have stayed, but she sent him away. For a while you would not have recognized her. For several weeks I thought I would lose her. It was not just the physical wounds, you see. I think she was consumed by all manner of fears, and she would wake up almost every night screaming. She is only now recovering, and I do not wish to see her harmed again."

"You need have no fear of that, Miss Woodruff."

"You know that plaguy cousin of yours has been circling around her like a giant cat coming in for the kill. Pegasus felt she had to get away from him, and that is why she has left this house and bought passage for America."

"Good God. If she is en route to America I shall never find her."

"I believe you could find her even in America, but it is not near so bad as that. She is still near Liverpool, and it will be days before she is scheduled to sail. If you ride there you are certain to intercept her."

He thought for a few moments—they were moments of planning, not indecision.

"I have an estate near Liverpool—it is called Mormount. I will arrange to have the postboys take you there today, and

I will go ahead on horseback. Will you be able to leave immediately?"

"Yes, of course, but perhaps you would like to finish your tea first and read a letter she has left for you. I was instructed not to send it out for a week or two, but I am so relieved that I will not be having to post it at all." Miss Woodruff handed him the letter. "I will leave you to read it alone."

He broke the seal and opened the letter slowly, holding it a moment before he began to read.

Dear Sir Hillary,

I have received your last letter, and it deserves a better answer than I am able to give it.

First, be assured that I would not have written you if I had known that my letter would be forwarded to the Continent and that you would be so disturbed by it.

The whole matter has become so difficult.

You must know that, if it were at all possible, I should wish very much to become your wife. But it is not possible. Marriage, to any man, is impossible for me.

I have decided to leave England, and when you receive this letter I shall already be en route to America, where I plan to take up a career in teaching.

You will always have a most special place in my heart, and I pray that you find some other woman more suited to make you happy.

God bless you.

Margaret Gorham

Miss Woodruff had returned to the parlor in time to see Sir Hillary crumple the letter and to mutter, "Damned unadulterated rubbish."

"I rather thought it would be," she said placidly as she took a seat.

"Where will she be in Liverpool?"

"We have arranged that she stay in Everton until the ship is ready to sail. I have a friend there whose husband keeps a respectable inn called the Swan."

He was up and shrugging into his coat when she continued,

"I don't mean to intrude, but are you sufficiently rested to start out?"

"Yes, yes, of course. I am used to traveling for days on end without rest. Appearance to the contrary, I am a soldier. Incidentally, later today my Cousin Claude will arrive in Yorkshire and go to Mansfield Manor. Robert Mansfield is just returned home."

"Yes, I know. Robbie is one of my boys, you know."

"To be sure. You have quite a collection of children to be proud of, Miss Woodruff.... Would you be kind enough to visit Mansfield Manor before you come west and explain the situation to Robbie and Claude? Tell them whatever you see fit or deem necessary. But explain to Robbie that I want Anthony kept under observation until my return. He is still in Yorkshire, is he not?"

"To my certain knowledge he was here yesterday. We have not broadcast Pegasus's departure, and even the manor does not yet know of it."

"Good. And tell Robbie that Anthony is mine. He will understand."

"Yes, even I understand, but I beg you to reconsider. After what my girl has suffered do you think it right that she should risk losing you because of *your* sense of honor?"

"Nonsense—it is only my sense of honor that has allowed Anthony to remain alive so long and to cause such suffering. I am a soldier and I have been a spy, and I can assure you that in situations such as these I have no honor—not a particle of it. I will not be hurt—Anthony has never been a match for me—he does better to prey on women and children."

"But here where you are personally involved you will not be the cold detached agent of your government."

"My dear Miss Woodruff, I can clearly see where my Pegasus has gotten her strain of moral perversity. I shall, in this, still be acting for my government. Killing people is never pleasant and often messy. I fail to see why I should leave Anthony to others when I am the only one who will derive any sort of pleasure from the act." Opening the door, he continued, "I shall see you in Mormount as soon as possible." He handed her a wad of bills to cover expenses. "And handle that pompous Phillip Gorham and his wife as best you can. He is one of your children I have yet to become fond of."

"Phillip was *not* one of my favorites. But one must settle for the appearance of virtue when the substance is impossible."

"Just so." And lifting her hand, he pressed it to his lips. "My dearest Woody, *au revoir*."

Chapter 20

Despite the deplorable condition of the roads, Sir Hillary was able to make good time riding through Lancashire, and he was fairly fresh and in good spirits when he arrived in the small town of Everton.

As he approached the Swan, however, he sustained something of a shock. Stationed across from the inn stood his old friend and sometime colleague Mr. Obediah Muggins. Mr. Muggins was strenuously engaged in acting occupied, and so Hillary merely quirked one eyebrow as he walked past, and the two of them met moments later behind the corner of a nearby haberdashery.

"Well, guv'nor, didn't expect you here so soon, but I don't mind telling you I am delighted by your arrival—properly delighted. This is no occupation for a man alone, don't you know."

"Before I commit myself to your enterprise, Mr. Muggins, I should like to know what you, my dear fellow, are doing in Everton."

"Aye, guv'nor, you're always one to play it coy—like a blushing maiden you are at times. Certain it is that you've put the sum of two and two together and gotten fourpence for your efforts. Yer no flat, sir."

"You are too kind, Obediah. Since you are unlikely to be following Miss Gorham, I have concluded that my Cousin Anthony is in the Swan as well."

"That he is. Has been for the better part of the day. Mr. Anthony Dillingham is a sly one, and there is no doubt of that. I have been sent flying all over England and Wales after that particular bird. I almost lost the scent there for a bit when I went harrying off to London 'stead of Yorkshire. But

Obediah Muggins sticks to his man, and consequently here I be."

"And what are your precise instructions from his nibs? Are you here merely in the capacity of an observer?"

"My instructions are to follow him and to take notice of anyone he talks to, and, finally, I am supposed to dispatch him to a better world—or a worse world, as will be the case for Mr. Anthony. His nibs believes, as I do meself, that Mr. Anthony being a gentleman it will not be good or seemly to see him topped public-like as we might for a more common sort of murderer and traitor. No, his being genteel and all, his nibs and I decided he should go quietly by the knife, and, incidentally, his nibs is most concerned that you not be involved in it."

"He does not believe I can dispatch my own cousin?"

"His nibs thinks that you might hesitate in the commission of your dooty, so to speak, and we would lose us a good Englishman and capital agent."

"I see. And what, Mr. Muggins, have you learned from your surveillance?"

"I have learned that Mr. Anthony is, at the moment, more interested in marriage than in spying for them frogs—at least for now. And I've also learned that I have no truck with the way he is pursuing this his latest interest. I had decided that I would have to intervene, so to speak, prematurely. That's why, guv'nor, I'm right pleased you made your appearance after all."

"You can safely leave the matter in my hands now, Mr. Muggins."

"Yes, I believe I can at that. But don't you go hesitatin' and lose me my commission with his nibs. His nibs is not a man to cross, you must know."

"I will not 'hesitate,' Mr. Muggins. But I prefer it to be a fair fight—with sabers."

Mr. Muggins turned and executed a gesture of mild distaste. "I will never understand you gentlemen. *I* should never give vermin like that the benefit of the doubt. I shall be properly angered, guv'nor, if you go an' get yourself killed and leave me to explain to his nibs and the blimey governess....Incidentally, guv'nor, your precious cousin is carrying a knife up his sleeve and a pistol in his boot. And, guv'nor..."

"Yes, Mr. Muggins?"

"If I had your cause I would be sorely tempted, sorely

tempted indeed, to make it slow. Ain't a man alive who would blame you."

"Yes, I am human enough to be sorely tempted to do so, but it is not my style, Mr. Muggins. Especially since there is likely to be a lady present."

"Oh, and guv'nor, the owner of the inn is an old friend of a friend of ours—Sergeant Tucker. He has seen my bona fides and there will not be a ha'penny worth of trouble losing Mr. Anthony after he is dispatched to a worser world. Them were his nibs suggestions—a disappearance."

"I will leave you to handle that aspect of the matter, Mr. Muggins. I will have other work to tend to."

"Righto, guv'nor—well, go to it."

They returned to the door of the inn, and after a brief exchange of information with the innkeeper's wife, Sir Hillary made his way rapidly up the stairs to Mr. Dillingham's chamber. Anthony was not there, but the sound of his voice was just barely distinguishable behind the door to Margaret Gorham's room. Sir Hillary stationed himself silently outside that door and opened it just enough so that he could see inside and hear every word of the conversation.

Anthony Dillingham had his back to the door, and Miss Gorham was doing her best not to look at anything in the room, least of all Mr. Dillingham. She was standing, almost riveted, to the window and looking out over the town, apparently totally oblivious to anything Mr. Dillingham had to say.

"Did you think you could escape me so easily, my dear Margaret?"

Margaret Gorham did not turn from the window. "How did you come to follow me here?"

"It was really pathetically simple, my love. You see, you are not so very clever as you seem to think. I knew you would have told your half-wit mother of your plans, and so I sought you there. Really, I disturbed her quite unnecessarily. It was all so obvious I had only to present myself as the rejected swain, as a gentleman of means and status hopelessly in love with her ingrate daughter. Your brother Phillip was there, and he agreed with me that you must be quite mad to so persistently reject such a superlative catch. I believe I have convinced him that you are planning, like Ophelia, to drown yourself in a bed of lilies. By the by, your precious Phillip will have you committed if I but say the word. What a charming family you have, my dear—and here I thought I had a monopoly of half-wit relatives. In any case, your family are all in the greatest sympathy with my cause, and your mother even fluttered romantically and deplored at length that wretched prideful madness which has led you to spurn such a handsome lover. Why do you, incidentally?"

"Why do I what?"

"Why do you spurn me when you know you have no choice, really?"

"You think I have no choice?"

"Just so. No *gentleman* will have you now. Certainly not my very fastidious Cousin Hillary."

Hillary saw her face turn in profile to him, and for a moment he fell back, stunned. He had left her a blooming, healthy almost pretty young woman, and he saw her now thin and tense, her face set in stone. She had never appeared so very beautiful.

Anthony continued, "Do you think I had not noticed how very fond of our Hillary was becoming of you and you of him? Piquant, is it not—and a pity that you are both gentleman of honor, so to speak. I shall gloat to see his eyes when you arrive in Devonshire as *my* wife."

"You have a vivid imagination, Mr. Dillingham. Sir Hillary has no especial affection for me, and I will not be going anywhere as your wife. I am quite resigned to the fact that I will marry no man—and certainly not you. Nor can I see, except for the specious sort of resentment you bear your cousin, why you should wish to marry me."

"Do you not see us as the perfect pair, my love?"

"I see that I hate you, and I am quite certain you hate me as well. I believe you are a vile, contemptible madman, and I will never cease to hate you and to fight you."

"Perfect, absolutely perfect. You must know I consider hatred a most gratifying passion. I have wanted women, taken them, and even forced them before—no man or woman has ever fought me as you did, my love." He removed a speck of lint from his sleeve and looked at her. "I can assure you it was the most gratifying experience of my life. There is no challenge, you see, in destroying weak people—my first wife was a very weak person—a dead bore after the first night. Most women are dead bores after the first night." When Margaret did not comment he continued, "You know, I have always resented having my children in that school. They are soft enough already. My first wife was an almost nauseating soft woman, and her children, I think, will break very easily.

209

By the by, I think you will cooperate with me for a number of very good reasons—one of them being that you do not want their destruction on your conscience."

"They are *your* children."

"Precisely, and like my wife they are completely under my legal and physical control. But I am not, truth to tell, very proud of that pair. Between us we shall make much better children. Our children will conquer worlds."

"Yes, well, you shall have to find a substitute—someone else to hate and make the mother of your children. I am sailing in a day or two for America, and I believe your brother, Claude, and your father now know what sort of a parent you are. *They* will not allow you to harm Sarah and Luke more than you have done already. While I shall be quite free of you in America."

Anthony stiffened in resentment. "I quite see whom you will be fleeing *from,* my dear Margaret, but I cannot like whom you are fleeing *to.* I have no intention whatsoever of losing you, and certainly not to some filthy savage."

"I beg your pardon?"

"In your village they speak of the American aborigine. They say he is like a devil and possesses your soul every time you mount a horse. I *cannot* have that, my dearest. I must be the only man to possess either your soul or your body. You are mine."

Still she did not turn to face him. "I do not mean to be dramatic," she answered, "but unless you mean to murder me you will not have me in any sense. Short of that you cannot stop me."

"Oh, I don't think it will come to that—not yet, at least. There is a house belonging to a friend of mine some distance from town, and we shall spend a delightful night there."

"Marriage is surely superfluous to your plans."

"*Au contraire.* Without marriage all my violence is superficial. I have no real control—no real power, so to speak. I think that after we have spent a few days alone, you *will* marry me. There are such a great multitude of fascinating ways in which to assure your compliance once I have your undivided attention."

"I am not leaving this inn with you."

"Now you *are* being dramatic. It is a relatively simple matter to render you unconscious—it will be a pleasure, really. And there are two very unsavory chaps belowstairs who will aid me in transporting your inert form into the
210

carriage. It will all be handled very quietly. Now, I really do insist that you look at me, Margaret. I am quite certain you have memorized the scene from that window. Turn around and face me, my pretty."

And saying this, he struck her viciously across the head before Hillary could move to intervene. She staggered and turned—a small pearl-handled pistol in her hand. Her back was rigid and her hand did not tremble.

"As always, magnificent, Margaret. But I do not believe that you would shoot an unarmed man at point-blank range, my love."

For a scant second Miss Gorham seemed unsure of herself.

"Perhaps Miss Gorham would not, but I would, Anthony." Hillary Pendragon's voice was almost devoid of expression. Margaret looked at Hillary, and now there was a ghost of a smile on her lips and a welcome in her eyes.

He spoke to her. "Move away from him carefully and come over to stand beside me. No, not you, Anthony. Anthony, you will be pleased to remain perfectly still—do not turn around."

Hillary grasped Margaret by the hand and gripped it firmly. "Now, Anthony, we will do very well if you continue to follow my instructions. The knife in your sleeve—very slowly drop it to the floor and kick it to the far wall."

"What knife?"

"I said drop it! I will not repeat myself again. Good. And now with your hands in the air...in the air, I said...kick off your boots and push them clear of you." Anthony complied with a shrug—almost too easily, Hillary thought.

"Miss Gorham, would you go very carefully and retrieve the knife and the boots—you will find a pistol in the right boot cuff."

She nodded to him and moved off silently.

"Good girl."

"Hillary, I don't mean to be a spoilsport, but if you have come to defend the lady's virtue you have come too late. She has no virtue left to defend, you know."

"No, my dear cousin, you are quite mistaken. I have not come to protect my lady's virtue. Her virtue is its own best defense, both in God's eyes and in mine—I have come to kill you, Anthony."

"At the risk of being *de trop*, might I ask precisely why you intend to kill me?"

"Ah, but there are so many reasons. I kill you for my king,

211

for my honor, and because you have become something of an annoyance to the woman I love."

"Noble, but something less than what I expected of you. I do not believe that you, any more than Margaret, will shoot me in cold blood."

"You deserve as much—and to die slowly—but it is not my style. I have brought your saber as well as mine."

"My saber. This is a well-thought-out plot."

"Yes, it is. Your father gave it to me, saying it was better than you deserved."

Hillary handed his pistol to Miss Gorham, with instructions to wait in the hall. And then, throwing the saber to Anthony, he called, "*En garde.*"

Miss Gorham could not bring herself to leave the room. She stood riveted, fear in her heart, as the two men began to parry. Before long, however, she became aware that though both faces were grim, Hillary Pendragon was in control of both himself and the battle. Anthony Dillingham was in control of neither.

Anthony's face was wet with perspiration, and the whiteness about his eyes now accentuated a look of fear, and not simply of madness. Within a very few minutes there was blood on his sleeve and on his leg, and as he was worked farther and farther into the corner of the room, he began to cower. Suddenly he threw his foil from him and raised his arms in an act of surrender, and then, almost miraculously, as Hillary hesitated a fraction of a second, Anthony Dillingham produced yet another pistol and discharged it at his assailant. Hillary feinted to his left and came up to drive his blade through his cousin's chest.

Sir Hillary removed his blade and wiped it clean while staring a moment or two at the quivering body. Only then did he turn his back on the helpless thing and go to Miss Gorham.

Almost in a dream, Hillary saw Pegasus, her left hand to her right shoulder, slowly sinking down the wall.

Muggins was through the door and saying, "Guv'nor, not to worry. You take the lady to the room across the hall. I'll look after cleaning up the mess here and clearing the debris."

Margaret felt herself swept into Sir Hillary's arms.

"I *can* stand," she said, and it came out a whisper. "It's the merest scratch, I can assure you."

Without vouchsafing her a reply Hillary took her into the other room and deposited her in the chair, then ripped the sheet from the bed and tore it into strips of linen. And then, still quite intent on the task at hand, he silently cut away the cloth from about the wound.

Then he spoke. "No, I don't think it is too serious, but the bullet will have to come out, and we must staunch the flow of blood. It is, I think, a very small piece of lead, but it must hurt like the devil."

She watched his long white capable hands wrapping the linen. "It hurts like ten devils." She grinned. "What will happen to Anthony?"

"I don't know and I don't care to know. If he is not already dead, he will be in moments, and Mr. Muggins is quite competent to dispose of the carcass."

"You heard almost everything he said, didn't you?"

"I heard."

There were several minutes of silence while he finished the bandaging. "Now, can you manage to stand? We are meeting your redoubtable Woody at Mormount, where we will find a doctor. By the by, we must think of some sort of silly excuse for the presence of the lead in your shoulder."

"You do understand that I *cannot* go with you. Please don't make it any more difficult for me than it is already."

"For a woman of sense you are behaving like a perfect numskull. Do you think I shall love you one whit less because you have been the victim of a maniac? I should have killed Anthony months ago. You have said you wished to be a soldier. Well, for the last two months you have been behaving like the silliest sort of schoolgirl. Like a pea-brained heroine in one of your damned stupid novels. Do you think that all of war is bravery and gallantry? I have had to kill farmboys who have died calling for their mothers. I have watched friends die, and I have had to make their passing easier. Do you think I do not bear the scars—that I don't have my horrible memories, my moments of excruciating pain? So you wake in the night in a blind panic—we all do."

"Anthony said you could not want me." She had lifted herself up into a standing position.

"Not want you! I worship you. I love you, I adore you, and you damned well better believe I still want you. Don't you understand I myself am to blame for that night? If you hadn't been so weak, so desperate—because of me—you would have killed Anthony. As it was he was bedridden for days. My dearest, most precious Pegasus. I'm the greater villain of the piece."

It is doubtful that Pegasus had heard him at the last. She had fainted dead away in his arms.

Chapter 21

Margaret recovered conciousness to see Sir Hillary sitting in a chair beside her bed. "Hello, my love, welcome back to the land of the living."

Her eyes were framed in great hollows, and her hair was loose about her on the pillow—a dark contour to her almost white face.

"Is this Mormount?" she asked weakly.

"Such as it is—yes."

"And Woody?"

"Your Miss Woodruff is a delight, my love. At the moment she is earnestly convincing our local practitioner of medicine that she herself is responsible for the bullet that was, until half and hour ago, lodged in your shoulder.... By the by, how do you feel?"

"Strangely weak."

"Yes, I imagine you do feel weak. It has been several minutes already and you have not contradicted me once." He stroked her hair gently away from her forehead. "Do you suppose we have set a new precedent, my love?"

"We have made quite a mull of it, haven't we?" She sighed.

"Have we really? I rather thought we were coming out of it quite well. You will not think it at all relevant, but I have never seen you so very beautiful before." Margaret looked back at him in muted curiosity, and he reached down and kissed her brow, and then, holding her hand in both of his, he suggested she have some dinner, adding by way of enticement, "I would not have believed it possible, but there is still a housekeeper—and a good one—in residence."

Margaret declined the invitation and managed to draw herself up in a creditable imitation of the old Miss Gorham by insisting she'd like to sit up. The effort cost her dearly.

The pain was excruciating, and she was just barely able to stifle a cry.

Hillary helped her to become more comfortable. "Is that better now, love? I've found that even relatively innocent little bullet wounds can be very painful. How bad is it?"

"It is bad, but the pain seems to be fairly well localized, and I don't feel it much unless I attempt to move."

"If you relax and allow yourself to be coddled a bit your shoulder will heal rather more quickly."

"I expect you think I have been very silly," she said.

"No, of course not. You could never be silly—it is not in your nature. You are the bravest and least silly woman I know."

"No, I used to think I was very brave, but I know now I am a wretched coward. Hillary, I would not make you a good wife. You deserve far better."

Hillary saw her meaning in her eyes and was quick to respond.

"And now you *are* indulging yourself, my love." Then he hesitated for a few moments. "I don't suppose you will believe me, but, like any other wound, that too will heal."

"Will it?"

"It must. How I curse myself for that night!"

"No, please, you must not be thinking that." They were both silent for another few minutes while she sipped some warm milk Woody had brought up.

"Hush now. We will talk about all this later. Now you must go to sleep or you will never get well, my love."

Within moments Margaret's eyes had closed. Slowly, very gently, he began to lift her hand from his own. Suddenly she was awake.

She spoke in alarm. "Where will you be?"

"Not to worry, my love. Your charming Miss Woodruff has rightly insisted that I cannot remain in this room, but I shall be across the hall, and you need only call me if you want me." Saying this, he tucked her into the down coverlet and examined the dressing to see if the bleeding had been properly staunched. Then, kissing her lightly on the cheek, he whispered, "Say your prayers now, child, and go to sleep."

During most of the succeeding days, Margaret remained in her room—much of the time with Sir Hillary. There seemed so much to talk about, so much to learn of each other.

They were both very content, but, by common consent, the subject of marriage was never seriously broached.

Monday into the second week, Sir Hillary decided that Miss Gorham might have visitors.

Characteristically, the Reverend Phillip Gorham was insistent on seeing his sister, and, with considerably more tact, Claude Dillingham, who had arrived in the area, was eager to pay his respects. Even Mr. Muggins had arrived in Mormount, and although he was officially carrying a request from his nibs, he would have liked to carry his own good wishes to Miss Gorham.

Hillary decided that while Claude was a welcome visitor, Phillip could be tolerated only in moderation, and Mr. Muggins not at all. In fact, that gentleman was graciously thanked and dispatched to London with the message that Sir Hillary would require some time in England to resolve certain personal matters. Margaret was not to know that Obediah Muggins had ever been to Mormount.

The visit with Phillip was not a success. The Reverend Mr. Gorham spent half an hour castigating his ramshackle sister for rejecting Anthony Dillingham and then for getting herself shot in a vicinity where she was virtually certain to become a nuisance to Sir Hillary Pendragon and an embarrassment to himself.

Sir Hillary came upon this scene, and after one brief glance at Miss Gorham, he sent her brother from the sickroom and politely denied him access in the future.

"Local opinion has it, my love, that as a minister of the Gospel your brother is good at funerals, moderate at baptisms, poor at weddings, and a disaster at the sickbed. What a pompous strutting little man he is. And I will not have the banns posted in his church. I can forgive you everything but him."

"Yes, I can see that he has not improved with time."

"Not improved! Like an indifferent wine he has simply ripened into vinegar. Thank the Lord for Claude."

"Claude?" She asked "What has Claude to do with my brother Phillip?"

"Claude is staying with a Lady Terbury, an old and valued friend of my Aunt Augusta. Unlike myself, Elizabeth Terbury simply dotes on sycophants, and Claude has convinced her she is in desperate need of a secretary and a private chaplain. She will offer Phillip two hundred a year, and I, with a great show of reluctance, will pension him off at a hundred and fifty a year. It is the bargain of the age, but I do not expect the fish to bite if he once learns that you have become the alpha and the omega of my world. Incidentally, my love, I believe you will have the pleasure of thanking Claude himself tomorrow."

Like a brightly colored butterfly, Claude Dillingham made his appearance the next morning. Mr. Dillingham minced across the sitting room, took her hand in his, and kissed it with great deference.

"But Miss Gorham, you are looking wonderfully well. I can assure you *I* would not be looking near so well if I were shot in the shoulder. I have the rather lowering conviction that, despite the best efforts to spare my tailor any unnecessary mortification, I would bleed all over everything, and at the sight of so much blood I would puke up my dinner and make the ruin complete." Sighing mournfully as he straightened the lace at his sleeve, he said, "I'm afraid I would have made a perfectly deplorable hero."

Margaret began to laugh, and Claude lit up delighted. "There, you see, you *can* laugh. I do like to make people laugh, you know. Even if they are only laughing at me, which of course you never did. Now, let me tell you about Sarah and Luke and the other children and how well they are doing at school. Children have the most remarkable recuperative powers, and we must all of us, I think, try to imitate them in this."

"But we are not all children."

"Your brother—what a trial that man is—would say that we are all children in the eyes of God—or some such thing."

"To be sure, Claude, in the eye of God it all makes sense. But it doesn't all make sense to me just now."

"What, doubt from Margaret Gorham! It is not at all like you. Of course it makes sense. The only thing that does not make sense is this nonsense of having the marriage of the year in Yorkshire."

"What marriage?" She had raised her voice, but Claude would not be stilled.

"It will, of course, be the marriage of the millennium in Yorkshire, but that is not saying much, is it? Yorkshire is such a dull place—positively provincial. Think of the wasted opportunity.

"The Mansfields themselves are up to snuff, although I can never approve of Robert's tailor—everything is a little too drab and three sizes too large. Still, for Yorkshire, what more can one expect? And you are to be married from their home, you know. I believe we will have my grandmother's gown for you—it will have to be recut, but it is simply loaded with pearls and the most delicate white lace. We shall have it quite *à la mode* in time for the festivities."

"Claude!"

"It's really too bad that Geoffrey's flibbertigibbet wife has the really big Barth diamond, but Hillary's mother's stone is the size of a *small* robin's egg and almost as blue. We will all be there. The children are coming, and my parents. Julia is bringing her new beau up from London, and Geoffrey and his wife will come from Cornwall."

"Please, Claude, stop it. I cannot, I will not, talk about such things."

He took her hand. "You know, Margaret, you are the very best thing that has happened to our family. We all love you."

"Thank you, Claude. But quite apart from any other considerations, your family cannot be thinking of a marriage so very soon."

"Because of Anthony?"

"Of course."

"But didn't you know, Anthony was caught smuggling and has been disgraced. We believe he has gone off to America. My mother is very upset, but she will live, you know—she positively dotes on gloom. I shall make a splendid regent, although I am, thank goodness, not at all given to fat. The best is that, unlike the fictional monster, we are all quite assured that *this* monster will not reappear. Margaret, won't you forgive us? Why should Hillary be asked to pay the price for Anthony's villainy?"

Miss Gorham was saved from the necessity of responding by the opportune arrival of Sir Hillary and Miss Woodruff with the teatray. No further mention of the matter was made, and the four spent the rest of the afternoon in idle conversation.

Except for occasional visits from the outside the three at Mormount spent the next few weeks in pleasant isolation. Most of the days were passed in light conversation and the evenings in Piquet. Miss Woodruff, Hillary, and Margaret had agreed to play for ha'penny a point. And while Sir Hillary and Margaret found themselves staring into each others eyes, they continued to lose heavily to Miss Woodruff, who seemed very intent on her cards. By the end of the month, Rachel Woodruff had amassed a a small fortune in ha'pennies together with the infinitely greater fortune of seeing her charge become hopelessly and very happily settled into love.

The days grew perceptibly warmer, and so did Margaret's heart. It was almost sufficient to spend hours and days together with Hillary in a kind of lazy communion. He had sent for her horse, and she began to ride and to teach him her skills. Slowly, almost imperceptibly, Margaret was regaining her strength. For once in her life she was not inclined to be demanding either of herself or of others.

It came as something of a surprise then when, one spring morning as they were walking hand in hand across the pasture, Hillary put her to the test. It seemed a perfect setting. They were, the two of them, alone in the world, enclosed in a soft morning mist, and they both knew themselves to be very much in love.

They had been laughing together about Claude's newest scheme for the wedding when Hillary, suddenly serious, turned to face her. "I don't mean to rush you, my darling, but as you must know, I love you very much..." He hesitated a moment, and then, finally, almost awkwardly, "Do you think you can see your way clear to marrying me?"

In an almost automatic sort of response she drew back and hesitated. And he, seeing the flash of fear in her eyes, hurried on, "No, no, my love. I can see I have been too hasty." He held her by the shoulders. "Margaret, I promise—I swear—you will have all the time in the world to answer. After all, there is no reason to rush our fences, is there? We will wait until you are quite recovered."

"You don't believe I am recovered now?"

"My dear Margaret, I love you to distraction, but I cannot think you are recovered. I first learned to love you as a tyrant governess—a little general—and while I should not like her as a steady dose I confess that I have come to miss that other Miss Gorham, the tyrant governess. I have determined that *she* is the woman I must ask to marry."

Hillary gently turned the conversation back to trivialities, and after about half an hour they returned to the house. But Margaret was unable to regain her earlier sense of tranquillity.

Later in the afternoon as Margaret was preparing for dinner, Miss Woodruff joined her.

Once the pleasantries had been exchanged, Miss Gorham noticed that her friend seemed uncharacteristically ill at ease. "Out with it, Woody. What is on your mind this afternoon?"

"I don't mean to interfere, Margaret. But when are you intending to marry Sir Hillary?"

"It is assumed, of course, that I will be marrying Sir Hillary."

"Don't quibble, my dear. I am assuming nothing of the sort, nor would anyone who had been fortunate enough to strike up an acquaintance with a certain Mr. Obediah Muggins."

"Mr. Muggins! Here!"

"To be sure he is here. He is a very fascinating little man. Come to carry off Hillary Pendragon, you see. But I don't suppose you would be interested."

"Do you mean to say that Hillary and Robbie are off to France—now?"

"Not Robbie. You see, his nibs, whoever that might be, will not use married men. Marriage impairs their judgment, so to speak. A young man must be quite fancy-free to indulge in *that* sort of work, you know."

"Woody, is that why Sir Hillary went alone on the last mission?"

"Just so. And Mr. Muggins, in his own picaresque way, explains that Sir Hillary very nearly didn't survive that last visit to France—'distracted as the guv'nor was and all.'"

Margaret was pacing the floor, and her voice was raised. "And is Hillary intending to go now?"

"He is planning to. Some driveling nonsense about giving you all the time you need—not rushing his fences. And of course he is determined to protect you even from the knowledge of Mr. Muggins's presence."

Pegasus had scarcely heard the last of this. White with rage, she had ripped the door open and gone in search of Sir Hillary. She ran him to ground in the library, where he was sitting in his shirtsleeves, writing a letter.

Miss Gorham, without a word, stalked over to the desk and snatched up the paper. The salutation read, "My dearest Pegasus." She did not read further. Instead she tore the paper in pieces and threw it in the fire.

"How dare you, Hillary? How dare you think of going off to France?"

He had stood as she advanced on him, but he made no effort to answer her. He simply stood quite still and waited.

If possible, Pegasus became still more angry. "You were going off to get yourself killed—without so much as telling me. All because of your damned stupid sense of stupid honor."

She was now pounding him on the chest, her eyes running tears. Half in fear, half in anger, she continued, "Well you can't do it. Do you understand? I won't let you go off and get yourself killed—and not without me. Do you understand? O God, Hillary. How could you ever think to do such a thing?" And she collapsed in his arms in tears.

Gently he stroked her hair and waited until she had cried herself out.

Afterward, still in his arms, she looked up at him. "Why, Hillary?"

He shook his head. "No, Pegasus. It is still your move."

She studied him for a moment longer, and then, placing her hands on his shoulders, she reached slowly up and, tentatively, kissed him on the lips. There was nothing tentative about his response.

A quarter of an hour later her head was nestled safely in his shoulder and he asked her, "What are you thinking, my dearest?"

"I'm thinking," she whispered, "that we really ought to post the banns as soon as possible."

"Just so, my love."

The banns were posted in Yorkshire the next Sunday. And, a few days later, with little fanfare and a great show of glee on the part of the resident staff of Mormount, Margaret and Sir Hillary left to make their way to Mansfield Manor to be married.

Let COVENTRY Give You
A Little Old-Fashioned Romance

CURRENT CREST BESTSELLERS

☐ THE NINJA
   by Eric Van Lustbader   24367 $3.50

☐ SHOCKTRAUMA
   by Jon Franklin & Alan Doelp   24387 $2.95

☐ KANE & ABEL
   Jeffrey Archer   24376 $3.75

☐ PRIVATE SECTOR
   Jeff Millar   24368 $2.95

☐ DONAHUE *Phil Donahue & Co.*   24358 $2.95

☐ DOMINO *Phyllis A. Whitney*   24350 $2.75

☐ TO CATCH A KING
   Harry Patterson   24323 $2.95

☐ AUNT ERMA'S COPE BOOK
   Erma Bombeck   24334 $2.75

☐ THE GLOW *Brooks Stanwood*   24333 $2.75

☐ RESTORING THE AMERICAN DREAM
   Robert J. Ringer   24314 $2.95

☐ THE LAST ENCHANTMENT
   Mary Stewart   24207 $2.95

☐ CENTENNIAL *James A. Michener*   23494 $2.95

☐ THE COUP *John Updike*   24259 $2.95

☐ THURSDAY THE RABBI WALKED OUT
   Harry Kemelman   24070 $2.25

☐ IN MY FATHER'S COURT
   Isaac Bashevis Singer   24074 $2.50

☐ A WALK ACROSS AMERICA
   Peter Jenkins   24277 $2.75

☐ WANDERINGS *Chaim Potok*   24270 $3.95

Buy them at your local bookstore or use this handy coupon for ordering.

COLUMBIA BOOK SERVICE
32275 Mally Road, P.O. Box FB, Madison Heights, MI 48071

Please send me the books I have checked above. Orders for less than 5 books must include 75¢ for the first book and 25¢ for each additional book to cover postage and handling. Orders for 5 books or more postage is FREE. Send check or money order only.

    Cost $_____   Name _____

Sales tax*_____   Address _____

  Postage _____   City _____

   Total $_____   State _____ Zip _____

*The government requires us to collect sales tax in all states except AK, DE, MT, NH and OR.

This offer expires 1 March 82   8177

CURRENT BESTSELLERS
from POPULAR LIBRARY

☐ INNOCENT BLOOD   04630 $3.50
   by P. D. James
☐ FALLING IN PLACE   04650 $2.95
   by Ann Beattie
☐ THE FATHER OF FIRES   04640 $2.95
   by Kenneth M. Cameron
☐ WESTERN WIND   04634 $2.95
   by Oliver B. Patton
☐ HAWKS   04620 $2.95
   by Joseph Amiel
☐ LOVE IS JUST A WORD   04622 $2.95
   by Johannes Mario Simmel
☐ THE SENDAI   04628 $2.75
   by William Woolfolk
☐ NIGHT WATCH   04609 $2.75
   by Jack Olsen
☐ THE GREAT SHARK HUNT   04596 $3.50
   by Hunter S. Thompson
☐ THE WOTAN WARHEAD   04629 $2.50
   by James Follett
☐ TO THE HONOR OF THE FLEET   04576 $2.95
   by Robert H. Pilpel

Buy them at your local bookstore or use this handy coupon for ordering.

COLUMBIA BOOK SERVICE
32275 Mally Road, P.O. Box FB, Madison Heights, MI 48071

Please send me the books I have checked above. Orders for less than 5 books must include 75¢ for the first book and 25¢ for each additional book to cover postage and handling. Orders for 5 books or more postage is FREE. Send check or money order only.

Cost $_____ Name _____

Sales tax*_____ Address _____

Postage _____ City _____

Total $_____ State _____ Zip _____

*The government requires us to collect sales tax in all states except AK, DE, MT, NH and OR.

This offer expires 1 March 82